"Cheye—————————————————
here? We are not friends of your tribe, but there are no
hostilities between us now."

"None between us," Touch the Sky agreed. "But the
Blackfoot murderer Sis-ki-dee has killed our peace chief. He
has escaped to the Bear Paw country. But by the sun of the
earth I live on, I mean to kill him."

One of the braves hooted in derision. "You? And what
makes you so intrepid, brave Cheyenne? Why should you
not die like the rest who have faced Sis-ki-dee? Who are
you?"

"I am called Touch the Sky," he replied quietly.

RENEGADE SIEGE

Touch the Sky fell silent, squinting at a spot on the cliff
just below them. It was foolish, of course, but Touch the Sky
could almost swear he had seen sparks fly from the face of
the—

Something tickled his left ear. More sparks flew into his
eyes. And then, with a sinking feeling in his belly like a
chunk of cold lead, he realized that arrows were pelting
them! And the sparks were ause these arrows were
special Comanche arro   vith white man's sheet
iron, not flint. Iron   inched when they hit
bone, making t

Touch t   how the renegades
had g   uld launch a large
han   , and the sheer number
com   deadly all around them.
Finall   and seemed to stop. Touch the
Sky, ho   breath, finally began to expel it in
relief. Su   he final arrow found them. And Touch the
Sky heard   sickening noise, like an ax cutting a side of
meat, as the iron-tipped arrow sliced into Little Horse's calf.

CHEYENNE

BLOODY BONES CANYON/ RENEGADE SIEGE

JUDD COLE

LEISURE BOOKS NEW YORK CITY

A LEISURE BOOK®

September 1999

Published by

Dorchester Publishing Co., Inc.
276 Fifth Avenue
New York, NY 10001

ISBN 0-8439-4586-9

COL   mg   4.99   9-15-99

BLOODY BONES CANYON

Prologue

Although Matthew Hanchon bore the name given to him by his adopted white parents, he was the son of full-blooded Northern Cheyennes. The lone survivor of a Bluecoat massacre in 1840, the infant was raised by John and Sarah Hanchon in the Wyoming Territory settlement of Bighorn Falls.

His parents loved him as their own, and at first the youth was happy enough in his limited world. The occasional stares and threats from others meant little—until his sixteenth year and his forbidden love with Kristen, daughter of the wealthy rancher Hiram Steele.

Steele's campaign to run Matthew off like a distempered wolf was assisted by Seth Carlson, the jealous, Indian-hating cavalry officer who was in love with Kristen. Carlson delivered a fateful ultimatum: Either Matthew cleared out of Bighorn

Falls for good, or Carlson would ruin his parents' contract to supply nearby Fort Bates—and thus, ruin their mercantile business.

Sad but determined, Matthew set out for the up-country of the Powder River, Cheyenne territory. Captured by braves from Chief Yellow Bear's tribe, he was declared an Indian spy for the hair-face soldiers. He was brutally tortured over fire. But only a heartbeat before he was to be scalped and gutted, old Arrow Keeper interceded.

The tribe shaman and protector of the sacred Medicine Arrows, Arrow Keeper had recently experienced an epic vision. This vision foretold that the long-lost son of a great Cheyenne chief would return to his people—and lead them in one last great victory against their enemies. He would be known by the distinctive mark of the warrior, the same birthmark Arrow Keeper spotted buried past the youth's hairline: a mulberry-colored arrowhead.

Arrow Keeper used his influence to spare the youth's life. He also ordered that he be allowed to join the tribe and train with the junior warriors. This infuriated two braves especially: the fierce war leader, Black Elk, and his cunning younger cousin, Wolf Who Hunts Smiling.

Black Elk was jealous of the glances cast at the tall young stranger by Honey Eater, daughter of Chief Yellow Bear. And Wolf Who Hunts Smiling, proudly ambitious despite his youth, hated all whites without exception. This stranger was to him only a make-believe Cheyenne who wore white man's shoes, spoke the paleface tongue, and showed his emotions in his face like the woman-hearted white men.

Arrow Keeper buried the stranger's white name forever and gave him a new Cheyenne name: Touch the Sky. But he remained a white man's dog in the eyes of many in the tribe. At first humiliated at every turn, the determined youth eventually mastered the warrior arts. Slowly, as his coup stick filled with enemy scalps, he won the respect of more and more in the tribe.

But with each victory, deceiving appearances triumphed over reality, and the acceptance he so desperately craved eluded him. Worse, his hard-won victories left him with two especially fierce enemies outside the tribe: a Blackfoot called Sis-ki-dee and a Comanche named Big Tree.

As for Black Elk, at first he was hard but fair. When Touch the Sky rode off to save his white parents from outlaws, Honey Eater was convinced that he had deserted her and the tribe forever. She was forced to accept Black Elk's bride-price after her father crossed to the Land of Ghosts. But Touch the Sky returned.

Then, as it became clear to all that Honey Eater loved Touch the Sky only, Black Elk's jealousy drove him to join his younger cousin in plotting against Touch the Sky's life. Finally, Wolf who Hunts Smiling's treachery forced a crisis: Aiming at Touch the Sky in heavy fog, he killed Black Elk instead. Now Touch the Sky stands accused of the murder in the eyes of many.

Though it divided the tribe irrevocably, he and Honey Eater performed the squaw-taking ceremony and now have an infant son. Now his enemies want to kill the boy as well as the man. Touch the Sky has firm allies in his blood brother Little Horse, the youth Two Twists, and Tangle Hair. Arrow Keeper has mysteriously disappeared, and now Touch the Sky is the tribe shaman.

But a pretend shaman named Medicine Flute, backed by Touch the Sky's enemies, has challenged his authority. And Wolf Who Hunts Smiling has crossed his lance with those of Big Tree and Sis-kidee, establishing the formidable Renegade Nation on Wendigo Mountain. They now mean to kill Touch the Sky and all who swear allegiance to the eternal outsider.

Chapter One

"Brothers," young Two Twists said nervously, "have you heard?"

Four Cheyenne braves, the other three older than Two Twists though still in the flush of young manhood, sat filing arrow points in front of Two Twists's lodge. This spot commanded an excellent view of the entire camp. Only strangers to the Powder River village might comment on the odd way the four sat: back-to-back, covering the four directions with weapons in hand.

"Go beg your mother for a dug," Little Horse teased him. "You act like the young girls in their sewing lodge, whispering over a secret. Have we not ears, buck? The camp crier rode across the clearing screaming it."

"Dress in a shawl," Two Twists shot back, "if you know so much about the sewing lodge."

"Let it go, brother," Touch the Sky warned Little Horse when he started to rise. The tall warrior enjoyed a wide grin at his two friends' harmless scrapping. Two Twists had learned his swagger from Little Horse—learned it too well, to hear Little Horse complain about the "young tadpole's" disrespectful mouth.

Tangle Hair, the most levelheaded and least boastful of his friends, said, "Why is Gray Thunder calling all the people together? The Council of Forty will meet in two sleeps anyway."

Touch the Sky kept a good eye on a lone tipi that covered a small hummock between the wide Powder and the clan circles of camp. By custom the tribe's shaman, and Arrow Keeper, always kept his tipi a little distance separate from the others, as did the chieftains. But in Touch the Sky's case it had always been so during his life among the Cheyenne. He could claim no clan and thus join no circle.

"Gray Thunder has something to tell the entire tribe," Touch the Sky answered. "That is why. Women are forbidden from council for fear they will reveal important secrets. But Gray Thunder has always included them in matters not involving any secrets. Whatever he has to say will touch on the entire tribe."

His three loyal followers watched, silent, as Touch the Sky's dark eyes cut for a moment from the tipi toward the northwest. The Great Plains swept toward the horizon in rolling brown waves, past the Little Bighorn, the Bighorn, and into the Yellowstone country. But his friends knew Touch the Sky's gaze flew over all that and sought the unseen: the lone, fog-enshrouded tip of Wendigo

Mountain in the Sans Arcs range.

"Brother," Little Horse said, laying a half-filed flint chip in the grass, "before he left, Arrow Keeper taught us that the hand of the Day Maker is involved in all things. Have you had some sign concerning this message Chief Gray Thunder has for us?"

"It may be," Touch the Sky said carefully, "that I have and do not yet know it. Signs are often indirect and misunderstood. But no, Maiyun has not called me into His plans. However . . ."

He nodded toward Wendigo Mountain. "You all know the worst trouble in the world is there. Big Tree with perhaps twenty honed Comanche fighters, each with several mustangs on his string and each mustang trained like a white man's circus pony. Camped with him is Sis-ki-dee and his band of Blackfoot Contrary Warriors. We have trimmed their numbers, bucks. Yet still there may be forty seasoned warriors total up there."

Tangle Hair saw where his friend was drifting and said, "Forty up there and perhaps that many again right here in camp. For that is how many Bull Whips lick the hand of their master, Wolf Who Hunts Smiling."

"The pretend Cheyenne," Two Twists said bitterly and Touch the Sky laughed.

"No, little brother," he said, "that name is taken. You were too young to remember, but Wolf Who Hunts Smiling used to call me that because I showed up wearing white man's shoes. But never mind that. You heard Tangle Hair just now. Eighty braves total stand poised to take this camp at any time, and perhaps only half that many—many of

13

them unblooded warriors—are able to defend it. Gray Thunder does not know what to believe about the renegades on Wendigo Mountain. Understandably, he finds it difficult to believe that Wolf Who Hunts Smiling has made common cause with Cheyenne enemies."

"But we four know he has," Tangle Hair said.

"We four, yes, you speak straight-arrow. And a few of the Bow String troopers also believe this. However, though he is unsure about Wendigo Mountain, he knows our wily Wolf is hungry for power."

Two Twists nodded. "You think this meeting tonight will touch on the treachery here in camp?"

"I do," Touch the Sky said. "Gray Thunder is weary. And with just cause. Under incredible circumstances he has kept this tribe together. He can no longer go alone to the river to bathe without guards or his life is forfeit. It is not that he fears to lose his life. Not fear—he knows the law-ways on this matter, for they are clear as a blood spoor in new snow."

"Indeed," Little Horse said. "His death now could be the death of the tribe, for while the death of a war chief is expected, the death of a peace chief must be avenged. If not, the Medicine Arrows are stained past all cleansing and the tribe doomed."

Touch the Sky nodded. "Your thoughts fly with mine. He will ask that a new chief be appointed before his ten winters as head councillor are served. Only think. Once he makes the request, his enemies will lose animus to kill him."

"Yes," Tangle Hair said, catching on. "For they will be curious to see if one of their own gets the nod. Which indeed might happen, for their numbers have augmented."

"True," said Touch the Sky. "But how long will it be before it happens?"

The rest grinned, understanding. They were now in the Moon When the Geese Fly South. The short white days of the cold moons were not too far off although daylight hours still got warm enough to break a sweat. Gray Thunder could not officially step down until the Moon When the Green Grass Ripens, well after the final snowmelt.

"That wily old warrior," Little Horse said, admiration clear in his tone. "He lowers the odds of being killed, and thus the destruction of the tribe, until the short white days are well behind us. The tribe will be between dog and wolf, neither with a chief nor without. We will not be exactly safe here in this place where trouble sleeps, but the powder keg will be pushed back some from the flames."

"Buck," Touch the Sky said admiringly, "you are learning to speak like a Councillor. Had you perhaps five more winters behind you, I think I would know our next peace chief."

"Good job for *him*," Two Twists scoffed. "Look at his belly! Have you ever seen a chief without a belly?"

"Yes," Touch the Sky said. "His name is Gray Thunder. Forty-two winters behind him, and still he grips like an eagle. Do you know that he wore the Medicine Hat at the battle of Wolf Creek? He had only eighteen winters behind him. Your age now."

"At Wolf Creek?" Two Twists said with awe, for his own father had died there, covered in glory.

"At Wolf Creek, buck. He stood beside Arrow Keeper and they smeared their bodies in Comanche and Kiowa blood. To this day the Comanche tribe has a saying when a man is beaten past all hope: 'He has heard the Gray Thunder.'"

All four braves were silent, and Two Twists was only a little ashamed of the wet film over his eyes for a moment. For any Indian worth his clout knew that bravery was the hardest thing and must always be told.

"I hope his plan has some effect," Tangle Hair said. "I watched you playing with your son this morning, shaman. You sat in the grass and bounced him on your knee and laughed like a man with no cares in the world—and then, in an instant, fear came over your face like a shadow. You hustled Little Bear into your tipi. It should not be that way, Touch the Sky. It should not."

This touched the tall warrior deeply, and in his surprise he held silent. Tangle Hair was right, he had indeed done that with his son. For it had come to him like a bad memory—the fact that hostile braves surrounded him in his very camp, many of them eager to kill his new son before his eyes. The same son they rightly feared, for his sire was the bane of their miserable, treasonous existence—and if one oak bears acorns, all oaks will. His son would grow to fight them alongside his father, and that thought turned their livers white with fear.

"You are right," he finally told Tangle Hair. "It is not fair. We have endured, bucks. They have tried to kill each of us, my wife and my son. So far, though, we have fought them off only when they bridged the gap. Arrow Keeper was right, the only way to destroy a boil is to lance it."

He fell silent at the abrupt sight of a pony cresting the long ridge north of camp: a pure black mustang with a roached mane. For a moment, even at this distance, the rider's profile was clearly discernible: the lean, hungry, lupine form of Wolf Who Hunts Smiling.

And in that moment fear iced his veins, for Touch the Sky realized he had not seen when this traitor slipped away. Yet now he was returning from the direction of Wendigo Mountain. Assuming he had left after the camp crier spread word of the gathering tonight, he could not have reached the Sans Arcs and come back in one full day.

But the Renegade Nation on Wendigo Mountain kept word-bringers stationed close to this camp. It had also been a sunny day, and they had a mirror station set up. The Moccasin Telegraph could be as quick as the white man's singing wires.

The rest saw it, too.

"When Sister Sun has gone to her resting place," Touch the Sky said, "the crier will call us into the clearing. You have seen the Wolf just now, riding back from the wrong direction. Bucks, when you are called, show up rigged for battle. Do not shed Cheyenne blood in this camp lightly, but if they move against Gray Thunder, they forsake the name of Cheyenne and become enemies. Kill them!"

"You will take this little packet of trouble here," Touch the Sky said, hefting his son, "to your aunt's tipi. She will not be alone—three junior warriors selected by River of Winds himself will be strolling along with you two. Don't be fooled by their youth,

I know each of them. You can never be truly safe in this camp, but they will all three die before you or Little Bear are touched. As for your aunt, Sharp Nosed Woman is worth at least one seasoned brave."

Honey Eater nodded, thinking how close to death her aunt had come defending her from the half-breed knife expert called Widow Maker.

"And my own wife," Touch the Sky added, "can match her great beauty with even greater courage. She is the daughter of our greatest chief, and his fighting courage is in her. I pity any man who tries to harm our little pup around you."

"So do I," Honey Eater said, "if *you* see him do it."

"We may swap praise, pretty one with the white flowers in her hair. But talk must give over to action. There will be trouble tonight, sweet Honey Eater. Take the present Caleb Riley sent you."

Honey Eater nodded. Touch the Sky meant the two-shot muff gun he had brought her to defend herself while he was out from camp.

"I have poked it in my parfleche," she said, "along with my love for you, tall warrior. You have warned me, and I have listened. Now just remember, while it would please your enemies to kill your wife or child and watch the agony on your face, they are more interested in killing *you*. Do not spend so much worry looking out for us that you trip into your own grave."

Touch the Sky sent an admiring glance toward his wife. She sat near the center pole of the tipi, sewing new moccasins with double soles for the cold moons to come. Warm buffalo robes were heaped everywhere. As protection from their vulnerability at night, when light from the firepit outlined them through the worn buffalo hide tipi cover, Touch the Sky had ingeniously "wainscotted" the tipi wall with a thick layer of elkskins— when seated, no one could be spotted from outside.

"Woman," he said, "you give good kisses and good advice. I will take some of the former and remember the latter."

She needed no further encouragement to seek his mouth with hers. He had taught her this odd white man's custom of brushing the lips close, and like many late bloomers she soon outstripped her teacher in bold skill and curiosity.

But though both had playing on their minds, Little Bear abruptly bellowed his displeasure at being ignored. He had only one winter behind him but could summon the lung power of a warrior. It was his roar, so like a grizzly cub, that had earned him his name.

"He will sleep later," Honey Eater promised her husband, "and we will not."

The desire in her voice sparked his own. But just then he heard the sudden drumming of unshod hooves. His eyes met Honey Eater's.

"Both eyes to the sides, little one," he reminded her gently. "Maiyun grant us strength for that which is coming."

"Cheyenne people! You know the way it is as well as I. A good peace chief does not dictate to his people. He attempts to voice the will of the tribe. It may truly be said that a chief often wields less power than the lowest warrior. And yet, I know he receives far more than his just ration of worrying."

Gray Thunder stood before a huge clan fire that sent long orange spear-tips thrusting into the black folds of darkness around the camp. Touch the Sky stood near him, his Sharps brazenly tucked under his arm and no apology written in his face. His men, too, stood armed and ready.

But so were many of the Bull Whips, who now went everywhere in camp fully armed—as if ready for battle at a moment's notice.

"Shayiena people! It is my duty to determine the will of the tribe. But there is no longer any collective will. Only factions ready to leap like slavering dogs the moment opportunity shows itself. Look here!"

He nodded toward Touch the Sky and then, facing one edge of the gathering, Wolf Who Hunts Smiling.

"See it? Are we not the Northern Cheyenne? Or have I eaten peyote and forgotten that we are, after all, heathen Comanches, who kill each other in their own camp?"

"Father," Wolf Who Hunts Smiling said, his swift-as-minnow eyes watching everything at once, "the Bull Whips are this tribe's policemen. We have no choice but to sully the law-ways because *that* one"—he pointed at Touch the Sky—"is a spy who has made common cause with our enemies."

"Don't stop there," Touch the Sky called out. "List all my sins. Tell how I cause the yellow vomit and bad hunts, how I make the new colts lame and dry up seeds in women's wombs!"

"Hear this?" Medicine Flute screamed. "Hear it, people? This is no mocking! You know how a guilty man sometimes makes light of the very crime he is trying to conceal? This is the dark magic this contrary shaman has worked on this tribe. He knows spells to pray you into the ground. I am the one who moved a star with my big medicine!"

"You move your bowels, you mean," a Bow String soldier shouted. "Every time you move your mouth."

"Did our chief die?" Gray Thunder demanded, anger clear in his voice. "If not, let him speak."

Touch the Sky might have apologized any other time, for he truly respected this overburdened chief. But the nape of his neck was tingling—a sure sign that bad trouble loomed. He was distracted, watching for danger everywhere. He spotted Little Horse doing the same.

"Danger has this tribe firmly by the tail!" Gray Thunder cried. "My old men counsel peace while my young men cry for blood. You know how the Dog Soldier, Roman Nose, has divided our Southern Cheyenne cousins. I fear the same thing is happening to us."

Despite his worry Touch the Sky could not help grinning when he tried to spot Honey Eater and the baby. The junior warriors had ringed her in so tight he couldn't even see her. But one of the youths was trying to extricate his elk-tooth necklace from Little Bear's fist, and Touch the Sky almost laughed out loud. That child would run the Wendigo ragged.

The impulse to laugh died aborning, however, when his eyes met those of Wolf Who Hunts Smiling.

Often, of course, he had seen those eyes gloating at him. But the look now could be called only absolute triumph. This was a man who was convinced deep down in his soul that he would soon command the very wind.

"Death stalks this camp!" Gray Thunder declared. "The old grandmothers keen long into the night, for they sense the tragic end of our nation. They, too, see the young bucks ready to sully our sacred Medicine Arrows by shedding the blood of our own."

What good was it, Touch the Sky wondered, to be a shaman—one selected and trained by Arrow Keeper? Yes, Touch the Sky had used medicine to save his people. But now, when he only needed to divine a simple answer, why were shamanic skills so useless? What treachery was in store?

Wolf Who Hunts Smiling's eyes cut toward the long ridge north of camp. It was merely a shadowy mass now in the pale light of a three-quarter moon.

Were the renegades massed there? Touch the Sky wondered. Perhaps ready to attack at a signal from Wolf Who Hunts Smiling?

But no, that could not be it. The wind was from the north, and he noticed the dogs were silent. Cheyenne camps were famous for their noisy dogs, kept for protection. A large group of warriors strange to their noses would have set them off barking by now.

A large group . . . but one brave could easily hide there.

Touch the Sky's eyes shot to the chief, boldly outlined by the fire behind him, then to Wolf Who Hunts Smiling, his lupine eyes mocking the tall brave. Then he looked to the ridge again, just as a muzzle spat an orange line of flame.

Bloody Bones Canyon

Chief Gray Thunder folded toward the ground even before the sharp crack of the high-powered rifle split the camp. Touch the Sky was standing close enough to feel a warm gout of blood slap into his face when his leader's skull was shattered like a clay pot.

Chapter Two

Later, after the tense events of that night had played themselves out, Touch the Sky understood why the traitors did not move an eyeblink sooner than they did: Even though at least some of them knew what was coming, most had not been told that their chief was about to be sent under. Violence in a Cheyenne camp was rare. The shock of seeing it froze them as it did the rest, just long enough for the camp defenders to rally.

It was not just the unexpected noise of the rifle firing, nor the sight of Gray Thunder lying dead on the ground, his life's blood draining back into the soil. It was also the taunt which reached them from the darkness enfolding the ridge:

"Cheyenne people! I have murdered your chief! He died unclean without singing his death song! And I swear to the four directions I will also piss on his scaffold! His mother was a whore, as are all Cheyenne women! Now there is blood on your sacred arrows, and it was the Red Peril who put it there!"

This blasphemy was spoken in the mix of Cheyenne and Sioux words that had become a lingua franca on the Great Plains. The insane, mocking laughter that followed caused Touch the Sky's band to seek each other's eyes. Fear marked all their faces, for each knew who boasted of the name "Red Peril," given to him by angry whites: the renegade Sis-ki-dee. The crazy-brave Blackfoot warrior who had once terrorized the Bear Paw Mountains of the north country.

And then Touch the Sky leaped into action.

Unbeknownst to Wolf Who Hunts Smiling, Touch the Sky and his band and River of Winds, the leader of the loyal Bow String soldiers, had practiced for just this emergency.

"Bull Whips!" Wolf Who Hunts Smiling roared. "Make it rain blood!"

Even as he shouted, he raised his Colt rifle to draw a bead on Touch the Sky. But the Sharps roared first, and there was a loud metallic *thwap* before the Colt flew from Wolf Who Hunts Smiling's hands, propelled by a slug to the breech.

Little Horse knew his part, too, and it was important. For he was armed with one of the most formidable—and loudest—weapons in camp. That was critical because Cheyenne Law-ways strictly forbade bloodletting within camp.

His revolving four-barrel flintlock shotgun was equipped with a mizzen and pan for each barrel. Now he rotated and fired, rotated and fired, four powerful blasts of rock salt aimed directly at the empty Bull Whip lodge. One entire hide wall was shredded to strings. The effect on the tribe was paralyzing.

Meantime, Tangle Hair and Two Twists did their part. Tangle Hair leaped close to Medicine Flute, the pretend shaman who played the dog for Wolf Who Hunts Smiling. Medicine Flute squawked like a prairie chicken under a hoof when the muzzle of Tangle Hair's British trade rifle prodded into his belly.

Two Twists dealt the same treatment to Rough Feather, leader of the Bull Whips since Touch the Sky had killed Lone Bear.

With the leaders of the traitors effectively trapped, the Bow Strings leaped into action. River of Winds had instructed each of them to draw a bead on the closest Whip.

The three junior warriors around Honey Eater and her child showed remarkable discipline for such young braves. Not one of them deserted his position.

For a long moment, while a coyote yipped and barked from the direction of the sacred Paha Sapa or Black Hills, the camp was frozen as if in a dreadful painting.

Touch the Sky spoke first.

"Cheyenne people! Now your shaman and keeper of the arrows is speaking! Do you see it? Do you need more proof? There lies your chief, heels still scratching the dirt, and this wily wolf was ready to add more blood to the flow! It was planned! He murdered our chief!"

"Bent words!" Wolf Who Hunts Smiling roared

out. "I moved only to defend our camp from White Man Runs Him! And good thing too! They were poised to slaughter us, but we Whips moved too quickly!"

Touch the Sky slid his finger inside the trigger guard.

"Then why not *keep* moving, *Whip*, and my next bullet will not stop short of your vitals."

"You two jealous stags lock horns once again," an elder complained loudly. "Is every tragedy that befalls this tribe merely one more excuse for you two to raise your battle axes? Not one of you has demanded to know who this Red Peril is, and there lies the issue of his treachery."

"We both know who he is, father," Touch the Sky replied quietly, his eyes never once leaving Wolf Who Hunts Smiling.

"Indeed!" Little Horse called out. "And Wolf Who Hunts Smiling has made common cause with him. Count upon it, Cheyennes! He rode out earlier today to plan this murder with the Red Peril."

This triggered more shouts and accusations. But the tension was reduced somewhat when an old woman from the Sky Walker Clan began keening for their dead chief.

"The old grandmother is right," Touch the Sky shouted. "This is not the time or place to settle matters of council. Headmen! Once the new sun has risen and traveled the width of four lodge poles, assemble at the council lodge. I command this as your shaman and will brook no more discussion now. Now let the warriors cut short their hair in mourning, for we have lost a chief whose like will not easily be found."

*   *   *

With River of Winds and his Strings on tense guard, Touch the Sky sent Honey Eater and her guards back to their tipi. Then, as Uncle Moon clawed his way higher across the sky, he met with his band, all of them huddled in the common corral for protection.

"Brothers," said an infuriated Two Twists, "even now Sis-ki-dee is fleeing back to Wendigo Mountain, laughing at our misery. I want to ride after him."

"Just like you," Touch the Sky said, "to wade in fast before you measure the water. Take the bait now and die, for they are waiting along the trail for us. No. We will take action. But first we make sure this camp is secure. As secure as we can make it, at least. For truly it has been like a dog devouring its own tail for too long now."

The level-headed Tangle Hair nodded at this. Even Little Horse agreed. He said, "Our shaman was not born in the woods to be scared by an owl. He is in charge now until the Councillors meet. They have killed our chief. This is no time to ride off with blood in our eyes. The white heat of emotion is worth less than the cold touch of cunning."

"Yes," Tangle Hair said. "When we strike, it must be sure and fatal. Against Sis-ki-dee, we will be fortunate to receive even one chance."

Touch the Sky held silent as his companions kept using the word "we." He would soon have unpleasant news for them. For already he realized something: This time it must be "I," not "we." This terrible crime was done in hopes of luring him *and his band* away from camp.

Bloody Bones Canyon

Yes, he must take the bait, and soon. For no one else could hope to catch Sis-ki-dee. And he *must* be caught, for only blood atonement could cleanse the Medicine Arrows. But if Touch the Sky left this camp now, including his wife and child, then he would do so *only* if his men were here—for no finer warriors were ever born of woman.

But he would break the news tomorrow, after the emergency council.

"For this night, brothers," he said, "sleep on your weapons. Two Twists!"

"I have ears."

"And a stout heart, Double Braid. Keep an eye on our wily Wolf. I want to know if he rides out from camp again. Tangle Hair, relieve him when the night sentries change shifts. Brothers, we are up against it. Keep your backs to a tree, circle your sleeping robes with dried pods, try never to be alone. We have no chief, and our enemies know it. The attack might come at any time."

"Brothers, do you know?" Medicine Flute said, peeking past the entrance flap of his tipi. "Two Twists is watching us."

"Watching me, buck," Wolf Who Hunts Smiling corrected him. "His master has given him his orders, and he will die carrying them out. Truly he is as loyal to Touch the Sky as Swift Canoe here is to me."

"As you say," agreed Rough Feather, leader of the Bull Whips. "Except that Two Twists is cunning and resourceful, while our not-so-Swift Canoe here has to pretend he has the brains of a rabbit."

The other three laughed while Swift Canoe frowned.

"Why is this thing humorous?" he demanded. "Never have I pretended to be a rabbit. Why would I? It is not logical, and—"

More laughter drowned him out. The events of earlier this evening had the Whips in high spirits, especially Wolf Who Hunts Smiling. True, they had missed their first opportunity to seize this camp once and for all. But well begun was half done— Gray Thunder was dead!

Wolf Who Hunts Smiling stuffed his calumet with moist brown white-man's tobacco, his special celebration blend.

"Stout bucks," he declared, "never mind slow boat here. He was stringing his bow with both hands when Maiyun handed out brains. But *all* of us were stupid this day! We should be dancing around the fires even now, with fresh scalps dangling off our clouts.

"However, no need to wring our hands and wail like the old women outside. For I have realized something. It is *better* that we did not succeed in a bloody takeover. Better that we waited."

"Have you been visiting the Peyote soldiers?" Medicine Flute demanded. "How better? Woman Face and his band still walk the earth. I am still not declared shaman. River of Winds will mount his squaw this night, a living man still. How better?"

Medicine Flute was so agitated that he had neglected to play his highly prized flute made from the leg-bone of a slain enemy. He held it silent in his hands now—a favor to the rest, for the monotonous notes made ponies nervous and children cry.

"How better?" Wolf Who Hunts Smiling's lips curled away from his teeth. He was small, but muscular and quick and blessed with the killing instinct of a wolverine. "This is how. Only think, bone blower. Sis-ki-dee is on his way north, riding into treacherous country he knows as well as you know that little willow grove where you sleep all day while pretending to chant prayer songs."

"So?"

"So?" Rough Feather repeated, mocking Medicine Flute's tone. "Our Wolf is on the right trail here. Sis-ki-dee heads even now for territory he can turn into a bloody killing ground. And White Man Runs Him has no choice but to follow."

"It looks grim, truly," Medicine Flute conceded. "But bucks, how many times has that one crawled out from his own ashes?"

Wolf Who Hunts Smiling shrugged. "Far too many. And he may this time, too. But it will not matter."

Now all three stared at him, confused.

"It will not matter," Rough Feather repeated, "if Sis-ki-dee fails to kill him?"

"Not at all, brothers. For think. Even if our white man's dog survives, he will surely be gone for many sleeps. How long can his men survive without him? It does not matter if Woman Face rides back to this camp if it is not the same camp when he gets here."

Swift Canoe wrinkled his face in utter confusion. "First you say I have pretended to be a rabbit. Now we are going to a different camp?"

"Buck," Wolf Who Hunts Smiling said, "it is a good thing you can ride and shoot, or I would sic the camp dogs on you!"

31

"He means, Pea-Brain," said Rough Feather, "that we will control this camp yet not suffer the taint of a violent takeover. Wolf Who Hunts Smiling will be our chief. Two Twists, Little Horse, and Tangle Hair will be worm fodder. So will any Bow Strings who oppose us. The rest will join my Whips or leave these ranges forever."

Wolf Who Hunts Smiling nodded.

"You have seen it written in the sand, Rough Feather, as have I. Touch the Sky preaches cooperation with whites. But there can be no cooperation with those who would exterminate us. We must exterminate them! It only remains for us to combine our force with Sis-ki-dee's and Big Tree's. Then we will wage the war of all wars! White man's blood will turn the new grass red!

"Rough Feather is right. I could order Big Tree to swoop down on this camp with his men. But our Sioux cousins would witness this, word of our cooperation with Comanches and Kiowas would reach the rest of the Cheyenne bands. Let us see what comes out of the council. I may end up chief by a vote of the stones."

By now Medicine Flute had caught on and fully endorsed this plan of action.

"And even if you do not," he said, finally bringing his eerie instrument toward his lips again, "the tall one will be riding out, quite possibly to his death. While he is gone, the worm will turn."

32

Chapter Three

When he was a half sleep's ride north of the Cheyenne hunting grounds, the Blackfoot renegade named Sis-ki-dee reined in his big claybank.

The gelding was trained to stop when he felt the reins dangling. Sis-ki-dee dropped them now and grabbed a handful of coarse mane, swinging down off the right side—the Indian side. He knelt for a long time in the grass that was lately turning brown, three fingertips placed lightly on the ground.

After a long time, the smallpox-scarred face broke into a wide grin. No one trailing yet. No groups, anyway. Those fingertips could feel a prairie dog moving beyond the horizon.

Of course, he would feel nothing when *that* one came after him.

The grin faded and Sis-ki-dee stood back up. He

made no effort to hide in the generous moonwash, for he was convinced by now that no one was chasing him yet. Big brass rings dangled from slits in his ears, heavy copper brassards protected his upper arms from enemy lances and axes. His face, once ruggedly handsome, had fallen victim to the pox. In defiance of the long-haired tribe that had expelled him, he wore his hair cropped ragged and short. A .44 caliber North & Savage rifle in a buckskin sheath was lashed to his claybank's rigging.

"This place hears me!" he shouted from atop a long rise in the pine country near the Bighorn River. "My name is Sis-ki-dee! I would face down the Wendigo himself, for I swear it now: *I* am the only devil in this country! I have murdered the Cheyenne chief whose name may never be mentioned lest his soul cry out in torment! And I vow by the sun, the moon, and the earth I live on that I will kill the tall bear-caller, Touch the Sky. But before I steal his last breath, I mean to skin off his face and wear it over mine while he watches me!"

Yes, he would come. He would ride to the Land Beyond the Sun in search of the man who freed his chief from his soul. But he would not need to ride quite that far. He would meet his death in the Bear Paws, at the border of the Blackfoot Nation and the Land of the Grandmother—Montana and Canada to the Crooked Feet, as Sis-ki-dee called whiteskins because their feet slewed outward when they walked.

Sis-ki-dee untied the ten-inch bowie knife from his belt. It boasted pearl handles and deep blood gutters along the blade to facilitate rapid bleeding. He pushed the tip against the hard muscle of his left thigh until it dinted the flesh.

He commanded a band of some twenty battle-hardened warriors, although they had been twice that number before they clashed with Touch the Sky and his Cheyenne brothers. They had once roamed the rugged Bear Paw country. The vast stretch between the Dakota and Idaho Territories had been protected by only one fort, and for a long time Sis-ki-dee had ruled the roost. Seemingly at will, his contrary warriors had attacked freight caravans, stagecoaches, couriers, even small patrols of Crooked Feet soldiers.

Then, quick as a blink, the winds of fortune blew in another direction. A newly organized Citizens Committee for Public Safety sent out circular handbills announcing a two-hundred-dollar cash bounty for his scalp. He had narrowly escaped several attempts on his life before fleeing into the safer regions here in the south.

At first fortune had smiled on him and his renegades down here. The sly Cheyenne named Wolf Who Hunts Smiling devised a brilliant scheme to form a Renegade Nation, and now Sis-ki-dee and the Quohada Comanche Big Tree were encamped with their bands on Wendigo Mountain. But every attempt to amass wealth, destroy the white miners friendly to Touch the Sky, or attack the Powder River Cheyenne camp had been thwarted by the tall one.

Until now.

Sis-ki-dee pushed harder on the knife until the point broke the skin, drawing blood. He grinned wide, his face frightening with its insane, murderous trance-gaze. At the very moment Sis-ki-dee had been born, a wild-eyed black stallion had raced past the tipi. And true to this awful omen, he had grown up wild-eyed, crazy, and dangerous.

When he had only thirteen winters behind him, a Cheyenne had shot his pony out from under him. Calmly, before escaping, Sis-ki-dee had first removed the hair bridle. The bridle itself meant nothing, this was only to demonstrate his reckless courage. Only later did the elders realize it wasn't just courage. The young brave was crazy-by-thunder and thus incapable of fear. At eighteen he was censured by his tribal council for leading other young braves in unauthorized raids against the pony herds of neighboring tribes.

But true to his nickname, the Contrary Warrior, he continued to defy the elders until he forced them to banish him forever. Since then his undisputed reign of terror had earned him his second nickname, The Red Peril.

Yes, the tall one would soon be coming. And it would be the ride of his life, for Sis-ki-dee meant to ensure a harrowing journey north. But first he must return to Wendigo Mountain and prepare.

"This place hears me!" he shouted again. "My blood now for his blood later!"

Never once wincing, Sis-ki-dee flexed his right arm and drove the tip of his bowie in deep, gouging out a huge gobbet of his own meat and leaving it as a gift to the place.

"Brother," Little Horse said impatiently, "there is no pleasing you. You will neither dance nor go home. Things went well at council for us this day, but look at your face. Did your best pony die?"

"I wish it had, buck, for then I would know what to mourn."

"Why mourn at all?" Two Twists demanded. "Except for our dead leader? All Behind Him here is right—things went well at council, for once."

Tangle Hair snickered when Two Twists alluded to Little Horse's recent weight gain. Little Horse scowled, but did not get up from the firepit. He nodded toward Honey Eater and her baby. They sat just beyond the little council circle formed by the four braves here in Touch the Sky's lodge.

"Double Braid," he said sternly, "if that pretty woman and her son were not present, I would flay your soles. Ride herd on your tongue, mooncalf!"

"You two jays," Touch the Sky snapped. "Save your fighting fettle, for you will soon need it. As for the council. You both speak straight, things went well for us. Too well, and that troubles me. Nothing comes easy for us in this camp except trouble."

"You are too seasoned against adversity," Little Horse argued. "Thus you suspect any good fortune. Wolf Who Hunts Smiling's supporters tried to persuade the Headmen to vote him new chief. Medicine Flute spoke his most eloquent lies, but all of it was in vain."

Tangle Hair said, "Your speech in favor of River of Winds as our new peace chief was better. River of Winds is a man of honor, and this entire tribe knows it. The Headmen voted for him, and there it is. How can you suspect anything?"

"This was a wise choice," Two Twists added. "Even many Bull Whips like River of Winds. He speaks one way always and has never hidden in his tipi when his brothers were on the war path."

"And now," Little Horse said, "our camp will calm somewhat. Enough that we may ride out together in search of the murdering Sis-ki-dee."

Touch the Sky shook his head.

"Nothing," he said, "is what it appears to be. Did you not learn at least this much from Arrow Keeper's teachings? I say it again. Wolf Who Hunts Smiling and the Whips did not try very hard to seize power this morning. A man who does not seize one opportunity is counting on another."

"Do you mean," Little Horse said slowly, "they are waiting for you to ride out after Sis-ki-dee?"

Touch the Sky nodded. "What else? They know I have to go. And they think you three cannot hold this camp in my absence. But they are wrong, and my warriors will teach them the error of their ways."

Little Horse, Tangle Hair, and Two Twists exchanged long glances. All four braves, as was the custom among blooded warriors, had cropped their hair short to mourn Gray Thunder. Touch the Sky was right, and they saw it clearly now.

"But alone, buck?" Little Horse said. "Against the Red Peril?"

Touch the Sky nodded toward Honey Eater and his son. "Yes, alone. For *they* will be alone back here. And River of Winds—do you think some of the Whips would not vie for the 'honor' of killing him as Sis-ki-dee did our chief? My job will be hard, and I will not honey-coat the truth. But you three will have the greater task. This is a two-pronged attack. You are all that comes between this troubled camp and bloody treason."

"We will hold it," Tangle Hair said, glancing at

Honey Eater as she brushed Little Bear's thick black hair with the rough side of a buffalo tongue. Right after he was born, and before the rest of the tribe had seen him, Honey Eater honored these three braves by requesting their presence to view him first. The child owed his existence to their vigilance, and Touch the Sky himself felt no jealousy when saying his son had four fathers.

"We will hold it," Tangle Hair said again, "or fall on enemy bones trying."

"So now begins the fight," Big Tree said.

Sis-ki-dee nodded. The Sans Arc range towered all about them, rising above steep headlands and deep gorges scrubbed by white-water rivers. They stood near the summit of the highest peak of all, Wendigo Mountain. Halfway back down, an eerie belt of mist circled it, caused by steam escaping from an underground spring. Only one narrow slope provided access to this camp—the rest of the mountain was rendered inaccessible by sheer cliffs and massive heaps of scree or by fallen and broken rock.

"The fight begins. By now they are washing their chief for his scaffold and the Bear Caller is preparing to track me."

Sis-ki-dee was busy stuffing his silver-trimmed Mexican saddlebags full of jerked venison and dried fruit. Below them, built in the lee of the mountain, was a stronghold of curved wickiups surrounded by rifle pits and pointed breastworks. A common corral made of poles stood off to one side, housing a cluster of magnificent mustangs. Blackfoot and Comanche braves dotted the camp, many of them gambling or sharing skins of corn beer.

"We have failed so many times," Big Tree said, "that I should despair of ever seeing him sent under. But this time it will be different, I sense it. Contrary Warrior, you and I may kill each other yet. But I am the first brave to say it: If that tall Cheyenne shaman has a match on the plains, I am speaking to him now."

"You are indeed, Quohada," said the shrewd Blackfoot, watching his ally closely. "I notice a thing. Now that we and Wolf Who Hunts Smiling have devised this plan, you have a honeyed tongue for me. You believe I am already dead, do you not? That I was a fool to take on this Touch the Sky?"

Big Tree was huge for a Comanche, with the rugged face and bowlegged walk that marked his Southwest tribe. But those bowed legs meant nothing when he was mounted on a war pony. Big Tree could string and launch twenty arrows in the time it took a good bluecoat pony soldier to load and fire his carbine once.

"A fool?" he repeated. "Perhaps. You have challenged him to the limit this time. Now one of you must die. But as I said, I sense that the winds of fortune are about to shift in our favor. He must trail you into country that would baffle eagles, country you know well. He must also come past this place on his way after you. I mean to have a good shot at him myself. I owe him."

Big Tree paused for a moment, bitterness twisting his features. He and his best warriors had laid siege to the home of Touch the Sky's adopted paleface parents down in Bighorn Falls. And somehow the tall one had rallied a group of wranglers and homesteaders to a defense so deadly Big Tree had lost seven men.

Big Tree said, "And there is the other part of the plan. Wolf Who Hunts Smiling's part. Do not forget. Even if the Bear Caller eludes death up in the Bear Paws and death passing this spot, he will return to a camp filled with his enemies. His loyal band will be carrion bait. He cannot be two places at once. But we can."

Sis-ki-dee threw his head back and laughed his crazy laugh. He lifted a leather flap to show Big Tree what was in his right saddlebag.

Big Tree grinned. "You had one left?"

Sis-ki-dee nodded. Several moons ago the renegades had derailed a U.S. Army munitions train. They had made off with hand grenades, Requa rifle batteries, and powerful nitro-gel packs. One of the canvas-wrapped gel packs—marked DANGER! HIGHLY VOLATILE—was tucked into the saddlebag.

"I have the perfect place in mind. Count upon it, Quohada. This is only one of the surprises I have in mind for that tall licker of white crotches. This will be the ride of his life. Even before he gets well north, he must clear you and this. From here on out his life will be a hurting place!"

Chapter Four

"Little Horse," Touch the Sky said, "I would speak with you."

It was early, the old grandmothers having just fallen silent after singing the Song to the New Sun Rising. Touch the Sky waited patiently, for Cheyennes, like all Indians, were late sleepers when in camp. Soon the entrance flap was thrown back and Little Horse stepped out into the morning mist.

His friend had passed a rough night, and exhaustion showed in his young face. Little Horse thumbed a rough crumb of sleep from one eye. Nonetheless, he was famed for his bravado, and he lived up to it now.

"Is today a good day to die?" he demanded.

"Not for a Cheyenne," Touch the Sky replied. Both braves grinned for a moment with the camaraderie of men who have entered the belly of the beast together and emerged victorious.

"Buck," Touch the Sky greeted him. "My wife has fed me, but your belly is still empty. Start a fire in the tripod and fix yourself a juicy elk steak. I will fill a pipe."

Despite the urgency, despite the danger breathing down on them from all sides, custom was strong. When two braves had something important to discuss, they never went at it directly. Now, while Little Horse fried himself some meat in fat and bone marrow, they smoked to the four directions.

They spoke of inconsequential matters for some time. Then Touch the Sky laid the pipe down on the ground between them—the signal that serious talk could begin.

It was cooler in the mornings now, and Touch the Sky wore a leather shirt. Little Horse gaped when his friend removed a coyote-fur bag from under his shirt. He opened it to show Little Horse four stone-tipped arrows dyed bright blue and yellow and fletched with vermillion-dyed feathers.

"Brother, these have been hidden under my sleeping robes. But I am riding out soon. I do not know if"—Touch the Sky corrected himself— "when I might return. My tipi will stand empty while I am gone, for Honey Eater and Little Bear will be staying with Sharp Nosed Woman. I cannot jeopardize them by asking my wife to keep these. The best thing would be to give them to a grizzly to protect. The next best thing is you. Guard them with your life, brother. Keep them forever sweet and clean, for the fate of the arrows is the fate of the people."

Even now the two braves felt hostile eyes watching them. Touch the Sky left the bag in the grass between them.

"I will hide them later," Little Horse promised. "I know those arrows were given to us by the High Holy Ones. I also know they are stained as we speak. Sis-ki-dee has shed the blood of our chief all over them. But this stain can be cleansed. I will protect those shafts with my very life, for nothing else must befall them."

"*Ipewa*," Touch the Sky said. "Good. How fared it during the night?"

"Quiet, but tense, buck. No one left camp except the night sentries and herd guards. But there was much activity between the tipis of Wolf Who Hunts Smiling, Medicine Flute, and Rough Feather. Count upon it, they have treachery firmly by the tail. Our chief may not make it into the ground before this camp explodes."

Chief Gray Thunder had been wrapped and placed on a scaffold high in a secret forest known only to the Cheyennes. By custom he would be left up there until nothing but bones remained. Then the bones would be buried. This was considered a vulnerable time for the dead—and for the living they left behind.

"You and Tangle Hair and Two Twists will be up against it, brother. But when has it ever been different? Those foolish enough to cross their lances with mine will never go hungry, for my followers always sup full of trouble and fighting and suffering."

Little Horse detected the bitterness in his friend's tone.

"You speak straight," he said. "But why blame yourself for being a good man? Is it your fault that your enemies have not given you a moment's peace since we took you prisoner so many winters ago? Shaman, you are far more sinned against than sinning. Yes, I have supped full of trouble since declaring my loyalty to you. And I expect to eat more, and gladly! I have no plans to die in my tipi, buck, nor do I cherish dreams of an old age.

"Never mind this camp. Never mind your wife and child. We three are here, and we mean to stand and hold. *You* are the one with the task of all tasks. Shaman, *kill Sis-ki-dee!*"

Kill Sis-ki-dee he meant to do, or die himself in the attempt.

With a buffalo-hair lead line wrapped around his arm, Touch the Sky walked out to the common corral. The tribe was rich in good mustangs this season. Touch the Sky had four ponies on his string, all of them good horseflesh. And like all horses, each had its individual strengths and weaknesses.

He must pick the best one for this mission. Only the best. A man would not get two chances against the Red Peril. There could be no remounts for he must travel light and fast and make the smallest possible target.

There was his new bay, enjoying a roll in a pile of fresh manure. Reddish-brown with a black mane and tail, it would be a good night horse—hard to spot.

On the opposite side of the corral he spotted his little pinto, white with irregular-patterned colored areas. More of a risk at night, but his strongest animal, powerfully muscled.

And here, trotting up to nuzzle his shoulder, was his friendliest horse, a sorrel sprinkled with gray. A long-legged animal and thus a good snow pony if Sis-ki-dee went far north.

And finally his albino, all white with blue eyes.

The mare was somewhat proud and aloof, grazing off from the rest of the herd. Touch the Sky liked that quality in her, for indeed it reminded him of his own status here in camp: in it but not really *of* it.

In some ways, she was a bad choice. She was pure white, which made her a risk at night. Yet she could travel over snow and not be spotted by an eagle.

She was temperamental and might rebel on him at a critical time. It was not the Indian way to water-starve and beat horses when breaking them, as white men did. Indians did not like to spirit-break their horses, for they knew spirit could be the winning edge in battle. And while that spirit might work against him, it might also prove an advantage.

But in the end he chose the albino. For of all his ponies, she was the most bullet-wise. Indeed, she eluded them the way most horses eluded bears.

It took him some time to catch her and get the hackamore and rigging on. Then he led her back to his tipi, deserted now, for Honey Eater and the little one had already moved in with her Aunt Sharp Nosed Woman. Touch the Sky gathered up his single-shot, lever-action Sharps, and the rawhide pouch containing cardboard cartridges of powder and ball.

He rigged them to his pony and returned for his new Osage-wood bow and foxskin quiver full of new, fire-hardened arrows. He also grabbed his stone-headed war club and his red-streamered lance.

During all these preparations he felt Honey Eater's eyes on him. He glanced up, while tying down his lance, and saw her standing in the entrance to Sharp Nosed Woman's lodge. Even from here her beauty made his breath catch in his throat. A soft doeskin dress clung to the coltish lines of her body, and fresh white columbine petals adorned her hair.

As was his custom when riding out, they had already said their good-byes earlier. But now, as he grabbed double handfuls of coarse mane and prepared to swing up onto his pony, she crossed both wrists over her heart: Cheyenne sign-talk for love.

He let go of his pony's mane long enough to cross his own wrists over his heart. And then he saw Little Bear crawl out from the tipi behind Honey Eater, looking for his father. The little boy loosed a bearlike roar that made the albino start nervously.

Touch the Sky grinned proudly. But it also felt like fangs were tearing into his heart. There stood the family he loved with every fiber of his being— the reason he kept on fighting. And there was a good chance he would never see them again.

For a Cheyenne, Arrow Keeper had once told him, *the end of one battle only marks the beginning of the next.*

Hardening himself for whatever lay ahead, Touch the Sky swung up onto his pony and rode off to an uncertain fate.

"Bear Caller!"

He reined in and glanced toward the center of camp. Two Twists was on guard, watching Wolf Who Hunts Smiling. He raised his lance, and Touch the Sky lifted one fist. Then he spotted Tangle Hair and Little Horse, both watching him.

But they weren't the only ones. There, gathered in front of the Bull Whip lodge, were Wolf Who Hunts Smiling, Medicine Flute, and their fawning dogs. Even from here Touch the Sky could make out the wide, lupine grin on the Wolf's face. This time, that grin said, no medicine can save you or this tribe.

"Hii-ya!" Little Horse yipped. "Hii-ya! Hii-*ya!*"

Touch the Sky, too, sounded the war cry, and his pony laid back her ears, eager for the run.

For some time the Comanche renegade named Liver Eater had watched dust puffs on the horizon to the southeast. Now he called over his shoulder to the brave behind him.

"Big Tree! A rider approaches. A Cheyenne. His hair is cropped short, but I recognize his black feather."

"If it is a Cheyenne," Big Tree said confidently, "it is *the* Cheyenne. Duck down, buck! That one sees all around most men."

The two braves were ensconced in a pile of scree at the steep base of Wendigo Mountain. Sis-ki-dee had already headed north for the Bear Paws, marking a clear trail for Touch the Sky. But the Cheyenne, unless he wanted to waste valuable time, would have to ride past this spot. And Big Tree meant to have one more chance at killing him.

Big Tree possessed a brand-new Spencer six-shot carbine, stolen from a blue-bloused soldier. He crammed copper-jacketed rounds through the trap in the butt-plate. Then he lay the rifle down and grabbed a double handful of arrows from his quiver, laying them in the dirt at his feet.

Below them, the trail Touch the Sky was riding debouched into the open for perhaps two hundred yards. Once the Cheyenne hit the middle of that stretch, Big Tree meant to rain death on him.

"First the rifle," he told his lackey. "If my bullets fail to score, I will switch to arrows."

"May I shoot at him too?" Liver Eater asked.

Big Tree nodded. "There was a time when I would have told you no, leave him for me. But that time is past. All I want now is to see his guts feeding the carrion birds, and I care not who spills them."

Touch the Sky could not fail to realize he was approaching the shadow cast by Wendigo Mountain.

Defying all odds, he and his band had once scaled the back cliffs of that formidable bastion. They had reached the summit, bloodied and weary, and fought a ferocious battle with the renegades up there. And somehow, they had returned with their sacred Arrows, stolen by Sis-ki-dee.

The renegades were not fools. They must know he was approaching. Sis-ki-dee would not return here, for clearly he was a lure—he was meant to draw Touch the Sky out from camp and keep him out. Only if Sis-ki-dee continued to flee would Touch the Sky follow, and he would only flee north. But would the renegades let him pass? Or would they be unable to resist an attempt on his life?

He broke out into the clear and carefully scanned the rocky slopes all around him. There were too many places for a man to hide. Touch the Sky did not attempt to spot shapes—in such terrain, it was slight movements that gave an enemy away. Nor did he look only straight on. He also turned his head to watch from the sides of his eyes, for sometimes peripheral vision showed things a full-front view could not.

And it was that last precaution which showed it: a very slight line of movement, as if someone were laying a rifle on a rock to draw a bead on him.

The albino was moving along at a canter. Touch the Sky abruptly whacked her on the neck. At the same moment she lunged forward, a plume of rock dust shot up just to one side of them. A moment later the sound of the rifle shot reached them.

The albino instantly recognized the ricocheting whine of a bullet. She automatically started crow-hopping and other evasive movements even as she continued to tear forward, hooves flinging up great divots of earth.

One after the other, whip-cracking rifle shots sounded. Touch the Sky, his heart leaping into his throat, instinctively slid into the defensive riding position invented by Cheyennes: He slid far forward and down, gripping his pony's neck with his legs and bending forward so that only his head showed when he peered back.

He counted five shots, a couple of them whirring by so closely, they sounded like angry hornets. Another whacked into his kit.

As soon as the rifles fell silent, the air turned deadly with arrows.

Fwip! Fwip! Fwip!

One slid across his neck, the fletching burning his skin. Arrows smashed into the rocks and clattered all around him, so many it seemed at least five men must be shooting at him. But Touch the Sky did not look for targets or try to fight back. He had selected this pony for just this type of emergency, and now she justified his faith in her.

Thanks to her savvy and agility, not one of the bullets or arrows scored a serious hit. Relief surged into the tall Cheyenne when they finally made it to the cover of the glacial moraine heaped past the mountain.

No, Little Horse, he thought, today is not a good day to die. But there was also tonight, and then tomorrow. And out there in that northern vastness, Sis-ki-dee waited to kill him.

In the meantime, there was trouble behind, too, for death stalked his village.

Chapter Five

"Aunt," said Laughing Brook, "why do you do that?"

Honey Eater, lost deep in reverie, only slowly became fully aware that both her little niece and her own aunt, Sharp Nosed Woman, were staring at her.

"Do what, sweet love?" she asked.

"Pretend to be working on your bead shirt."

"Why, you little sprite! Pretend? Here it is in my hands. See? I am doing what is called the rickrack braid."

Laughing Brook solemnly shook her head. "No. You are thinking of Uncle Touch the Sky. Your eyes are not looking close."

Honey Eater flushed and Sharp Nosed Woman, who was rocking Little Bear's wicker cradle, snorted.

Bloody Bones Canyon

"Little one," Sharp Nosed Woman said to the youngest, keeping her voice down so as not to wake the sleeping child, "how many winters have you? Six?"

"Seven," Laughing Brook corrected her with great dignity.

"Oh, forgive me, *old lady*. Whether it is six or seven, you have too many brains for a woman. Trouble will be the ridge you camp on. But you are right. This aunt of yours, she will ruin that shirt yet if she does not force her thoughts to fly back home."

The two women and the little girl sat in clear view of the rest of the camp, following Touch the Sky's instructions. Although the immediate tension had lessened somewhat recently, to the greatly troubled Honey Eater, menace seemed to mark the very air.

Bow String soldiers, like the Bull Whips, were authorized to patrol the camp with weapons, and they did. Night and day. They worked in pairs, brother covering brother in this camp divided against itself.

Honey Eater felt reassured when she glanced past the council lodge. There sat Two Twists, showing some junior warriors how to clean a rifle. Indians had a bad habit of thinking guns worked by "medicine" and did not require care. But Touch the Sky, indoctrinated by white men, had taught his band deep respect for proper cleaning and care of weapons. His men would not lose a battle due to stoppages in a filthy rifle, as did too many red men.

However, what reassured Honey Eater were his constant glances in her direction. And there, down the slope and past the Wolverine Clan circle, sat

Little Horse, his revolving-barrel shotgun tucked under one arm. Wolf Who Hunts Smiling would not shake him unless he somehow turned invisible. Tangle Hair was likewise sticking to the Bull Whip leader Rough Feather, yet also managing to watch her.

Any one of these three loyal braves would die for her or the child. They were especially nervous, she knew, because they had failed once before despite their best intentions. The renegades, assisted by the criminal bluecoat Seth Carlson, had lured them from camp and she and Little Bear had been stolen by the murderous half-breed Widow Maker. They had sworn on their lives it would not happen again.

"Child," she said gently to Laughing Brook. "What is it?"

The little girl had turned pale. Now she pointed across the clearing. Honey Eater glanced where she pointed and felt her skin go clammy: Medicine Flute was coming up from the river, his close-cropped hair still soaked from bathing.

"He scares me," Laughing Brook said defiantly. "When he blows his bone flute, the little babies cry. Some girls in the Crooked Lance Clan told me a thing. They say dead fish choke the river after he bathes. You heard him tell me he was going to send Rawhead to get me!"

Rawhead was the most feared bogey among Cheyenne children. Laughing Brook had burst out sobbing when Medicine Flute told her that lie. Honey Eater flushed with anger now as she thought about it.

"He has no power, child," Sharp Nosed Woman assured the little one. "Only Maiyun can send anybody to get you, and He loves little children. He made the days and gave them to the Cheyenne people."

"This man only pretends to have power," Honey Eater said. "But his medicine is all tricks."

For a long moment Medicine Flute stared at Honey Eater, his heavy-lidded eyes and fleshy, girlish mouth making her shiver with disgust. But beyond the filthy lust Honey Eater saw there—for his loins were on fire for her—she read something else: his gloating assurance that *this* time her husband was worm fodder.

"Ahh, the little one sleeps?" he called over. "If he wakes up crying, his mother will slip him a breast. I would like to see one myself."

He lifted his leg-bone flute to his lips and piped a high, shrill note. Little Bear woke instantly, and though he was not one to show fright, now his round little face contorted with fear. He howled as if red ants were after him.

"Shush, Aunt!" Honey Eater said quietly when Sharp Nosed Woman started to scream at the pretend shaman. She scooped her son out of the cradle and began patting the small of his back, calming him. "Leave it alone. This just now was nothing. They have something terrible planned," she added, thinking out loud.

"What?" said Laughing Brook. The sensitive child was alerted by her aunt's tone.

"Nothing, child. Do me a big favor? Run see Coyote Woman and tell her I need some red thread."

"You have plenty of red thread," Sharp Nosed Woman said after the child tore off, her braid flying out behind her.

"I know," Honey Eater answered. Little Bear, calm now that Medicine Flute was gone, had quieted. Honey Eater laid him back in his cradle. "I wanted to talk with you alone."

"Why, niece?"

"Aunt, do you not see it?

"See what, pretty one? The future, the past, or the back of my eyelids? Speak words I can pick up and examine."

"The danger in this camp," Honey Eater said. "Something is about to happen."

"Yes, I do see it. Have I not eyes? This looks like a camp of heathen Comanches, all armed to kill their own fathers."

"Yes, of course. That. But I mean something else. They intend to move soon, to seize the village. Wolf Who Hunts Smiling and the Whips have a plan. That is why they are so content to be quiet right now and not make trouble. Did you not see how smug Medicine Flute looks? As if his future greatness is assured."

Sharp Nosed Woman shrugged. "You may be right, you may be wrong. So? Things are the way they are with men. It is none of our doing. They have no use for us. We are not welcome at their councils, only when the rut-need is on them. We cannot concern ourselves with their plans."

"Yes, we can," Honey Eater said firmly. "Medicine Flute has already told me his plans for *me* if the Whips seize power. He means to take his dirty pleasure, then leave me out on the prairie for any Bull Whip who will have me. What about the rest of the women and children? What about Laughing

Brook? And you say we cannot concern ourselves with their plans?"

Sharp Nosed Woman lay her beadwork aside for a moment.

"What can we do except get ourselves killed?"

"I don't know, Aunt. We can't answer that until we try. But look there. Little Horse, Tangle Hair, and Two Twists have sworn their lives and honor to protect us. This time they cannot do it alone, I fear. We must look sharp, Aunt, and be ready to help. Never mind the danger. Either we fight and *perhaps* survive, or we play the 'good' woman and die worse than dogs!"

After the ambush attempt by Big Tree, Touch the Sky began a stretch of quiet, uneventful riding toward the Yellowstone.

The trail was easy enough, for Sis-ki-dee made no effort to hide his tracks. Indeed, he took time now and then to mock his Cheyenne enemy. Once, rounding a butte, Touch the Sky found crow feathers—symbolizing the Cheyenne people—scattered in a circle made by animal blood. The message was unmistakable: The Shaiyena nation was on the verge of destruction.

At least the country was open here, vast, rolling brown plains that changed only when nearing rivers. It was not good ambush country, and Touch the Sky relaxed somewhat.

On the other hand, Sis-ki-dee was a contrary warrior. He took great pride in doing the unexpected. Recalling this, Touch the Sky realized the ambush could come at any time. Most especially when it seemed safest.

Touch the Sky made no camps, stopping only to water and graze his albino. He ate while riding, chewing pemmican and fruit from his legging sash. Wherever he grabbed a bit of sleep, he made no fires. This was not to ensure that he eluded Sis-ki-dee, for that one was far out ahead of him and heading north. He was now riding through Crow Country, and the Crow tribe were enemies of the Cheyennes.

It would take him perhaps two sleeps to cross the Crow hunting ranges. If he continued due north, he would reach the land of the Assiniboin; if he veered east, he would be in Hidatsa country near the Knife River. But he meant to bear northwest, straight into the heart of Blackfoot country.

The albino's pride was working in his favor. She would not, like other ponies, rebel at hard use. Cheyenne ponies were forced to get used to rugged ways to ensure their survival in a cold, harsh land where grass could be scarce to nonexistent during the short white days. Where a white man's pony would demand grain, a Cheyenne pony would rip the bark off a cottonwood; while cavalry ponies starved after winter storms, Cheyenne ponies broke through the ice crust to gnaw the frozen, brown grass beneath it.

What lay ahead Touch the Sky could not say. He knew only that it would be a bloody, terrible business—for him and for those he loved. This was confirmed anew when he debouched from a deep cutbank south of the Yellowstone.

Sis-ki-dee had left a sign for him. And seeing it made the fine hairs on his nape rise up stiff.

In the dying grass to the right of the trail was a

circle of rocks about ten hands wide. The grass had been burned out, leaving charred earth. On the scorched ground was a rock painted red and black, a dead mouse with a ragged hole in its breast, and crude stick tracings depicting a bear and a cub. Entrails had been spread on these last.

Touch the Sky, under Arrow Keeper's expert eye, had become adept at thinking in and reading symbols. The charred earth, of course, symbolized the destruction of the Cheyenne homeland. Red and black were the colors of blood and death. The "lowly" mouse was in fact highly prized by Cheyennes, and this dead mouse symbolized him, Touch the Sky. The ragged hole in the mouse's chest was where Sis-ki-dee ripped out its heart—as he meant to rip out Touch the Sky's, perhaps even taking a bite of it while it still pumped. For by ingesting an enemy's heart, some tribes taught, you also ingested his courage.

All that was disturbing enough, and proof of Sis-ki-dee's insane mind. But when he translated the stick drawings covered with real entrails, Touch the Sky felt his palms throbbing. What was a bear, after all, but a "honey eater"? And the cub, of course, was a "little bear."

His wife and son. And each step he took behind this murdering, crazy-by-thunder renegade carried him that much farther from those who needed him most.

Chapter Six

Unlike most Plains Indians, who were easily awed by spiritual matters, Sis-ki-dee had no patience for supernatural foolishness. His philosophy was simple and direct: A true man kept his weapons to hand, for he feared no god but the gun.

And *this*, he told himself, his eyes aglitter with the sickness in his soul.

He held the tight, canvas-covered pack carefully in both hands. It was about the size of a white man's Bible, and, he carried it with the care accorded a religious object. The pack was labeled in bold yellow letters: NITROGLYCERIN GEL. CAUTION: EXTREMELY VOLATILE. HANDLE CAREFULLY. EXCESSIVE HEAT OR SHARP, CONCUSSIVE CONTACT WILL DETONATE.

Ghost warrior, they called the tall Cheyenne. And Bear Caller. But Sis-ki-dee knew how it was with these clever fakes. Their deft tricks were taken for magic by gullible souls. He had heard several stories about this "great battle" up in the north country of his own birth, where Touch the Sky supposedly turned Bluecoat bullets into sand. But who had claimed to see it besides those who followed him?

No. You could lay a feather on a rock and call it a bed, but only a fool would sleep on it. And only a fool would believe this Cheyenne was a medicine man.

The brass rings dangling from his ears glinted in the sun. Sis-ki-dee, following easy trails, had just crossed the Yellowstone at a wide gravel ford. He could still see the river from here, winding down below and behind him in the westering sun.

This place where he stood now, deep in Crow Indian country, was known as Two Moon Ridge. It rose suddenly beyond the tableland of the river and paralleled the trail below for some distance. The steep ridge, almost a cliff, crowded the trail, massive piles of scree and glacial moraine heaped along its length.

Sis-ki-dee bent down to tuck the nitro pack in a natural opening among a pile of boulders that rose as high as a paleface lodge. It was a straight drop from here to the trail below. Above this spot was a comfortable place where he could watch the trail and also get a clear shot at this nitro.

One bullet, while the "bear caller" was riding below, and Sis-ki-dee could unleash enough rocks to rival the Front Range of the Great Stony Mountains, known as the Rockies to hair faces.

This was the way Sis-ki-dee liked things to be:

treacherous and dangerous, with worthy enemies locking horns in a bloody fight to the death. But he also sensed a thing. He sensed that time was running out. The game had been good. It must, however, draw to its close.

And more than anything else in the world, he wanted this tall Cheyenne sent over forever. Touch the Sky had once, in front of the Red Peril's entire band, defeated him in a Blackfoot Death Hug: a knife fight with the two opponents' free arms bound together at the wrists. Not only did Touch the Sky win the fight, he humiliated Sis-ki-dee by knocking him unconscious but not killing him—saying, in effect, that he was on a level with soft-brains and women, unworthy of killing.

And that, Sis-ki-dee told himself now, had been a serious mistake. For it was always better to kill a man outright than to humiliate him, to leave him alive to seek revenge.

For a long moment he glanced toward the southeast, knowing his enemy was coming even though he could not see him yet. Then he went to take up his position above, waiting for the moment when one shot would send the entire world crashing down on Touch the Sky.

"Count upon it," Wolf Who Hunts Smiling assured his companions. "The worm is finally turning. Woman Face has taken the bait. Not only will we soon fly our streamers over this camp, but we will do so without shedding a drop of blood."

He, Medicine Flute, Rough Feather, and Swift Canoe sat in a council circle within Wolf Who Hunts Smiling's tipi. A pipe of kinnikinnick had made the rounds, and now the sweet smell of red willow bark hung thick in the air.

Rough Feather started to speak, then glanced irritably at Medicine Flute.

"Stop that infernal piping, you skinny jay!"

Swift Canoe snickered at this rebuke while Medicine Flute scowled. But Rough Feather was no brave to fool with, and Medicine Flute reluctantly lowered his leg-bone flute.

"You should show more respect," Medicine Flute complained, "for this tribe's new shaman and keeper of the arrows."

Rough Feather laughed. "Shaman! Stuff all your 'medicine' into a quiver, and you would have an empty quiver!"

However, he quickly returned to the meat of the matter, turning to Wolf Who Hunts Smiling.

"How," Rough Feather demanded, "can you guarantee a bloodless takeover? And indeed, why is that so important? We have attempted attacks in the past."

"We have. And failed. For once, let us try the easy way across the river. Only think. If we rebel as Roman Nose has, we will be outlawed by the other nine bands of the Cheyenne. Yes, we can now force the tribe. But our Sioux cousins, too, will turn their back on us, even count us among their enemies."

By now Rough Feather was nodding. "I see how your thoughts drift. With so many former allies turned enemy, how can we hope to launch a combined attack against the white soldiers and settlers and drive them from our ranges?"

Wolf Who Hunts Smiling thumped Rough Feather on the chest, a rare sign of respect. "This is why you will go far in our new Renegade Nation, Rough Feather. Unlike Not-So-Swift Canoe here, you can take a small piece and finish the entire painting. A violent takeover leaves us covering our flanks when we should be mounting an attack in force. But a peaceful change of power, especially in our present state, would not be taken amiss."

Rough Feather nodded. "It rings solid enough. It is good strategy. But why are you so sure we can do it?"

Wolf Who Hunts Smiling's furtive, swift-darting eyes did not slow down even in the relative safety of his lodge. Always, even in sleep, those eyes stayed in motion, watching for the ever-expected attack. And often enough, it came.

"Buck, those who would seize the reins of power cannot afford womanly hand-wringing and debates about the various causes of the winds. A man with a good plan stands halfway to the finish. This next council will be ours, for we will rehearse our every move. We will select good speakers from among the Whips. We will coach them in advance on what to say. In the most persuasive and reasonable manner, we will force the leadership issue to a vote of the stones."

Medicine Flute, who had been pouting since Rough Feather insulted him, could not resist a grin of admiration for his leader.

"Brother, this is excellent! River of Winds has no legal claim to the title of chief. Our votes outnumber theirs. It is unusual to force a vote of the stones, but not unprecedented. We will put you up for chief. And once the stones have spoken, no man may question them."

"As you say. And once we have the reins, the pony either obeys or tastes the whip. The Whips will confiscate Bow String weapons until further notice. We will move quickly, smoothly, methodically. We can have the Headmen bent to our will before anyone sees the game."

All of this had been too many words, too quickly delivered, for Swift Canoe to follow. Now he frowned in confusion.

"What game, brothers?" he asked. "And must we whip our ponies? Mine becomes very sulky if I—"

"Cheyenne," Wolf Who Hunts Smiling warned him, "there are times when your soft brain fails to amuse me. This is one of them. By Maiyun, close your feeding-hole now or your guts will string my next bow."

He turned back to the other two. "As for Woman Face, he would be better off following the Wendigo himself into the middle of a blue-blouse fort than trail Sis-ki-dee into the bear paws. But even if he eludes death once again, he will return to *my* camp."

"Our camp," Medicine Flute reminded him. "And his woman is now *our* woman."

Rough Feather found this worthy of a deep-chested laugh. "You squaw-boy! My nephew has twelve winters, and his chest is thicker than yours. Honey Eater is now *ours?* And would you mate with a grizzly, too? Never mind what *he* would do to any man who touched his wife. She will open you up from rump to throat."

This left Medicine Flute outraged, for his sense of dignity far outstripped any muscles or courage to back it.

Wolf Who Hunts Smiling found all of this amusing. Rough Feather was right, of course. Medicine Flute was worthless as a man. But he was quite adept at faking the shaman traits, and among superstitious Indians, men such as he were quite useful.

"Put it away, brothers," Wolf Who Hunts Smiling said, pouring oil on the waters. "A needle and a thread are two very different objects, are they not? Yet both together are required for sewing. You, Rough Feather, and you, Medicine Flute, are two very different braves. But like needle and thread, you will combine to sew up this tribe."

All Indians respected a good speaker, and this was impressive indeed. Medicine Flute calmed down, especially when Rough Feather graciously said, "After all, our bone blower here is quite adept at putting the trance glaze over his eyes."

"Brothers, I have ever been loyal," Swift Canoe put in. "But this talk of needles and threads—I refuse to stoop to such womanly work as sewing."

This time Wolf Who Hunts Smiling joined his other two friends in a howl of laughter at Swift Canoe's stupidity. The Wolf broke out a bladder bag of corn beer and passed it around.

"Brothers," he told them, "Honey Eater is not the issue. Seizing this camp is. One world at a time! For now, Rough Feather, let us list the Whips who speak well, then send word to them. The councillors meet in one sleep."

A twig snapped outside the tipi, and Wolf Who Hunts Smiling instantly had his knife in hand. He threw back the entrance flap and stepped out into the coppery light of a westering sun.

Bloody Bones Canyon

No one was nearby. But there, as usual since Touch the Sky rode out, was one of his men: young Two Twists, perhaps a double stone's throw away. But that twig snapping—Two Twist's chest was heaving, as if he'd just made a great exertion. Such as running away from the back of the tipi, where he might have been eavesdroping. From now on, Wolf Who Hunts Smiling resolved, he would keep a sentry around his tipi.

"You, Double Braid!" he called. "You are a good fighter. But your loyalty to White Man Runs Him will send you to your scaffold. Cross your lance with mine, and I will make you a councillor. Otherwise, die hard with your master, white man's dog!"

Well to the northwest of his troubled camp, Touch the Sky continued to cut sign on the one man he feared most in the world yet must kill to appease the law-ways of his people.

The Yellowstone was low this late in the season, and fording had been child's play. Crossing Crow country, however, was not. His tribe was not currently engaged in a bleeding war with them, and hostilities had abated somewhat of late. The two tribes had begun to make common cause against the blue blouses. Nonetheless, old hostilities rankled deep on both sides. Crow warriors were highly territorial and did not deal kindly with trespassers.

He had no intention of fighting, so he played a constant game of avoidance. Touch the Sky excelled at finding cover where none seemed to exist. He could move rapidly, yet mainly unseen, by searching out cutbanks, runoff seams, hidden defiles; by sticking to shadow masses, he cut down on danger from his own shadow.

However, it was one thing to elude Crow Indians, another to escape the vigilant eye of the Red Peril.

If Sis-ki-dee chose, he could play with him. He had done it before. The Blackfoot defied natural laws somehow, moving soundlessly where a mouse would make noise. Touch the Sky had once spent the worst night of his existence trapped on a derailed train with that mad man. He would gut a child as quickly as he would a rabbit, and nothing pleased him more than to drive his enemies wild with fear before killing them.

No, he would not resist the chance to kill his enemy along the way. For one thing, Sis-ki-dee was wanted up in the Bear Paw country. Why not make the kill sooner and turn back before risking himself?

This last thought made Touch the Sky rein in and carefully check the terrain around him. He had been through this way only twice before. But he knew that long ridge looming up over him on the right was called Two Moon Ridge because it took so long to ride its length.

Sis-ki-dee could hide anywhere along its length.

True, another inner voice answered the first, but what do you do? Hold your pony to a walk and scour every inch, hoping to see the sun glint on Sis-ki-dee's brassards? And move so slow you give him a perfect target?

Or do you do *this*?

Whack!

"Hii-ya! Hii-*ya!*"

The albino, surprised by the sudden slap of his

hand on her rump, bolted forward. She was tired but far from exhausted and welcomed this challenge from her master. She laid back her ears and lowered her mass even as she quickened her pace.

The rapid beat of unshod hooves echoed off the high, steep ridge that flew by to Touch the Sky's right. Sis-ki-dee was a good marksman, as his killing of Gray Thunder had dramatically proven. So Touch the Sky did not assume he was safe—just that he was making it more difficult for the Red Peril to let daylight into his soul with a bullet.

Sure enough, just as he pounded through a long turn, a shot rang out. The bullet did not come anywhere near him. But before he could rejoice, there was a noise so loud that he was sure the world was exploding apart. One moment the ridge was towering over his right shoulder. An eyeblink later, it was crumbling down all around him.

The albino nickered in terror as something huge and heavy smashed into Touch the Sky and he saw the light bleed from the sky before his world went dark.

Chapter Seven

"You did well, young brother," Little Horse assured Two Twists. "Sneaking up to the tipi was foolish. Had a Whip spotted you, he would have killed you on the spot. But I do not wish your foolishness undone. Now we know their plan."

"We do," Tangle Hair said bitterly. "But it is like knowing a drought is coming. It will come nonetheless."

Little Horse nodded. "True enough. Yet, one may also store water and trick it. Forewarned is forearmed."

The three braves crouched in the common corral to the north of camp. This allowed a good view of the village while affording a measure of security. Below them life went on, if not normally. All three youths recalled the better days when hope told a flattering tale for the Powder River Cheyennes.

Bloody Bones Canyon

In better times this village had raised its shout to the hills. All night long the clan and lodge fires had sent their orange spear tips into the sky. Younger braves bet goods on foot and pony races. Older braves sneaked behind their lodges to drink weak corn beer and recite their coups to any who cared to listen. The women hovered near the cooking pits to roast elk and antelope meat for the upcoming dance feasts. The children had run wild everywhere, playing at taking scalps and counting coups. Stirred up by all the activity, the camp dogs had howled and barked as if moon crazy.

And now, the troubled faces of these three young warriors said silently, only look.

With Touch the Sky gone, more menace than ever seemed to mark the air. Though hated beyond measure by his enemies, they also feared and respected him. His presence had been the best policeman of all. As soon as Sister Sun went to her rest, the women and children took to their lodges. No one had time to gamble or race or wrestle—all braves with twelve or more winters either packed a battle rig or kept one handy.

"Less than one sleep now until the council," Tangle Hair warned them. "Time is a bird, brothers, and well into his flight."

Little Horse nodded. "Straight words. Our enemies keep up the strut now with a new confidence. Have you noticed it? It is as if, in their minds, Touch the Sky is already dead."

Two Twists said, "Any other man foolish enough to trail Sis-ki-dee would be by now. But our shaman is a match for him, brothers."

"We know that," Little Horse said. "But our enemies, respect him though they must, know the facts. This Sis-ki-dee. True it is, he has failed several times to kill Touch the Sky. But equally true, Touch the Sky has failed to kill him. This fires our enemies here in camp with a bottomless confidence. They will move swiftly and well at council. However, as Two Twists reports, their plan *must* take place at council. Am I right?"

His friends watched him closely, recognizing the shrewd glint in his eyes.

"You usually are, All Behind Him," Two Twists said, "though I chafe to admit it. Less chatter and more matter. What are you saying?"

"I am saying, insolent pup, that if there is no council, there will be no takeover. Not tomorrow."

Tangle Hair snorted, sounding remarkably like one of the ponies around them. "So? Just because River of Winds is in danger does not mean he will cancel a meeting of the Headmen. He means to be a good chief, and good chiefs do not lightly deny the right to council."

"Of course not, Stone Skull. But what if the Medicine Hat is missing?"

His friends instantly saw the brilliance of this. By strict decree of the law-ways, no council could be held unless the sacred Medicine Hat was worn by the Keeper of the Hat. When Cheyennes entered battle, one brave selected for his courage and fighting skill always wore the Medicine Hat. And indeed, braves wearing this fur hat topped by buffalo horns had performed great deeds under its influence.

"Who is the Keeper?" Two Twists demanded.

"High Road of the Antelope Eaters Clan," said Little Horse.

Tangle Hair frowned. "No brave to fool with."

"Nor will we," Little Horse said. "But we *will* get that hat. Bucks, we are the best among the tribe known as the Fighting Cheyenne. Even now, Touch the Sky is fighting the battle of battles to cleanse our arrows. Let his bravery set the mark for our own!

"Now, enough womanly whining. Quickly, let us hone our plan for seizing that hat. I know where to hide it once we get it—the same place where I have hidden the Medicine Arrows. Either we fox High Road, or this camp goes to the Whips and we will be lucky to ride out with our scalps."

For an unknown period of time Touch the Sky lay motionless, his mind playing cat-and-mouse with awareness. His body alternated between dull throbbing and fiery pain. Consciousness became a narrow place surrounded by patches of dense fog. His mind passed from fog to clarity and back in an endless pattern.

His uncle the moon took over the sky, the long night passed, and still the pain drove lances deep into his flesh, crushed him, pinned him like a physical force. However, with his body trapped and helpless, his mind was freed as it once had been on the Spirit Path at Medicine Lake. And once again images from his past were sprung from memory.

He glimpsed the unshaven, long-jawed face of Hiram Steele's wrangler Boone Wilson, again saw him unsheathing his bowie while Kristen Steele screamed a warning. He flexed another memory muscle, and now he saw the smug, overbearing sneer of Seth Carlson, the Bluecoat lieutenant who helped Steele ruin the Hanchon's mercantile business.

There was more—images flying past like quick geese in a windstorm. He saw his own people torturing him over fire; he saw the white whiskey trader again slaughtering white trappers and making the killings look "Indian"; he saw himself on the verge of death in the lethal grip of the Cherokee called Mankiller; he saw himself leading his terrified but determined band up the steep cliffs of Wendigo Mountain; he saw those given up for dead, victims of deadly mountain fever, rising from their death beds after he and a white medicine man combined their skills to save the dying Cheyennes.

And mixed in with all the fragments from his past were glimpses from his vision quest at Medicine Lake, glances stolen from the future. He saw his people freezing far to the north in the Land of the Grandmother, saw Cheyenne blood staining the snow. The screams of the dying ponies were even more hideous than the death cries of the Shaiyena.

It all led to one huge battle. And then the warrior leading the entire Cheyenne nation in its last great stand turned to utter the war cry, and Touch the Sky recognized the face under the long war bonnet as himself.

But the pain, always the pain . . .

Sis-ki-dee waited, patient as a wolf behind a buffalo herd, content to take his prize when the danger was past. For he knew this one. Knew how he had crawled out of his ashes so many times before.

Uncle Moon took over the sky, and still Sis-ki-dee waited. He gnawed a leathery chunk of venison and washed it down with good river water from the bull's-eye canteen he had stolen from a soldier. Now and then he pinched a louse from his scalp and crunched it between his strong white teeth.

His eyes seldom left the jumbled mass of rocks and boulders blocking the trail below him. It had been a perfect shot, his bullet detonating the nitro with devastating effect. Touch the Sky's pure white pony had somehow clambered to safety, the most amazing animal Sis-ki-dee had ever seen. He meant to catch her up if she showed herself.

But clearly, he had seen a good chunk of mountain fall straight down on the hapless Cheyenne.

Nonetheless, he meant to wait even longer. He was in no hurry. Not where that one was concerned. Either he was dead, or he would be soon.

Sis-ki-dee smiled as he thought of it. If nothing else, in just a few sleeps he would know for certain—the smell would tell him.

By day the sacred Cheyenne Medicine Hat usually rested on a pole in front of the dance or soldier lodge of the current keeper. While always highly protected when it was among outsiders, the hat was not at risk among the people themselves. Why would anyone take it? Such an act would ensure severe punishment and, even worse—bad medicine for the offender.

After sunset, however, the Medicine Hat was always found near the keeper. This was the custom, not so much to protect it as to ensure the keeper would have it to hand in case of surprise attack.

High Road, who would be keeper until the next Spring Dance, was a warrior in his prime who had distinguished himself at the Tongue River battle. He had lost his wife in the recent outbreak of mountain fever, the second good woman he had lost to deadly plagues. Now, until he sent the gift of ponies to another woman's clan, he was alone and fending for himself.

The eve before the first council with River of Winds as chief was brisk, with a steady, cold wind down off the northern ice. Shivering in a thin leather shirt, High Road knelt at the cooking tripod outside his tipi. He quickly built a fire with the ends of the sticks poked into the fire and lit first, not the middle, which was the white man's style and, of course, wasteful, like most things white men did out here.

He heard voices approaching and glanced up.

"I tell you this thing right now," Two Twists was saying to Tangle Hair, "I have *never* tasted coffee this good! Those beans we get from the Mexicans, they are often bitter. But this is rich white man's coffee. The finest."

"As you say, buck," Tangle Hair said. "And they are simply giving it away, first come, first served. It will not last long."

"You two," High Road called out. "What will not last long?"

"This coffee, buck," Two Twists answered him, proffering his pottery mug. "Two Bow Strings, Bear Hump, and Hawk in Flight were caught taking meat rations. Their troop leader has assessed a punishment. They had some fine coffee they were hoarding. Now they have brewed it for all comers."

"With sugar and the new white man's canned milk," Tangle Hair put in.

"With sugar and milk?" High Road repeated. A can of this would be tasty indeed with his evening meal. "Where are they, stout braves?"

Two Twists pointed. Indeed, the braves in question knelt in plain view, stirring the coffee now. High Road could smell it from here, fragrant beyond belief.

He never gave a thought to the Medicine Hat, nor should he have. The odds of an attack in the short time it would take him to fill his can and return were so remote as to be ridiculous.

It was a moment's work to duck into his lodge and obtain the old tin can he had found along a trail and used for drinking. He was only twenty paces from his tipi when Two Twists, flashing a triumphant grin at his companion, ducked inside.

Touch the Sky wasn't really sure when he regained consciousness.

It did not come to him all at once, but in slow accretions. As awareness grew sharper, so did his pain. Finally, when he was fully aware, the pain made him wish he was not.

He remembered it now, remembered why he was still alive. There had been an explosion—Sis-ki-dee's work, of course. Then the slide. He was still alive now for one reason only: Even as the weight of a displaced ridge smashed him to the ground, he had managed to roll into a slight runoff fissure. It was just deep enough to lower him beneath the lethal mass. But now he was trapped, battered and bruised, beneath uncountable tons of rock.

He could move his arms and his legs, but only mere inches and only one at a time. And always with incredible effort. He could not rise more than an inch or two, not even enough to turn over onto his back.

How long had he been trapped here? He wasn't sure. Thirst had swollen his tongue until it felt like a dry husk in his mouth, and hunger gnawed at his belly. But he had no water and could not get at the food in his legging sash. He assumed the albino mare was dead, smashed to a paste and his weapons and water with her.

Not that it mattered. He was trapped as surely as the insects calcified in stones along the banks of the rivers.

And where was Sis-ki-dee? That hardly mattered, either. For whether he had lingered around here or ridden on to the land of the short white days, he had finally made good on the boast of his life. He had defeated, finally and forever, his worst enemy in all the world.

Was it even true, Sis-ki-dee dared to finally ask. Was it? Had he finally killed the Bear Caller?

Elation had begun to hum in his blood. Nevertheless, he moved with extraordinary caution as he climbed carefully among the rocks he had unleashed on top of his enemy.

His rifle was unsheathed and lay across the crook of his arm, capped and ready. Again and again he studied all the openings, looking for signs of a body. But then, any man trapped under all of that would not be easy to spot.

He glanced up toward the trail, reckoning the spot where Touch the Sky had been knocked off. That way, he was able to guess the approximate place where he must be trapped.

He sighted a cleft in the mass of rubble. He aimed his North & Savage into it and fired off a round. The bullet splatted against rock deep beneath him. He fired several more rounds into what might be openings leading to his enemy.

"Mighty Bear Caller!" he shouted. "Will you summon grizzly bears to move these rocks? I only look for you now because I would still like to skin off your face and wear it. You white liver. If you are alive to hear this, believe it also, I will top your woman and kill your baby in front of her."

A sudden skittering noise behind him made Sis-ki-dee's heart turn over. But with battle-honed reflexes, he whirled. There was the white mare, watching him from a defile.

Sis-ki-dee made the mistake of aiming at a pony who was savvy about rifles and bullets. She sprang just as he fired, and the bullet whanged into the rocks around her.

"There lies your pony, Woman Face!" he lied. "The blood is truly beautiful against her snow-white coat."

But now Sis-ki-dee was tiring of this child's game. He was convinced that Touch the Sky was feeding worms. Nonetheless, he would take no chances. One or all of his band still might follow. He would resume his flight into the north country until things had calmed somewhat.

But first, one last touch. Just to make Touch the Sky's world a hurting place in the rare event that he was trapped alive under those rocks.

Sis-ki-dee took the time to drag plenty of damp, green wood up from the river. He took crumbled bark from his saddlebag, for he always kept emergency kindling at hand, and set a huge pile of the wood ablaze. It poured thick black smoke into the cracks and openings between the fallen rocks.

A smudge fire. Useful for keeping off insects at night near water. Or for slowly, miserably suffocating a man trapped in an enclosed space.

Chapter Eight

"This High Road," Wolf Who Hunts Smiling said in a dangerously quiet tone. "Who knows him? What manner of brave is he?"

"A good warrior," Rough Feather said promptly. "I tried to talk him into bringing his gift to the Bull Whip Troop. But he will take the initiation with neither the Whips nor the Strings."

"In this," Medicine Flute put in sarcastically, "he is like Woman Face. I have noticed a thing. There are more and more independent braves in this camp since Touch the Sky refused to join a soldier society."

"Soon," Wolf Who Hunts Smiling swore, "there will be none. Every brave who has trained for a warrior will fly the black and red streamers of a Bull Whip from his pony's tail."

Rough Feather said, "Despite what has happened, wily Wolf, I say it now and this place hears me: High Road was foxed! He is not one of ours. Nor is he a brave to cooperate easily. So I cannot ask him this thing. But count upon it. He did *not* conspire to lose the Medicine Hat."

"I believe you," Wolf Who Hunts Smiling said. "I know his Antelope Eater Clan. A shirker or two in the lot, but no cowards or fools. You speak straight-arrow, buck, he was duped. It was Little Horse, Two Twists, and Tangle Hair, the lick-spittles of Touch the Sky. It has the duplicitous hand of their master all over it."

Wolf Who Hunts Smiling scowled and fell silent, brooding as he gazed out over the greenish-brown quiltwork of the plains. He, Medicine Flute, Swift Canoe, and Rough Feather had ridden well out from camp to parley. Clearly there were too many ears in camp.

"There can be no council without that Medicine Hat," he said. "All of you know me. You have smoked the common pipe with me. Now have ears for my words, for they are the kind you can put in your sash and examine later."

Wolf Who Hunts Smiling suddenly stopped speaking and stared at Swift Canoe. This feckless brave had swung down from his pony and was walking away toward a clump of hawthorn bushes.

"Buck," Wolf Who Hunts Smiling demanded, "have you eaten loco weed? Where are you going? I am speaking, fool!"

Swift Canoe looked confused, his most common expression.

"Brother, you just said we should examine your

words later. So I am going to make water. Why do you—?"

Rough Feather and Medicine Flute laughed so hard they were forced to slide down from their ponies.

"Slow Boat," Rough Feather jeered, "your brain is smaller than the hole you piss through. Your mother should have drowned you at birth."

"She did," Medicine Flute said promptly. "But she forgot the afterbirth."

This sent Rough Feather and Medicine Flute into new gales of mirth while Swift Canoe stood uncertainly, dancing from one foot to the other in his urgency to void his bladder.

Wolf Who Hunts Smiling frowned so deeply that his eyebrows touched. "This," he said with cold, quiet rage, "is why we are not already the lords and masters of our own domain. Look at you three fools! Am I done speaking?"

Now they were all silent. Something made one of the ponies sneeze.

"Now have ears," Wolf Who Hunts Smiling commanded. "I tried. You all know it. My plan was to take this camp at council, without bloodshed. Our enemies have made that impossible by stealing the Medicine Hat. So be it. Things are the way they are."

In an eyeblink his obsidian knife was in his hand, and then flying through the air. It thwacked into a cottonwood tree and stuck deep in the gnarled bark.

"I tried the peace road," he repeated. "The next move will be violent."

"Simply attack the Strings?" Rough Feather said

doubtfully. "I think we can win, but brother, think on this thing. It would be a bloody victory, one in name only, for more of us would be killed than would survive."

"We will attack," Wolf Who Hunts Smiling confirmed. "But only after we have sent a word-bringer to Wendigo Mountain. Never mind discretion, we will simply get a nasty job behind us. Big Tree is waiting with some of the best warriors in the Red Nation. When his men join the attack, victory will be swift and certain."

Despite being pinned almost motionless, Touch the Sky found room to flinch when Sis-ki-dee fired his first round.

He had assumed his enemy was gone by now. The Cheyenne had no way of knowing if the renegade could glimpse him from above. There were tiny air shafts, clearly, for he had not suffocated yet, though the air was certainly close and stale. And there was some light filtering through. Enough that he could barely discern height of day from total darkness.

None of the bullets came lethally close. But it was an eerie sensation to a red warrior, this being completely trapped while under fire. Over and over again, relentlessly, Cheyenne braves practiced a pattern: Fire, and then immediately move to a new position. Always stay in motion, and never let your enemy pin you down.

As the bullets splatted and ricocheted, he had felt the depths of his helplessness.

And of course, because it was Sis-ki-dee, there had been the inevitable taunts about topping

Touch the Sky's woman. Sis-ki-dee, like his comrades on Wendigo Mountain, scorned the rigid code of the warrior and its demand that an enemy be killed with dignity. Killing was a miserable disappointment to them if they did not first see their victims humiliated in the final moments of their lives.

Touch the Sky had far more important problems than Sis-ki-dee's childish vulgarity. He had assumed his albino mare was dead by now, so fury lanced through him when he heard her approach, then Sis-ki-dee's shot.

"There lies your pony, Woman Face! The blood is truly beautiful against her snow-white coat."

Touch the Sky hoped it was a lie. If not, she had died as a result of her loyalty and training. For Cheyenne ponies were trained to return to the last spot where they were with their masters.

Then came a trouble bigger than all these: the thick black smoke that licked into the tiny air shafts of the rockslide, devouring the precious oxygen.

At first Touch the Sky had been aware only of a stinging heat growing behind his eyelids. Then he started to feel lightheaded. At the same time he noticed, dimly, a familiar sound. It took him only a few heartbeats to recognize it as the crackle of green brush burning.

A smudge fire!

Panic was utterly useless, yet for a moment panic he did. Once again a warrior trained to skirmish on the move was trapped against a new danger. He could not hope to grab this one and throw it to the ground. That helplessness seemed to sever his will from his nerve, and cold sweat erupted all over him.

His lungs filled with acrid, burning air that felt like thousands of tiny ants biting him from the inside. He wanted nothing more in the world than to get up and run to open air, yet he could not even roll over. Oh, Maiyun, he needed to breathe, he needed to get out, he must!

The stern, calming voice of Arrow Keeper came to him then from the hinterland of memory, words the old shaman had spoken to him when he almost gave up during his grueling initiation rites:

If you cannot endure this small thing here today, little brother, how will you stand and hold when the war cry sounds? When the blood of your people stains the earth?

Those words had shamed and rallied him then, and they did so now.

Because it was late in the fall moons, and he was riding north, Touch the Sky had worn his leather shirt. Now, as the bitter smoke stole the air from his nostrils, he turned his face into his shirt and pulled it tight around his head.

This trapped a little air and, at the same time, protected him from the smoke. He forced himself to pretend he was hiding under water, something he had done often to avoid enemies. This helped him to slow his heart rate and breathing dramatically.

Willing himself almost to the verge of unconsciousness, he breathed very slowly and shallowly. Gradually, the acrid smoke dissipated. Finally, the grateful brave felt a tiny lick of cool, clear air from above the pile of scree. The fire had gone out.

Bloody Bones Canyon

But surviving that smoke and hearing Arrow Keeper speak to him renewed Touch the Sky's determination. The light was at its best right now, so it must be the middle of the day or so. That light allowed him to peer out ahead a little and survey the scree through a small opening. And as he looked, he recalled Caleb Riley telling him about something called the "angle of repose."

Caleb, younger brother of Touch the Sky's blue-coat friend Tom Riley, was a miner in the nearby Sans Arcs range. Touch the Sky had served as pathfinder when Caleb's Far West Mining Company needed to build a railroad spurline through the mountains. And watching them blast out slopes and level grades, Touch the Sky had learned some useful information.

The "angle of repose" referred to the critical balance point where any massed rocks or scree would lose the fight with gravity and start sliding. There was always one linchpin rock, Caleb had explained—disturb it, and the whole mass was in motion.

Touch the Sky couldn't be sure now. No doubt only hope made him even think it possible. But that chunk of oval basalt just out ahead of him—it looked like a good candidate to be the linchpin. And if it wasn't, so what? Better to die attempting a plan than bemoaning his fate.

But could he reach it? There was only one way to find out.

He had no idea how long it took him to work his knife out of its sheath and slowly force it toward the rock. His muscles cried out at the exertion and the terrible cramping. Many times he stopped and closed his eyes tight, for sweat poured into them and burned them over and over.

But eventually, rewarding his long patience and effort, his blade was wedged securely under one end of the rock. He could not yet budge it, of course. It was only the tiniest ray of hope. But he seized it anyway.

Slowly, methodically, he began digging at the gravel and crushed scree under the rock.

"Take this to Wendigo Mountain," Wolf Who Hunts Smiling said to one of his favorite Bull Whip soldiers, Ties the Rope. "Give it directly to the Comanche called Big Tree. Do you know that one, brother?"

"Does a fit buck rut?" Ties the Rope answered. "Of course I know that one. On foot he is as ungainly as a drunk bear. But put him on a pony, and death is the name that is on him. A big man, for a Comanche, and even uglier than most of them. And he wears a bone breastplate."

Wolf Who Hunts Smiling nodded. He handed Ties the Rope a small round piece of black marble.

"No message?" Ties the Rope said.

"This is it, buck. He will know what it means. But have ears, Cheyenne. Our enemies are all around us, lurking, watching. I picked you because you are a good man to ride the river with. And your horses are the best. Pick your fastest, and ride hard. Do this, and I swear by the four directions, you will be a far more important man than you ever dreamed."

Ties the Rope placed the marble in his parfleche and then cut out his best pony, a ginger with a roached mane. He tied the Bull Whip streamers to her tail, stuffed his legging sash with pemmican and dried fruit, and rigged his weapons to his pony. He left camp by the north trail, watching carefully all around him. He was convinced that no one followed him.

Nor would anyone catch him. Not on *this* speed demon.

"Hi-ya!" he shouted, lashing the ginger with his sisal quirt.

She laid back her ears, eager for the run.

Little Horse and Tangle Hair did not need to follow Ties the Rope. They merely had to wait for him.

Touch the Sky had urged them to creative thinking to win this battle. And it was Little Horse again who saw the right course. They must not play catch up, but cut off. Logic told him what Wolf Who Hunts Smiling's next move would be: He would send for Big Tree and his killers.

So well before Wolf Who Hunts Smiling's word-bringer rode out, the two Cheyennes went on ahead and found a good spot where the trail passed through scrub pine on both sides. Tangle Hair took one side, Little Horse the other. They laid a strong buffalo-hair rope across the trail. Each brave held one end in readiness.

When Ties the Rope came flying down that slope, his pony blowing foam, the two braves timed it perfectly. Just before he reached the rope, each brave snubbed his end quickly around a tree. The ginger hit it so hard, and so fast, the rope snapped. But not before the hapless pony crashed to the ground hard, throwing Ties the Rope.

The brave bounced hard into a tree and lay

stunned. His pony, less fortunate, broke her right front leg so hard that splinters of bone penetrated the ginger coat. Grim-faced at the task, for no tribe loved ponies more than Cheyennes, Tangle Hair asked Maiyun's forgiveness even as he shot a bullet into the poor animal's head, ending its suffering.

"Quickly, Cheyenne!" Little Horse urged him. The stout warrior was untying the black and red streamers from the dead pony's tail. "Catch up your pony and tie these to his tail. I would go in your place, but Big Tree knows me too well even with my hair cut short. Are you sure you know the message? Repeat it."

Tangle Hair did.

Little Horse grinned. "If it works, none dare call it foolish. I am not easy, sending you to that mountain of death. But Two Twists is back in camp alone and I must return before they move. May the High Holy Ones ride with you, Tangle Hair. And remember, wipe that decency off your face. You are now a Bull Whip!"

Chapter Nine

Weakness fueled his desperation as Touch the Sky raced against time to somehow move that rock. The same chunk of basalt he hoped against hope was the critical linchpin, the one rock upon which the rest of the mass hinged.

He had made some progress, although at great cost to his endurance. Once or twice he thought he felt, through the handle of his knife, the rock shifting a bit as he dug and gouged under it. But this angle was terrible. He could barely get the tip of his knife under the rock, much less put any real pressure on it.

He had thanked Maiyun for a sudden rain squall and the trickles which flowed down to him. But a few swallows of water only made him want more. Nor could he eat to sustain his strength— he could not quite force his hand low enough to get at his legging sash, where his rations were.

Dark, dizzying waves of exhaustion flowed over him. His arm would tremble, drop. Once he dropped the knife and it almost skittered out of his reach. His heart had leaped up into his throat, for that weapon-turned-tool was his last—albeit very slim—hope.

Daylight gave way to darkness, and now and then, exhausted, he snatched a few moments of uneasy sleep. But his slumber was filled with disturbing images: a full moon turned blood red; a snake devouring its own tail; and most disturbing of all, the moon and the sun appearing in the sky at the same time—the sign, according to ancient Cheyenne lore, that the People would be chased back through a hole in the earth and doomed to the nether regions.

Each time, he woke from his sleep physically stronger and determined anew to escape this early grave.

But nothing in his warrior's experience had prepared him for this gruelling, agonizing struggle—one that reduced weapons to a mockery and rendered fighting skill useless.

He gouged harder, wincing at the effort, and then fate dealt him a crushing blow: His obsidian blade snapped off clean.

Oh, by all the high holy ones, what had he done?

Frustration, fear, anger, and exhaustion suddenly welled up from deep inside him. Touch the Sky shouted—a loud, powerful bellow that sounded the depths of his misery. And then he slumped, defeated.

So this was to be the ultimate fate of the warrior

whose destiny had been told in a medicine vision? To die slowly and miserably under a pile of scree? No one would find him in time. He would not be expected back at camp for some time, nor would anyone—except his enemies—be riding this way soon.

He had always been one to fight. When the bullets were gone, he emptied his quiver; when arrows gave out, he went to his lance and war club and blade. And when they were gone, he had fought on with rocks and raw courage.

But how could he fight this enemy now? And when it came time to sing his death song, he would not miss the bitter irony: *Nothing lasts long,* began the simple death chant, *only the earth and the mountains.*

The same earth and mountains that would soon kill him.

"Liver Eater!" Big Tree called out to his favorite toady. "Bring us a pipe! A word-bringer's arrival is always an important occasion."

Tangle Hair cursed his luck. The long ride up the steep front slope of Wendigo Mountain had been uneventful. The renegade sentries knew the Bull Whip streamers and recognized him as an ally. He had hoped to deliver his message quickly and leave. But no such luck. Big Tree and his men had been drinking heavily. Now the Comanche terror was in an expansive mood.

It would go hard when he finally asked for, and received, his unexpected message. But Tangle Hair knew the custom. Big Tree was the leader, and only when he decided it was time would they turn to business.

Big Tree had grown quite adept at the Cheyenne language. When he couldn't think of the right word, he switched to Sioux or used a sign.

"So?" he demanded. "You are one of Wolf Who Hunts Smiling's Bull Whips?"

This galled Tangle Hair. But what else was there for it?

"One of his best," he boasted.

Big Tree grinned, eyeing his heavy coup stick. "I see you have counted coup many times. You Cheyenne men are no cowards. But you place too great a value on this childish game of touching your enemy before you kill him. No one touched your mighty Chief Gray Thunder before his brains were blown out all over his people."

Big Tree roared so hard with laughter that he doubled over, clutching his own knees for support. Rage swelled within Tangle Hair, but he contained it in time.

Unfortunately, habit was strong. Big Tree's sacrilegious pronunciation of Gray Thunder's name made Tangle Hair automatically make the cutoff sign for speaking of the dead. Big Tree roared again.

"Oh, poor little Cheyenne maiden! Does she fear the dead? Gray Thunder was a dung heap. May that white-livered coward wander in the Forest of Tears forever."

This blasphemy surpassed anything Tangle Hair had ever witnessed. The shock of it held him silent.

Now Big Tree, sobered somewhat, narrowed his eyes suspiciously, staring at Tangle Hair.

"I could swear I know you, all right. But not from seeing you with the Bull Whips. It was when I tried to steal the white children from the iron horse. I could swear it was you I saw up on that ridge, covering Touch the Sky."

"If I ever cover *that* one," Tangle Hair scoffed, "it will be with dirt in a shallow grave. We all look alike to you now because our heads are shorn. We Whips did not want to cut short our hair for this weak old woman Sis-ki-dee killed. But we must keep up the appearance of loyalty."

Big Tree considered that and seemed to find it reasonable.

"Never mind your silly superstitions," he said, finally growing impatient. "Give me the message from Wolf Who Hunts Smiling."

Tangle Hair pronounced it. Big Tree stared as if he had just announced that horses could fly.

"Say it again," he commanded. "For surely I did not hear you straight."

"You heard me, Big Tree. Many soldiers are coming to Wendigo Mountain. An entire regiment. They mean to slaughter every Indian here. You must flee to your homeland at once."

In his delirium, Touch the Sky dreamed of ponies.

They raced, wild and free, in the high-country meadows where the grass grew up to their bellies. Bays, buckskins, calicos, chestnuts, claybanks, duns, pintos, piebalds, roans, every imaginable color and marking. He saw himself in the midst of them, bouncing with practiced ease on the back of his albino as she joined her wild kind and carried him high into the snow-capped mountains.

So much space and air and freedom to move. Unlike this prison that would soon become his tomb.

The horses nickered and snorted. Somehow the sound seemed even more real than the images, so much closer.

Pain shot spear-tips into him, and the dream images faded. But the nickering continued, close by, insistent.

Touch the Sky blinked and woke to cold, aching pain.

Hunger had knotted his stomach tight as a fist. Thirst worked at him again, and he slipped a few pebbles into his mouth to work up some moisture.

The dream. All those ponies . . . they had sounded so real.

Then he heard it, no dream this time, the familiar, ringing impact of unshod hooves on rock.

Again the insistent whinnying, and instantly he recognized his albino. Sis-ki-dee had lied to taunt him. She was still alive!

Few Indians ever named dogs or ponies. But they did teach them distinctive whistles to identify and locate their masters in the dark. He worked up what moisture he could and managed his whistle, a little fluting warble like a wren.

Immediately the clattering clamor of hooves grew closer as the albino ascended the slope of scree.

Touch the Sky whistled again, hope putting more volume into it this time.

She came closer, and now he could glimpse her through a chink in the scree. Still a stone's throw too far down. If only he could get her close enough to step on that rock—and if only it *was* indeed the linchpin. . . .

He whistled again. Desperation prodded him to add in English, "You'll get the oat bag, sweetheart, if you come just a little bit higher."

As if someone were indeed shaking an oat bag to tempt her, the mare took one, two, three steps, then stopped.

Frustration welled up in Touch the Sky. She was still perhaps a hand's width away from that oval chunk of basalt.

"A rubdown with sage clumps," Touch the Sky tossed into the hotchpot. "And then green ears of corn!"

The albino surged up, her right foreleg planted squarely on the basalt. Touch the Sky's heart sank when she heaved up effortlessly, the rock sustaining her weight. He had been wrong, hope had driven him to delusion—that was not the linchpin.

"All right, then!" he shouted out boldly to the world, defeated but never destroyed. "We will see how a Cheyenne can die!"

His last word was still reverberating in his ears when the albino snorted in fright. A heartbeat later Touch the Sky pressed himself as flat as he could while the whole world seemed to shift and heave around him.

But when the dust cleared, his pony stood unharmed just below him. And Touch the Sky was free to fight on.

Ties the Rope fell silent and turned his battered face away in shame. His collision with the tree had left one cheek bruised the color of grapes.

"So that explains it. All of us have been here waiting, sleeping on our weapons, for Big Tree's men to swoop down on this camp. Then the sentries come to me with the report that Big Tree's Comanches have fled to the south, driving their ponies before them."

Wolf Who Hunts Smiling fell silent. It was bad enough when he flew into a rage, but when he spoke quietly like this, even the boldest warriors quavered. Once, all of a sudden while in a mood like this, he had beaten a pony to death with a war club.

"The failure is not yours, Ties the Rope," the wily plotter said. The braves gathered around him in the Bull Whip lodge breathed a sigh of relief. Ties the Rope was a good man, and they had feared for his life when Wolf Who Hunts Smiling and Rough Feather heard of this failure.

"The failure was all of ours," Medicine Flute spoke out. "For we should have killed White Man Runs Him when we first had him prisoner over fire. See what happens when only one smallpox blanket slips into a camp?"

Swift Canoe turned pale.

"What is it, rabbit brain?" Wolf Who Hunts Smiling demanded.

"Brothers," Swift Canoe said uncertainly. "I, too, want to see the Whips in control of this village. But this is going too far, this business with a smallpox blanket. What if some of us die?"

This caused a hoot of derision throughout the lodge.

"This one," Rough Feather said, "was stringing

his bow with both hands when Maiyun passed out brains."

This broke the tension, but not the troubled frown that wrinkled Wolf Who Hunts Smiling's brow.

"Big Tree and his men are gone, brothers," he said. "We will send a man after them. But you know Comanches once they are fleeing toward their beloved Blanco Canyon. It will be many sleeps before we can get word to them."

He was sharpening his knife as he spoke, on one edge only as Indians did.

"So never mind the renegades. We have been too indirect, bucks. When a bull is charging you, you do not strike at his flanks. You take him by the horns! We have three bulls rushing us, and their names are Little Horse, Two Twists, and Tangle Hair. From here on out, we waste no time with rigged councils or massed attacks. We focus on those three. Close, unrelenting, like cats on rats, until we have killed them!"

Chapter Ten

The big claybank gelding performed like a well-oiled machine, spiriting Sis-ki-dee ever northward toward his homeland.

Well north of the Yellowstone, the renegade swerved west to avoid the bluecoat mirror stations near Fort Union. Normally sentries would not bother to relay word about one Indian. But they would recognize this one, and the word would spread as quick as fire through prairie grass. The man who killed Sis-ki-dee could sell his teeth alone for a small fortune.

Especially when the word spread across the plains: This Sis-ki-dee had killed Touch the Sky of the Northern Cheyennes!

Now and then, when he thought of what he had done, elation swelled inside him. How many men had found hard death trying to send *that* one across the Great Divide? The very thought of it made the mad Blackfoot renegade toss his head back and scream out to the heavens, challenging the very gods on high.

But Sis-ki-dee was a cunning man who had survived this long by seldom taking anything on faith. The man who laid down his rifle also laid down his life.

That thought made him rein in his horse from time to time and carefully scour his back trail for any signs of being followed. He watched for moving shapes, dust puffs; he dismounted and placed his ear close to the ground and felt it with his fingertips.

Nothing. The only thing chasing Sis-ki-dee was fame and power!

Finally. At long last it was done, smoke behind him. He had killed the greatest obstacle to his success. Now it was time to begin the next phase, for Wolf Who Hunts Smiling was right, these were good times to be alive for any red man smart enough to capitalize on the suffering.

The Renegade Nation would rule the Powder River country the way Big Tree's Comanches had once ruled the Llano Estacado or Staked Plain of the southwest. White man's gold would bring them fine weapons and equipment, and white man's blood would wash away the paleface's brief history in the West, returning the land to the red men who originally owned it.

But first, Sis-ki-dee knew, he must hole up and see which noble follower of Touch the Sky came to avenge his death. He had the perfect hideout in mind. However, he might be there a long time, and he knew he would need a woman. Sis-ki-dee believed men were like volcanos—if they did not relieve the pressure, they would explode.

He knew where to get a woman. A beautiful woman. Besides relieving his pressure and cooking for him, she might come in handy as insurance.

There was a crow village near Crying Horse Creek, and the Crow women were renowned for their beauty throughout the plains. He touched up his pony with his sisal quirt, bearing right toward Crying Horse Creek.

Touch the Sky's problem was not that of cutting sign on his enemy. Sis-ki-dee, clearly confident he had finally killed his man, took no pains to disguise his flight.

No. The trail north was as clear as mountain runoff. His struggle was even more difficult, for it was a struggle against himself.

His warrior's instinct told him he must keep driving on. Once a man set out for the kill, his only task was to get it done. It had always been his way to fire and move to a new position, fire and move, always drawing closer to his enemy until the final movement that brought death.

And now he was battered and exhausted, terribly weakened from his gruelling ordeal in the rockslide. Not only did he have a long, hard ride into mostly unfamiliar country—he was chasing the Wendigo himself. When that red devil turned to fight, he would need every reserve of strength.

Yet strength was lacking in him now. And since strength was the first virtue, making all other virtues possible, his will to fight was also weak. Touch the Sky knew this thing could not stand. Not if he were to survive the next encounter with the Red Peril.

So before he resumed the hard chase, he returned to the Yellowstone and waited near a salt lick. He killed an antelope and faced the frustrating problem of trying to dress it out without his knife. He made do with the stone tip of his war lance, which he sharpened first.

The nutritious liver and brains he boiled together in a stew, adding rosehips, bone marrow, and a few wild onions for flavor. He carved out a hindquarter of meat and cut the best steaks from it. For one full sleep he ate and rested, making restorative teas of yarrow root.

During this period, while he holed up in a pine-needle–carpeted thicket, the albino grazed on a long tether, likewise resting. She had already saved his life once, and Touch the Sky knew her part in the fight was not yet over. To a Cheyenne, a pony was never just an instrument of war—it was a battle partner. Even the bravest warrior might cry openly when a favorite pony was killed in battle, and none called it weakness.

When his resting was over, Touch the Sky again pointed his bridle toward the north country. Despite his urgency to get a hard job behind him, he moved slowly at first, resting more frequently and gnawing on the last of the antelope.

Steadily, his strength—and fighting fettle—returned. And steadily, he moved north, nearing the Bear Paw country. He never forgot that this was hostile Crow territory. Once he spotted a Crow hunting party, their thick, long hair trailing down below their hips and made even longer by gluing horse tails to it. He hobbled his pony in a copse and waited until they were gone.

During all of it, he thought often of Chief Gray Thunder, sent to an unclean death. The only fate worse, to an Indian, would be drowning, for everyone knew a drowned Indian's spirit remained trapped in water forever.

And thinking of Gray Thunder meant also thinking of the man who killed him. How many times had Sis-ki-dee made his life a hurting place since the ill-fated day he first encountered him in the Sans Arcs three winters ago? And even now, each time he passed through a potential rockslide area, he could not help cringing. For who knew how many of those nitro packs that mad killer possessed?

Again, as he neared the Land of the Grandmother to the north, Arrow Keeper's words whispered in his memory: *Keep white man's cunning on one flank, red man's cunning on the other.*

"They always look more like the father than the mother," Sharp Nosed Woman assured her niece. "Even the girls. You have your mother's great beauty, Honey Eater. But true it is, your face takes more after your father's."

Sharp Nosed Woman made the cut-off sign, slashing her hand quickly in front of her.

"So it is with your son," she added. "Maiyun bless him, he is the mirror image of Touch the Sky."

The two women sat in Sharp Nosed Woman's tipi playing with Little Bear. He was beginning to fuss a bit, so Honey Eater knew he would soon take a nap. That troubled her. For then she would have more leisure to worry herself to death about her brave.

There was enough to worry about right here in camp. But thanks to some very brave and vigilant work by Little Horse, Two Twists, and Tangle Hair, as well as some loyal Bow Strings, serious violence had so far been avoided. River of Winds still presided as chief. Angry braves from the soldier troops were still scouring the area in search of the Medicine Hat. Though no one gave her the details, Honey Eater suspected that her husband's band knew right where it was. No council could be held until it was found, and these days no council meant fewer chances for treachery.

All that was bad enough. But where was Touch the Sky? This Sis-ki-dee, she only knew of him indirectly. Her husband told her little about his troubles, for he did not want to worry her more than she was forced to worry already. And truly, he knew she had her own hard battles to fight. That made it even harder—knowing he, if he was still alive, must be worried sick about her and Little Bear, too.

Little Bear sighed a long sigh as he slipped into slumber. She admired his tiny but strongly wrought features, but seeing those limbs that were destined for strength made her sad—this one, too, would know little of peace and comfort. He was his father's son, and it was his destiny to struggle for the mere right to existence.

"Niece?"

Startled out of her reverie, Honey Eater glanced at her aunt.

"I have noticed a thing," Sharp Nosed Woman

said, keeping her tone casual as she shelled peas into a bowl.

Honey Eater smiled. Her aunt was not skilled at dissembling.

"You know what the big, tough warriors always say, Aunt. If you have something to say, speak it or bury it, for only women play coy games."

Both women laughed. "Yes," Sharp Nosed Woman said. "They abuse us worse than dogs, and yet we love them. We are as crazy as they are. At any rate, this thing I have noticed. It is a mark. Buried just past your son's hairline. An arrowhead birthmark. You can see it when his hair is wet."

Honey Eater nodded. Had her thoughts been that clear in her face?

"Yes. The mark of the warrior. And before you say it, I will. Touch the Sky has one, too, in the same place."

"As I said, most often they resemble the father. But this mark?"

Sharp Nosed Woman stopped shelling and glanced at her, her copper face serious now. "You know I am a practical woman, not given to nonsense about visions and magic. But I do believe in Maiyun, and I tell you now, those birthmarks are His doing. He has marked these two out."

Honey Eater was about to reply when a voice called out urgently from outside the entrance flap: "Sisters, I would speak with you!"

"Two Twists," Honey Eater said quickly, rising to throw back the flap. But dread warred with hope. What if he brought bad news about Touch the Sky?

"Come in quickly," she told him, glancing behind him to make sure it was safe.

Bloody Bones Canyon

"Have you seen Little Horse?" he demanded.

"Little Horse? No. Why?"

A frown brought the young warrior's brows closer together. He looked vastly different to the women now that his head was shorn.

"By the directions, this has a bad odor to it. I had hoped to find him here. Little Horse has disappeared. No one knows where he is. And two Bull Whips are gone, too—two of their best killers!"

Sis-ki-dee was not foolish enough to actually approach the Crow village near Crying Horse Creek. He had once terrorized this region with a band that, in its prime, boasted forty warriors. The Crow Crazy Dogs, their fiercest warriors, had set up a vengeance pole against him. If they captured him, he would be tortured for days before his belly would be slit and his entrails fed to the dogs while he watched himself being eaten alive.

But it was not necessary to actually enter the village. He knew Crow customs well. Their women, considered even more beautiful than the stunning Cheyenne maidens, were intensely modest. A bathing pool, well away from the camp, had been dug from a natural sink behind the creek.

Sis-ki-dee ground-hitched his mount in a cutbank out of sight of the camp and the bathing pool. Taking cover behind clumps of juniper and little copses of pine, expertly sensing the best places to crawl, the renegade moved gradually closer to the pool.

He parted some rushes and then felt his lips easing back from his teeth in their crazy-brave grin. The young woman just then twisting water from her long black hair made his blood sing with lust. Still young enough for taut, supple skin. But every bit a woman, as those swollen breasts proved.

In a heartbeat his pearl-handled bowie was gripped in his right palm. Ducking back, Sis-ki-dee did an excellent imitation of a puppy whimpering in distress.

Chapter Eleven

Clearly there was bad trouble in Crow country.

Touch the Sky sat his pony in the lee of a butte, sheltering them from a brisk wind and watching smoke messages fill the sky. Each tribe used its own secret signals, so he could not read the actual messages. But from the patterns and timing, he could tell that separate groups of warriors were remaining in touch as they followed someone—the signals were progress reports.

As to who that someone might be—they were riding in the same direction he was taking, following Sis-ki-dee's trail.

So the Red Peril had managed to get the Crow tribe on the war path. No surprise, knowing Sis-ki-dee. But now Touch the Sky's task was infinitely more difficult. All these riders made travel across the Marias River country more risky. He had enough to worry about just watching for ambushes by Sis-ki-dee. Now he also had to contend with Crow warriors sporting blood in their eyes.

He touched up his pony and resumed his northward trek, careful to keep to all the shelter he could find. The country around him now was mostly rolling foothills. The snow-capped peaks of the Bear Paws were clearly visible, the chief landmark of Blackfoot country.

Touch the Sky stuck to defiles and cutbanks, rode behind ridges and along dry streambeds sheltered by trees. Long ago, Arrow Keeper had taught him an important lesson about survival in the wilderness: Keep speech and thought to a minimum and listen to the language of the senses. And for a long time he did just that. He forced his "inner eye" to close and looked only through the outer.

But Arrow Keeper had little advice for a man worried sick about his wife and child. And it was thinking about Honey Eater and Little Bear that caused Touch the Sky's vigilance to slip.

He had debouched from a narrow coulee and was passing between two shoulders of red rock when he heard a sickeningly familiar sound, the metallic *snick* of a rifle bolt sliding home.

At this moment he faced the same options a wild animal faced when in danger: fight or flight. He didn't know yet if he had a fighting chance or not. But flight was out of the question. There was nothing out ahead to come between him and a bullet to the back.

So Touch the Sky halted his pony with a slight pressure of his knees and glanced overhead.

His heart sank. Five Crow warriors, hair hanging

long behind them, held rifles trained on him from one of the stone shoulders.

They scrambled nimbly down, never once lowering their rifles. One seized his pony's buffalo-hair bridle and held her. Touch the Sky noticed that several of the warrior's fingers were missing—the Cheyenne tribe called Crows Stub Hands because they lopped joints from their fingers as a token of mourning, and some hardly had the use of one hand. This one had saved only his thumb and trigger finger—but that was enough, Touch the Sky thought grimly, respectfully eyeing his Colt musket.

The others moved in close, examining his weapons and kit. Clearly they intended to kill him and were already dividing his possessions.

"Are you lost or have you gone Wendigo?" the brave holding his pony's bridle demanded. He spoke in a clear dialect of Lakota Sioux, easily understandable to a Sioux's Cheyenne cousins.

"He has come to steal ponies," another said. "These Cheyennes are great horse thieves."

This one pulled Touch the Sky's rifle out of its scabbard and began examining it. One of the braves carried a white man's blacksnake whip. He snapped the popper hard, and the tip stopped just a hair's breadth short of Touch the Sky's face.

The Cheyenne knew he was being tested and never once flinched. "You missed," he said calmly. "Try again."

The brave frowned and snapped his popper again. This time it opened a cut across the bridge of his nose.

"I thank you heartily, Absaroka friend," he said,

using the ancient name of the Crow tribe as a mark of respect. "There was a fly itching my nose."

Despite the hostility stamped into their features, this made several of them smile grudgingly. A man who showed fear when captured, as whites foolishly did, was doomed. But most Indians were reluctant to maltreat a man they respected. They might still kill him, of course. But it would be a quick death and worthy of his character.

"Shaiyena," one of them said. "Why are you here? We are not friends of your tribe, but there are no hostilities between us now."

"None between us," Touch the Sky agreed. "But the Blackfoot murderer Sis-ki-dee has killed our peace chief. He has escaped to the Bear Paw country. But by the sun and the earth I live on, I mean to kill him."

When he mentioned Sis-ki-dee, all five braves exchanged troubled glances. The one holding his bridle nodded. This explained all the Cheyenne and Sioux smoke signals recently to the south.

"Is it even so? Then, Cheyenne, you are a much bigger fool than you look. A man would do better to chase a grizzly into its den than to follow Sis-ki-dee. Look ahead."

Touch the Sky looked where he pointed. Another group of Crows approached from the north.

"Our comrades, too, were after Sis-ki-dee. The Red Peril has stolen one of our women, Gliding Hawk, who has been promised in marriage to one of our subchiefs. But see, they are returning. Do you know why?"

Touch the Sky shook his head.

"Because, as we feared, he has ridden into

Bloody Bones Canyon. No man will follow Sis-ki-dee into that place. Many have tried, and many have died."

"I have heard of it," Touch the Sky said. "But I do not care if he has fled into the white man's hell— he will not shake me. If you let me ride on, I will kill him *and* get your woman back."

One of the braves hooted in derision. "You? And what makes you so intrepid, brave Cheyenne? Why should you not die like the rest who have braced Sis-ki-dee?"

"So what if I die? A man does not take the war path only when he can win. If an Indian thinks on all the ways he might die, he will not leave his tipi. Our law-ways demand his death. Therefore I mean to kill him. What could be simpler?"

The brave who had just hooted in scorn was now squinting at the mounted Cheyenne, trying to place him. "Why were you sent to do this?" he asked. "Who are you?"

"I am called Touch the Sky," he replied quietly.

His words affected them like canister shot. The brave who had hit him with the whip turned pale. For all knew of this one, this legendary warrior whose medicine could summon the grizzly to his aid.

The brave with the whip offered it to Touch the Sky. "You owe me a good crack, Cheyenne," he said. "I did wrong to hit you. Now strike me back."

Touch the Sky knew it would insult the brave and his gesture if he simply refused.

"You are a good man and have no fear of a lash. I can see that. I might do it anyway, just for sport, but bucks, know this. While I sit here wasting words with good men, one who shames the Wendigo himself is fleeing."

The stub-handed brave holding his bridle now let go. "Then ride on, Cheyenne, and see if you can succeed where legions have failed. I respect your courage, and we do not call your tribe the Fighting Cheyenne for nothing. But I would not ride into Bloody Bones Canyon to save my mother, for only devils come out of that place alive. Go, Touch the Sky, but first make peace with your god!"

Little Horse was about to be murdered, and he knew it.

He had known it even before he spotted the lone Bull Whip following him through the scrub-tree country east of the Bighorn River.

He had known it by simple process of elimination. Wolf Who Hunts Smiling had failed to usurp power through the council. Nor could he call a council until the Medicine Hat was found. He had also failed in a bid to take the camp by force, and by now Big Tree's men were far south of here, taking that dream with them.

So it did not require a shaman's think-piece, Little Horse decided, to guess the wily Wolf's next move.

He had not originally intended to ride this far. Earlier, he had ridden out of camp to check on a group of Bull Whips, making sure they were indeed working their ponies and not massing for an attack. As he took the long route back to camp, making a general scout, he noticed one of the Whips break off from the rest and slip into the trees.

He recognized the brave by the markings on this

pony: Scalp Cane of the Bull Dancers Clan. And knowing of his clan of bullies and petty thieves, he knew immediately what was happening.

Instead of fleeing to camp, he set his cayuse at an easy lope toward the Bighorn.

Little Horse, like any brave who had ridden with Touch the Sky, had been forced to kill many foes in the eternal struggle to survive on a hostile frontier. But killing was never easy for him, only something he did well because as a warrior it was his duty to ensure the survival of his tribe. Of course he boasted and made light of death, pretending he was eager to die himself. That was the way of most warriors. But down deep in his secret well of feeling, he not only feared death but loathed killing.

So this path upon which he was setting out now gave him great pause, for he was setting out to not only kill, but kill fellow Cheyennes.

In the Cheyenne tongue, the same word was used for "murderer" and for "putrid," because it was believed that murder began the internal corruption of the spirit. And because murder of a fellow Cheyenne was so heinous, the High Holy Ones gave their people the sacred Medicine Arrows to protect. If Cheyenne blood was spilled by another Cheyenne, that blood stained the arrows and thus the tribe.

Indeed, he thought, it was Gray Thunder's blood that was on them now. And Touch the Sky, if he still lived, was attempting to cleanse those arrows even now. For all these reasons, Little Horse would not lightly set out to kill enemies within his own tribe.

But even old Arrow Keeper, who counseled for the peace road and once told Touch the Sky to swallow insults rather than shed tribal blood, agreed on one point: Cheyennes who coldly, maliciously planned to murder their fellows ceased to be protected by the law-ways. And thus their blood would not stain the arrows.

I will wait, Little Horse thought, refusing to glance back and alert his enemy that he knew he was back there. *I will be sure beyond all doubt of his intentions. And then it will be one bullet for one enemy.*

"Today is a good day to die," he assured his pony. "But not for us."

"Hold on tight, pretty one," Sis-ki-dee said in the Crow tongue, for most Blackfoot warriors knew some of it. "If you fall off now, I will get no pleasure from you. Only the buzzards will get to enjoy you then."

The insane renegade threw back his head and roared with wild laughter. It echoed far and wide, bouncing off the barren turrets of the basalt badlands known as Bloody Bones Canyon.

Gliding Hawk did indeed cling to her captor tightly, despite her loathing for this scar-faced monster. She had never once set foot in Bloody Bones, though all her life she had grown up hearing stories about it. Crow mothers, wishing to control wild children, would threaten to "send you to Bloody Bones Canyon if you can't behave."

And now look, this red devil, who perhaps ruled this place as the Wendigo rules the Forest of Tears, was taking her into its bleak and wild heart.

It was not so much a canyon as a deep wound in

the earth. White men claimed it had been the work of huge ice floes coming down from the Land of the British Grandmother to the north. Crow legend taught that it was the first hole in the earth, through which came and went the evil spirits that governed men. Either claim made sense, looking at the place.

Only one trail led in, the same one that led out, if indeed anyone could leave. The surrounding walls were dangerously precipitous, at some times turning into sheer cliffs. There was no plant life—indeed, not even dirt for it to spring from. The floor of the canyon was cooled magna from centuries-old volcanic eruptions.

The big claybank's hooves rang sharply on this magna floor. Gliding Hawk had no idea where this cruel, stinking Indian was taking her. But he kept reminding her of what he had in store for her.

"I will make you howl like a she-bitch coyote," he promised her. "You are used to Crow men. Wait until Sis-ki-dee has topped you. Never again will your own men satisfy you."

Thus it went. She stayed numb with fear and apprehension while he seemed to be in festive spirits. But that soon changed.

Toward the end of a long day he halted and quickly scurried up a small turret of basalt. She watched him remove a pair of brass binoculars from the parfleche on his sash and train them out toward the south country.

A moment later he cursed sharply in his own language. When he returned to his horse, his mood was hardly festive.

"Bad news, woman! A Cheyenne I was sure was

dead is alive and tracking me. I tell you now, he is a noble red man who has sworn to kill me. We will see how noble he is when it comes down to this: Either he rides off, or you die."

Chapter Twelve

Now he is mine, Scalp Cane gloated.

The Bull Whip soldier had been trailing Little Horse for perhaps as long as it took the sun to travel the width of four lodge poles. He had no idea where Touch the Sky's lickspittle was heading—perhaps to the secret place where he had hidden the Medicine Hat and the Medicine Arrows.

That thought twitched his lips into a grin. How Wolf Who Hunts Smiling and Rough Feather would howl his praises if he returned to camp with those arrows and that hat—and Little Horse's bloody scalp.

And now that scalp was as good as dangling from his clout. For Little Horse had just made the mistake of taking the long trail through Beaver Creek Valley. It would emerge between two high walls of red rock—and there was a shorter game trail which led from here to the caprock of those walls.

Wolf Who Hunts Smiling had finally realized that so far they had merely been hacking at the branches. Now it was time to strike at the roots. Sis-ki-dee was taking care of the main root. Now Little Horse, Tangle Hair, and Two Twists must be "rooted out."

Scalp Cane rode a fast hunting pony, a well-muscled buckskin. He also owned a Spencer carbine captured from a blue-blouse and was an excellent shot with it. He chucked the buckskin up to a run, bearing left toward the slope that would take him out over the spot where Little Horse would emerge.

He reached the caprock in good time and swung down from his mount, hobbling it with strips of rawhide. A quick glance to the winding trail below showed that his prey had not yet emerged.

Scalp Cane grinned again as he took up a prone position and found a good spot to set his left elbow for aiming. It would be a fairly long shot, but an easy one: The light was good, Little Horse would be riding slowly coming out of a dog-leg turn, and the Spencer was an excellent gun with good rifling in the barrel to minimize bullet drift.

Faintly, he heard the hollow rhythm of hooves approaching. Scalp Cane thumbed rounds through a trap in the butt plate and jacked one into the chamber. Little Horse's cayuse emerged below. Scalp Cane drew a bead on the rider's back as he slipped his finger inside the trigger guard and took up the slack.

The Spencer's stock slapped his cheek, there was a sharp whip-cracking sound, and the rider flew from his pony, sprawling motionless to the ground.

"*Ipewa,*" Scalp Cane said out loud. "Good!"

"Very good shooting," a voice behind him agreed. "Now turn around, Scalp Cane, for unlike you I won't shoot a man in the back unless he makes me."

Scalp Cane felt his heart jump into his throat. He whirled to confront Little Horse. The brave stood naked except for his moccasins—even his feather and headband were missing.

"Look closely at my 'body' below," the sturdy warrior told him.

Scalp Cane did. Only now did he realize his mistake. That "rider" was a buckskin suit stuffed with grass, complete with Little Horse's feather.

Little Horse held his four-barrel shotgun trained on the Whip.

"No," Scalp Cane begged. "It was not my idea."

"Those who hold a torch for the Wendigo also do his work," Little Horse said. "Now, I will be better than you. I will let you sing your death song first."

"No!" Scalp Cane said again.

Little Horse reached one thumb up and clicked the hammer from half cock to full cock.

"Yes," he said. "If this were the end of it, I might show mercy. But my tribe hangs in the balance. I am not killing you for personal vengeance or glory, though I have that right. Now act like a man for once in your life and let your dying be the best thing you ever did. Sing! For I am sending you over, traitor!"

This is the way it must look, thought Touch the Sky, across the ranges of the moon.

He had never even imagined land this desolate.

He had ridden the alkali flats of the scorching Llano Estacado, negotiated the Bisti Badlands of New Mexico, even survived the treacherous cliffs of Wendigo Mountain. But none of them compared to this desolate place.

Wind whipped through the many nooks and crannies of the basalt turrets, sending up an eerie, high-pitched whistling reminiscent of Medicine Flute's leg-bone flute. He could see little in either direction, for the trail wound tortuously. Now, as Sister Sun went to her rest, Bloody Bones Canyon took on an eerie, blood-orange tint.

The tired, cold, but determined brave paused often to listen and consult his shaman eye. The wind rose in howling shrieks like berserk ponies; then it would trail out in a whispering moan, and the word it whispered made his fine hairs rise:

Sissss-ki-deee . . .

The Red Peril had a hostage now. That should slow him. Even so, he failed utterly to garner any signs as to his whereabouts. This stone floor of the canyon left no helpful signs. He did learn, from breaking open the claybank's droppings, that Sis-ki-dee packed grain for his horse. That was more bad news, for there was no forage in this place of death. Touch the Sky's pony would soon need graze as well as water.

This last Touch the Sky was able to find in small amounts thanks to his past ordeals in water-scarce country. Now and then he would stop and climb atop a jumble of boulders. These retained small amounts of water in their hollows, which he could suck out by lying flat on his stomach.

Indeed, this quest had forced him to use every

survival skill he knew, and would exact more before it was over—he knew that by now. For he knew the Red Peril. That one relished human misery, thrived on it the way goslings thrive on plump berries. Indeed, his eyes grew bright with the pleasure and life it gave him to cause others suffering and death.

And because he knew that, Touch the Sky forced himself to eternal vigilance now. The death traps were waiting.

And so was the taunting.

He knew that when he first heard the improbable sound of a rattlesnake buzzing.

This was not rattler country. And this late in the fall moons, a snake would be out where there was sun else it could not get its temperature up enough to hunt.

He heard the sound again, somewhere behind him.

Suddenly, directly in front of him, a stone bounced off a spire of basalt.

Again the buzzing rattle. But it had changed location.

The next stone bounced off his albino's flank and made her shy in fright. Nervous sweat beading on his back despite the cold, Touch the Sky quickly calmed his mount and urged her forward. The last thing he could afford to do now was let Sis-ki-dee panic him or his pony.

It troubled him. He had not let his mind wander, and yet once again Sis-ki-dee had gotten close to him unobserved. Mocking, taunting, the way Touch the Sky had humiliated the Blackfoot in the eyes of his followers—by not killing him when he had the chance. Touch the Sky had refused that kill then because Sis-ki-dee had been knocked unconscious, and the warrior code did not sanction killing a sleeping enemy. Even so, Touch the Sky now regretted that decision. It had brought more harm to his tribe and him, and would bring more—indeed, it might be about to kill him now.

He fought down his fear, for fear was like anger—it got in the way of a warrior's best killing skills. This was Sis-ki-dee's way of counting coup, reducing a man to gibbering fear before he made him die a hard death. But Touch the Sky meant to deny him that coup.

His Sharps was ready in his hand, a primer cap behind the loading gate. But where was he to aim it? He would grease any enemy's bones with war paint—indeed, when he first rode into Bloody Bones, Touch the Sky had marked his face with a piece of charcoal. Black, the symbol of joy at the death of an enemy. But against Sis-ki-dee, a man never saw his enemy until he decided to show himself.

This was not fight-or-flight, he could do neither. The terrain kept him from either moving quickly or holing up.

Again, the angry buzzing sound.

Sweat beaded on his scalp, tickling like insects. He concentrated on his breathing, on mastering his fear. He must not let Sis-ki-dee unstring his nerves or he was lost—and if he was lost, so were Honey Eater and Little Bear and the rest of the Powder River Cheyenne village.

There was a sudden noise right behind him.

Touch the Sky whirled, his heart skipping a beat.

Moments later he realized it was only another stone. But the Red Peril's little game was starting to work. His nerves were getting frazzled. And the mocking laughter that now erupted all around him confirmed that his enemy knew it.

"Aunt," Honey Eater said nervously as Sharp Nosed Woman threw back the flap and entered her lodge after a visit to her clan women. "Any word?"

Sharp Nosed Woman handed the baby a rattle made from snake's teeth and a dried gourd.

"I suppose you mean any word on Touch the Sky or Little Horse?" her aunt said. "And the answer is yes."

The white columbine petals she was braiding into her hair now fluttered from her fingers, unnoticed. Honey Eater turned a shade paler.

"Oh, what is it?" she demanded. "What do you know of my husband?"

"Niece, by the directions! Settle down, do not bite your lip off for worrying. I have heard nothing of Touch the Sky. It is Little Horse. He has returned."

Honey Eater was disappointed that it wasn't Touch the Sky whose safety was being confirmed. Nonetheless, it relieved her to know Little Horse was safe after all. Not only did she share her husband's admiration for the loyal brave—he was this camp's best hope of survival while Touch the Sky was gone.

"I am glad to hear it," she assured her aunt.

Sharp Nosed Woman nodded. "So am I. With Little Horse here, Tangle Hair and Two Twists have a better chance at keeping our new chief alive. But he has returned to camp with plenty of trouble. Come here and see."

Her aunt's tone was ominous. Dread heavy in her belly, Honey Eater crossed to the entrance flap.

"Look," the older woman told her. "See over by the Bull Whip lodge?"

"Yes," Honey Eater replied. "A huge knot of men. All Whips. And there is Wolf Who Hunts Smiling and Medicine Flute. They look grim as death. But why are they all so silent? And what are they looking at?"

"There," Sharp Nosed Woman said. "Rough Feather just moved out of the way. Now do you see it? It was left there as a warning."

Abruptly Honey Eater did see it—a fresh scalp, still dripping blood, had been mounted to a pole in front of the lodge.

"That hair once belonged to Scalp Cane," Sharp Nose Woman said. "And it was Little Horse who lifted it from him."

"I sent one of my best men," Rough Feather protested. "I would have done it myself if Two Twists had not dogged my shadow. Do not accuse *me* of weak leadership, buck! If a man's best shaft cannot penetrate the wood, then why blame the man for hard wood?"

"Your 'best shaft,'" Wolf Who Hunts Smiling answered, scowling so deep his jaw ached, "was a pinpoint against a spear! You should have sent several braves to do it."

"I am telling you straight-arrow, I could not! Tangle Hair and Two Twists and a few of the Bow Strings have got us covered like shadows on rocks.

I cannot walk to the river to relieve myself without one of them counting the drops!"

"Why," Swift Canoe demanded with utter confusion, "would they care how many drops of piss you—?"

With a snarl of frustrated rage, Wolf Who Hunts Smiling lifted his coup stick and smacked Swift Canoe soundly on the side of the head. The stick lost the battle and snapped, while Swift Canoe appeared unfazed. This enraged Wolf Who Hunts Smiling even further.

In a moment his knife was in his hand. He drew it back to gut the lame-brained idiot when Rough Feather, grinning with pleasure at the sight of it, caught his arm.

"Give over, buck," the troop leader advised. "We need Swift Canoe."

"I will 'need' him onto his scaffold," the ambitious schemer vowed, "if he again opens his mouth and lets more dung fall out of it!"

Medicine Flute watched all this in shrewd silence, and he was worried. This was not like Wolf Who Hunts Smiling—this loss of temper. He had always been a fiery brave, one to anger quickly, but it was not his way to let trifling matters, such as Swift Canoe's legendary stupidity, work a burr into him. No. The pressure was getting to him. And if Wolf Who Hunts Smiling could break, so could the rest on his side. It was time for decisive action.

"Brothers, have ears," Medicine Flute said boldly. "Either we act together, or we die one by one. Rough Feather was right. We are covered close—by day."

This alerted Wolf Who Hunts Smiling, and he

glanced at his skinny but resourceful "shaman." "I like the taste of it, buck," he encouraged him. "Feed us some more of this food for thought."

"See it clear? They are on us by day. But we are Cheyennes. It is not our custom to work our plans at night. Our enemies know this, and their night-time vigilance is much less. And of course, they too must sleep sometime."

Wolf Who Hunts Smiling nodded. "I take your meaning. We must toss custom to the wind and make our move after dark."

Medicine Flute nodded. "A bold nighttime coup. Quick, efficient, we rise up as one man and kill River of Winds and his loyalists while they lie naked in sleep!"

Chapter Thirteen

Touch the Sky finally reached the opposite end of Bloody Bones Canyon, and all he found for his efforts was frustration.

Always, since the fateful day his trail first crossed the Red Peril's, it had been thus. He recalled the Sioux Chief named Trains the Hawk. He knew all too well about Sis-ki-dee's treachery, and he had once said:

"Battling Sis-ki-dee is like fighting against a fire in a windstorm that constantly changes its direction. Just when you think the flames are out on one side, you are singed on another. And when he decides to hide, he is like Maiyun in the universe—everywhere felt but nowhere seen."

Everywhere felt but nowhere seen . . . that neatly summarized the essence of this consummately evil Blackfoot warrior. He had no honor, but, unfortunately, neither did he feel fear as most men did. Truly insane, he did not fear the sting of death. And such men were especially dangerous.

Everywhere felt . . . Touch the Sky hunkered down behind a rock spine and sent a long, scouring look around at the sea of basalt turrets and piles of scree and glacial moraine—a gray, unbroken mass surrounding him. He had taken the trail to its end and rode up out of the canyon. But though there was plenty of soft dirt once the canyon floor rose up to the surrounding plain, Touch the Sky found no sign.

Sis-ki-dee and his hostage had not ridden out of the canyon.

So they must still be here.

But where?

Again he fought down a welling sense of rage and frustration—and deep apprehension for Honey Eater, Little Bear, and the rest back down at the Powder River camp. While they might very well be locked in the struggle of all struggles, sorely missing him, he was chasing shadows up here in the northern wastes.

Where? Where could Sis-ki-dee be holed up?

Touch the Sky had found precious few places that offered any shelter. There was a small limestone cave now and then—each of which he searched, his heart in his throat. But nothing. How could two Indians and a big seventeen-hand claybank just disappear?

Easily, when one of the Indians was Sis-ki-dee.

"I'll have to do it all over again, girl," he said wearily to his even wearier albino. Fortunately, there had been a heavy rain earlier, and Touch the

Bloody Bones Canyon

Sky had stretched his leather shirt out between rocks to form a reservoir for water. He had gathered enough to give his pony a few good swallows. She had supplemented these with smaller amounts from tiny depressions in the stone floor of the canyon.

But she'd had next to nothing to eat for two sleeps now. Occasionally Touch the Sky saw a scrub brush growing out of a crack in a rock. He would break these off and give them to the albino, letting her nibble the bark. Unlike spoiled white man's horses, who would starve in winter if they weren't grained, Indian ponies learned to be resourceful and to expand their diet. But these tidbits were hardly adequate sustenance.

Touch the Sky himself was running low on provisions. He had not weighted himself down with too much food, planning to shoot rabbits and forage for roots and plants. But both were out of the question on this lunar landscape.

So was the option of giving up and returning to his camp. He was his tribe's shaman and the keeper of the arrows. This Red Peril had killed his chief. That crime could not stand, not by the law-ways given to the people by the High Holy Ones themselves.

Cautiously, glancing all around him first, he moved out of the cover of the rock spine. Yes, he'd have to do it all over again. But this time he'd do it without his pony. She was too tired to trek this entire canyon again. Besides, he would have to do more climbing this time to examine spots in higher elevations—climbing by hand and foot, not pony.

"C'mon, girl," he said, so tired and preoccupied

that he didn't even realize he'd slipped into English—something he did when he approached the feather edge of exhaustion.

He had spotted a fairly secure cave about a triple stone's throw from this spot. He would hobble his pony there, then continue his search.

"Now comes some good sport," Sis-ki-dee gloated, watching his enemy's every move through his field glasses.

The wind howled and shrieked all around him, whipping his hair about like writhing black worms. He watched the Cheyenne below him, leading his beautiful albino pony into a small cave.

"That wily Cheyenne makes few mistakes," Sis-ki-dee assured the frightened Gliding Hawk. "But he has made one here. For he was too stupid to look up as well as all around."

Sis-ki-dee, his Crow hostage, and his pony were all atop a huge basalt pinnacle crowned by a flat top softened by eons of wind-blown dirt that had accumulated on the rock. Ingeniously, so subtly that one hardly noticed them from below, a series of shallow steps had been carved into the pinnacle. They wound around it like a white man's winding staircase. To anyone on the ground, they appeared to be natural depressions in the rock.

Sis-ki-dee and his comrade Plenty Coups, who had been killed by Touch the Sky in the Sans Arcs, had made those steps years before. That was in the days when they still terrorized this region. Many, many times they had fled into Bloody Bones Canyon and taken refuge up here. Surprise attacks were impossible, for there was only one way up—the winding steps.

Sis-ki-dee was tempted to go for a quick kill. He could have done it many times by now. But while that would certainly end his present danger, it would be terribly unsatisfying. This tall one humiliated him! Let him sup full of sorrow and suffering before he crossed. It was not Sis-ki-dee's way to merely kill an enemy this important.

Sis-ki-dee watched the tall Cheyenne Bear Caller emerge from the cave without his pony. Then he moved quickly out of sight behind a jumble of scree. The search was on all over again.

But this time the Cheyenne is minus his pony, Sis-ki-dee thought with a grin that stretched from ear to ear.

He checked the girl's ropes—made from human hair, which Sis-ki-dee had discovered was stronger than buffalo-hair ropes when wet—and the strip of cotton gagging her mouth. Satisfied, he bent to pick up his North & Savage in its buckskin sheath. Then, thinking better of it, he set the gun back down. He'd take just his bowie for this little mission. He could move more quickly that way.

"Try not to cry hard at my absence," Sis-ki-dee goaded Gliding Hawk. "When I return I shall take my pleasure again. I know how much you enjoy my tender attentions."

A visible shudder ran through her willow-slender body, and Sis-ki-dee had to stifle his insane bray for fear of alerting the Bear Caller. Then, stooping so he wouldn't skyline himself for his enemy, he headed toward the steps that would take him down to the canyon floor and more bloody terror.

* * *

It all felt wrong somehow, but Touch the Sky couldn't pin the feeling down.

Several times, as he threaded his way slowly through the basalt turrets and scree, he stopped to look back toward the cave where he'd left his albino. The last of his pemmican was also cached back there. It was risky, but what were his options? For now the scouting had turned to the arduous task of climbing, and he must be unencumbered.

It hadn't occurred to him to pay much attention to the numerous basalt formations, for of course they could not be climbed. But he did concentrate on the numerous piles of scree and moraine, some of them piled as high as hair-face lodges. One by one, skinning his hands and shins raw, he ascended them.

The climbing was hard enough. But not knowing what to expect at the top made it doubly fearful. Absolute silence was vital, for even a loud breath would warn Sis-ki-dee.

The piles were unstable, and each hand- or foot-hold had to be tested. Nor could he always take the easy way up, for that was the most obvious. Sometimes he was scaling virtually perpendicular surfaces.

One pile secured, then a second, while Sister Sun tracked further across a bottomless blue sky. He lost his chill in the sweat of exertion, though sometimes the arctic wind blasting his sweat-soaked skin felt like a knife digging in. Hunger gnawed at his belly like a rat. His limbs, still sore from the ordeal under the rockslide, now trembled as they neared exhaustion from all this climbing.

He neared the top of his third pile of scree. Inches at a time, he brought his face up close to the brim to glance over.

A hideous screech, a fast rush of motion, and Touch the Sky fell backward, expecting death from Sis-ki-dee's blade. Instead, a hawk tore off into the sky, its deadly talons missing his eyes by inches. The startled Cheyenne very nearly plunged to his death, but at the last moment he flexed his legs and back muscles hard, breaking his fall.

For the space of perhaps ten heartbeats he clung to a rock, letting his pulse return to normal. But that was it for this day, he resolved. He would return to the cave, eat some of his dwindling rations, then snatch some badly needed sleep.

This struggle was wearing him down like no other, and yet, how little fighting he had done so far! How he longed to finally find that crazy-by-thunder savage and either kill him or be killed. Either way, this madness would end.

He had just begun his descent to the stone floor of Bloody Bones Canyon when he remembered: As long as he was up this high, best to make a complete search from the side of his eyes, too. Soon after he began scouring the canyon walls with his peripheral vision, Touch the Sky spotted a momentary glint of light, off to his right.

A glint just like the setting sun might make if a ray caught one of the brassards on Sis-ki-dee's arms or one of his brass earrings. And it came from atop that tall basalt pinnacle whose very top was well above this position. As if Sis-ki-dee had peered over the edge just for a moment to check on him.

The discovery did not fill him with elation. It

might well have been the momentary glint of quartz or mica or feldspar. For truly, thought Touch the Sky, how would anyone climb that towering shaft of stone? From here he could not make out much about its surface features.

He glanced around, but saw nothing close that would take him high enough to look at the top of that turret. That fact alone gave him pause. For indeed, the turret's very invulnerability made it a prime spot for an innovative killer like the Red Peril.

Yes. The more he thought about it, as he worked his way slowly down, the more sense it made. Siski-dee had to be here in Bloody Bones somewhere. And unless he could turn himself, his hostage, and his mount invisible, that big, secure turret must be the somewhere.

But how? How could it be scaled? He could not see all of it. Perhaps the other side would explain the mystery. At any rate, he would be committing suicide if he tried now. He was too tired and weak. No, first he would eat and rest.

He worked his way back toward the cave, sticking carefully to as much cover as possible. It had already occurred to him that, despite his care to leave the cave unseen, he might well have been spotted from the vantage point of that basalt tower. If so, his safety was woefully compromised. As tired as he was, he determined to lead his pony to another cave further away.

He could see the cave entrance now, a dark opening in the gray wall of the canyon. Touch the Sky was perhaps ten feet from the entrance when the brisk wind wafted a familiar smell to his nose. The sheared-metal stink of fresh blood!

Heedless of his safety, he rushed into the cave and almost tripped over his dead pony. She had been savagely throat-slashed, and his food cache was gone!

Chapter Fourteen

"It was Scalp Cane's death that has pushed them," Little Horse declared. "I knew it would when I killed him and lifted his hair for them to view. I meant it to. Our shaman has said it more than once, and he speaks straight: 'If you would destroy a boil, you must lance it.'"

"You did what must be done, buck," Tangle Hair assured him. "And I back your decision. But things are the way they are. A badger backed into its hole bites twice as hard."

Two Twists nodded across the clearing toward the chief's lodge, now occupied by River of Winds and his squaw. A well-armed Bow String soldier sat on either side of the entrance flap.

"None of the Whips has been showing much interest in our new chief. Yet, something new is in the wind. They have been talking among themselves and putting the word around."

"They always have new treachery on the spit," Little Horse agreed, watching thoughtfully as yet another Bull Whip trooper went down to the river and lay on his belly for a long drink.

"As you say," Tangle Hair said. "But what is left to them? Our scouts tell us Big Tree and his marauders are still flying on the wind toward the Blanco. The Medicine Hat is still missing, so they cannot call a council to seize the tribe by vote. Do you think, then, they mean to strike on their own? It seems a foolish plan, for though they slightly outnumber Touch the Sky's followers, he has enough left to make it a bloody and pointless victory."

Another Whip headed toward the river to drink. Little Horse watched him, and a foreboding came to him.

"They mean to strike on their own," he confirmed. "Tell me, bucks, have you noticed a thing? Have you seen how thirsty the Whips have suddenly become?"

Little Horse had never been one to waste words in idle observations. Two Twists and Tangle Hair followed his glance toward the Powder.

"Indeed," Two Twists said, also wondering. Indians were not great drinkers of water except on two occasions: for storing in their bellies when it was scarce, or when they needed the urge to urinate to wake them up in time for some important occasion, for Indians were notorious late sleepers.

"They are drinking much water," Tangle Hair speculated out loud, "because they need to wake up during the night."

During the night! Against all tradition, violating

the highest tabu, the Wolf Who Hunts Smiling meant to strike after the sun went down. Even more heinous, he meant to kill the loyalists in their sleep, drenching Cheyenne campground with the blood of the people!

All three braves exchanged long and troubled glances. It was hard for them to accept, for old habit was strong. Indians were taught from birth to fear the night, for it was believed that a brave lost much of his medicine in darkness. Cheyennes were among the red men who were especially loath to risk an important undertaking after sunset.

Yet there went two more Bull Whips after water.

"Now we know," Little Horse said. "Thank the Day Maker for that. With surprise on their side, it would be over quicker than a hungry man could eat a hump steak. But we have been warned. Let us put the word out to all the Bow Strings. Tonight every man sleeps on his weapon. If we are quick enough, we may do the hurt dance on them yet."

His companions nodded and rose from the ground to do as Little Horse suggested.

"We must take things as we find them," Two Twists said. "Yet, I wish our shaman would ride in. He, too, has gone to lance a boil. As grim as things seem here, I have looked into Sis-ki-dee's eyes. Thus I know that Touch the Sky has the greater battle."

"The Cheyenne's idea of hell," a Cavalry soldier once wrote in his journal, "is being forced to eat his own pony."

Nonetheless, Touch the Sky faced that hell. He used the stone point of his lance to butcher out a hindquarter of the dead albino. Unfortunately, there was no fuel for a fire, so he was forced to chew the tough, stringy meat raw. Once or twice he felt his gorge rising, but he fought it down. There was no choice. He could not set out after Sis-ki-dee without strength in his limbs. And the meat gave him strength.

Even in death, he thought, the albino was helping him to fight on.

The night, at least, was perfect for this grim mission. A quarter moon was obscured by a thick raft of clouds, and few stars blazed in the sky. Touch the Sky finished his unsavory meal, then prepared himself for the ordeal ahead.

He could not locate mud, so he used his nubbin of charcoal to completely darken his face and neck. Next he used his blanket—after a great struggle to pry it out from under the dead pony—to wrap his head completely. Patiently, he lay for one full hour, letting his eyes adjust to absolute darkness. When he removed the blanket, his night vision had improved dramatically.

He regretted the loss of his knife. This climb would not permit the bulk or weight of his rifle or throwing axe. He settled for untying the lance point, which he tucked into his legging sash.

It was cold and windy when he emerged from the limestone cave into the dimly lit landscape of Bloody Bones Canyon. This northern chill sliced deep down to his bones. Thanks to his dilated pupils, he had a good, if daunting, view of that huge basalt turret.

It rose straight up, wider at the base than at its summit but still huge at the top. Big enough to hide

a horse, even, but how would it—how would anyone—get up there? Yet he was sure Sis-ki-dee had
managed it.

Sticking to cover, he quickly approached the
base of the turret. Thus it was, feeling around, that
he discovered the man-made steps carved in the
side. They rose up gradually even as they wound
around—big enough to accommodate a horse.

That explained the how. Now came a more important question. How else? For surely it would be
suicide to use those same steps.

Even as he thought this, he heard a slight scrap-
ing sound above him. A moment later a huge boulder crashed down only a few inches away from
him, making Touch the Sky's heart turn over.

Then came that crazy-brave laughter, echoing
out over the lurid lunar landscape of the canyon.

"Careful, Bear Caller! I dropped something!"

More laughter. "Cheyenne! Hurry on to the top.
I have a fine woman waiting for you. I will let you
top Gliding Hawk as I mean to top your Honey
Eater after I kill you."

Another rock crashed down, so close that Touch
the Sky felt the wind from it. Nonetheless, he continued his desperate search. There was nothing so
easy as steps, but he did find, by careful feeling,
slight hand-and footholds that did not follow the
winding steps.

It would be a long, difficult climb. And perhaps
he would run out of holds further up and be forced
to come back down. But there was nothing else to
do. Going up those steps meant sure death. The
choice was between probably dying and surely dying, and so it was really no choice at all.

His mouth formed its grim, determined slit. Touch the Sky fought for his first holds, feeling the coarse basalt tear at his skin.

"Woman Face!" Sis-ki-dee roared out above him. "Hurry! I have a skinning knife ready. I mean to wear your face when I poke your woman."

"That is all I know, sister," Two Twists assured Honey Eater, whom he truly did love as a sister. "Little Horse sent me to tell you. Be ready this night for treachery. I know Touch the Sky has left you a gun. I also know you have the fighting fettle to use it. Keep it to hand. You, also, Sharp Nosed Woman—be ready. These Bull Whips have lost all honor, and I think they would not scruple to kill women. Especially you two."

"After darkness?" Sharp Nosed Woman repeated, incredulous. "They would move then? Shed blood in the evil of nighttime?"

"Of course they would," Honey Eater said. She, among all of them, had found it easy to believe of these dungheaps. "Wolf Who Hunts Smiling has already killed our own. Why stop now or respect *any* of the law-ways? He is as low as the bloodthirsty Comanches."

Later, Honey Eater noticed a curious thing. Her little boy refused to sleep in his usual place near the center pole of the tipi. Instead, he insisted on crawling toward the entrance flap, taking up a spot very near it.

Almost as if he were being . . . vigilant. Of course that was foolish. Still . . .

She almost moved him after he finally fell asleep, but thought better of it. He was his father's son, and what appeared to be odd behavior usually had its good reasons. So she left Little Bear where he was.

His father . . . Oh, how terribly she longed to feel her tall, strong husband pressing her against the flat, hard muscles of his chest. Yes, they faced a world of hurt here in the Powder country. But they were united. She, Sharp Nosed Woman, Little Horse, Two Twists, Tangle Hair, and the loyal Bow Strings who even now protected her tipi.

But Touch the Sky? All alone he faced a foe worthy to be the Wendigo's nemesis. It had always been that way since he joined the tribe. Whenever misery and suffering and danger were doled out, he got double portions.

On the other side of the center pole slept Sharp Nosed Woman, a war club lying near her robes. She snored softly, occasionally muttering in her sleep—silly little snippets to her long-dead husband Smiles Plenty, killed by Pawnees in the same attack that killed Honey Eater's mother.

And near the flap, unperturbed, Little Bear slept on, his hands balled into tiny fists.

Be ready this night for treachery.

Honey Eater made sure the two-shot, over-and-under parlor gun was near her right hand. Outside, an owl hooted, and another answered. That made her feel better because she knew those weren't owls—they were Bow String sentries relaying the all clear.

Slowly, still thinking of her husband, Honey Eater tumbled down a long tunnel into sleep.

* * *

Get Four Books Totally
F R E E* –
A Value between
$16 and $20

Tear here and mail your FREE* book card today!

PLEASE RUSH
MY FOUR FREE*
BOOKS TO ME
RIGHT AWAY!

LeisureWestern Book Club
P.O. Box 6613
Edison, NJ 08818-6613

AFFIX
STAMP
HERE

By the time he was halfway up that stone pinnacle, scrabbling for each hold, Touch the Sky's fingernails were all torn out. The ends of his fingers were raw and bloody and screamed with pain each time he forced them to find another hold where none seemed to be.

Slowly he inched his way up, sheer will and determination impelling him. That, and the knowledge that he had also scaled Wendigo Mountain's cliffs—much higher than this, and in winds strong enough to knock an eagle from its flight. What Cheyennes have done, Arrow Keeper always told him, Cheyennes will do.

Though he was paying for it dearly, his strategy was working so far on one count. Sis-ki-dee, utterly convinced those steps were the only way up, had focused his attention at the spot where they approached the top. Touch the Sky could not see him, but he could certainly hear him. His taunts—and the woman's screams of pain when Sis-ki-dee tormented her for entertainment—were clearly audible. They were Touch the Sky's only way of judging his progress.

The meat he had forced himself to eat earlier had given him valuable strength. But now fatigue licked at his muscles, and up here, fatigue meant more than just halting—it meant losing his hold and falling back to that rocky floor. He willed himself to continue upward, knowing he somehow had to gain the top—he could not make it back down now, this way, if he had to.

Another thing troubled him. He could not speak up or Sis-ki-dee would know his plan. Yet clearly Sis-ki-dee was becoming suspicious as he heard no noises on the winding steps. Now Touch the Sky heard him moving around up there, and his stomach sank. He must hope the night was dark enough and avoid glancing up, to keep his eyes from reflecting light.

A long, tense silence followed while he willed handholds to take him higher. Then, turning his blood to ice, came the chilling words from straight overhead:

"Are you down there, Woman Face? Come closer, let us hug."

Touch the Sky held still, not even breathing. He expected each blink of his eyes to bring death. Instead, he heard Sis-ki-dee move back to his original position and begin his taunting again. Clearly he had reassured himself all was safe elsewhere.

"Nothing lives long," Touch the Sky whispered. "Only the earth and the mountains."

When he finished uttering his death song, he resumed the arduous climb.

Honey Eater wasn't sure exactly when she woke up.

Or why. For all seemed peaceful enough. Little Bear's tiny chest, which enclosed such powerful lungs, still rose and fell rhythmically in sleep. Sharp Nosed Woman, too, still slept peacefully, her faint snores whistling in her nostrils.

Nor did anything seem amiss from without the tipi. The camp dogs were quiet. A breeze sighed in the tops of the cottonwoods down near the river. Old Crazy Quilt, an addled grandmother of the Coyote Dancers Clan, was keening softly from her tipi—a token of grief for her husband and two sons, all three slain at the Washita battle. Some nights she went on all night, and most in the tribe found it comforting.

Everything was calm enough. But Honey Eater lay there tense, watching, waiting. Her slim hand snaked out and gripped the checkered stock of the pistol.

Still no sign of danger, nothing to justify this tension. She willed herself to relax, breathing as Touch the Sky had taught her to do when she faced trouble—deeply, from low in her belly, not high in the lungs.

Yes, it was all right, she told herself. They were not foolish enough to strike without help. Not with the likes of Little Horse, Tangle Hair, and Two—

Honey Eater's face drained cold at what happened next.

With no warning and no transition from sleeping to waking, her little boy suddenly sat up. His eyes were wide open, but he saw nothing inside the tipi. Unbelieving—for he was too small to be going through these deliberate motions—she watched Little Bear reach out to lift the entrance flap.

He stared out into the vast darkness. So did his mother. The adult saw nothing to excite alarm. But the child did.

His bear-like roar of warning, ear-splitting in that silent camp, made Honey Eater wince even as her skin goose-pimpled. Later, when the elders compiled the annual Winter Count in pictures that were the only Cheyenne history, Little Bear's roar would become known as the Shout that Saved the People.

The camp defenders were literally sleeping on

their weapons. This roar brought many of them out of their tipis, the war cry on their lips. Honey Eater, too, bravely leaped outside, ready to kill the first Bull Whip who meant to hurt her aunt or her child.

And now she saw the chilling sight: a long, thin line of armed Bull Whips crossing the central clearing!

But her son's roar had alerted one other key player in the drama, the ever-vigilant Little Horse. This sturdy warrior had not gone to sleep. So he was the first defender to leap up to the line.

He had planned it out carefully with Tangle Hair and Two Twists. In order to save this tribe, they would need to seize the element of surprise and use it to create an illusion of massed defense. Honey Eater watched them now, pride swelling her throat. They had learned this white man's trick from her husband.

Little Horse raced up and down, discharging all four barrels of his fierce, revolving barrel shotgun. Loaded with buckshot, it sent a virtual wall of death hurtling across that clearing. At the same time, Tangle Hair and Two Twists emptied their rifles on the far flanks, creating the sense of a wide line of fire.

This bold gamble worked magnificently.

The cowardly Medicine Flute, who had not wanted to participate in the attack anyway, suddenly found buckshot ripping into his flanks like rattlesnake fangs.

Screeching, "I am dead, they have killed me!" he turned tail and ran, making amazing progress for a dead man.

When Swift Canoe, who was no coward, also

threw down his rifle and turned to run, Wolf Who Hunts Smiling roared out, "What are you doing, rabbit brain?"

"Medicine Flute is dead!" he shouted back. "Yet he spoke and ran! The Wendigo is loose among us!"

Several other braves, missing the main meat, heard only the shouted, hysterical words, "The Wendigo is loose among us!" Honey Eater, Little Horse, and the rest watched—amazement starched into their features—as the Bull Whip charge turned into a rout. Shrieking in fear like little children in a thunderstorm, they scattered into the surrounding woods.

Chapter Fifteen

"I will tell you how it is, pretty one," Sis-ki-dee said in a low, intimate tone to his prisoner. "You are in for what the Crooked Feet call a dog-and-pony show. That Cheyenne has the guts of ten men. But he does not credit Sis-ki-dee with enough brains. Many dead men have made this same mistake."

A cheerful fire blazed, for Sis-ki-dee had cached plenty of buffalo chips up here, and they made for excellent fuel. Nor was there any reason to fear a good fire—this was the highest point in Bloody Bones Canyon. Gliding Hawk, gagged and tied at the wrists and ankles, lay well back from the fire and the rim of the basalt platform.

When next Sis-ki-dee spoke to the girl, it was much louder. The words were meant for Touch the Sky's ears, not hers.

"Do you know, little goose? I have heard many

men debate the proper way to kill this Touch the Sky. Most argue for a fast, humane kill. True, they hate this tall Cheyenne who licks crooked white feet. But most Indians, steeped in honor are not eager to see such a capable and courageous warrior suffer an unmanly fate."

The Red Peril tossed back his head and roared with crazy laughter.

"Torture, they argue, is wasted on this buck anyway. Many have witnessed it with their own eyes—nothing, they say, will break this one. Nothing. Under pressure, they say, there is no soft place left in him."

Sis-ki-dee kept his head turned toward the direction of the ascending steps as he spoke. But his thoughts drifted the other way—toward the direction from which he knew the Cheyenne *really* approached. He would play along with the noble red man.

"But do you know, play-pretty? Sis-ki-dee believes *any* man can be broken. Can be reduced to gibbering and begging and crying and making water all over himself in fear. Any man, this Cheyenne shaman included."

Waiting near the spot where the Cheyenne would soon be challenging this position was a coiled net. Sis-ki-dee had it all laid out, ready to throw down when his prey was close enough.

"Any man," he repeated. "I make all of them beg."

Sis-ki-dee had a pile of rocks glowing in the embers of his fire. He used two sticks to scoop one out.

"Bear Caller!" he shouted. "Here is something to make you think of your woman!"

He crossed to Gliding Hawk and dropped the

glowing rock onto the exposed expanse of her stomach. Immediately there was the crackle and stench of flesh cooking and a fierce scream of pain that rivalled the death shriek of an eagle.

"Hurry, Noble Red Man! Perhaps you can save this one from the Contrary Warrior!"

Touch the Sky was long used to Sis-ki-dee's taunting. It was not his way to feel the barb of sharp words. Sis-ki-dee could enjoy his child's game. In fact, the Cheyenne welcomed it. The constant insults told him where his enemy was.

It was exhaustion that he was up against now. He knew his climb was almost over. Somehow, he had avoided falling, and now the holds were even fewer at a time when his every muscle trembled with the effort of this arduous climb.

But one thought drove him on, past any possibility of failure: At the top waited his worst enemy in all the world. Or at least one of them, for he knew Big Tree and Wolf Who Hunts Smiling were the other two poison stingers in an unholy triumvirate.

But neither of them had killed his chief. That was Sis-ki-dee's doing. And now Touch the Sky meant to be his *undoing*. He had only his will, his depleted strength, and the lance point in his sash. However, he meant to kill Sis-ki-dee even if he must dash his brains out on the rocks.

More taunts, and the captive Crow woman screamed. Touch the Sky smelled the stench of human flesh, and anger flattened his lips. Glowing rocks. How well he knew that fiery horror. For hours Henri Lagace, the whiskey peddler, had tortured him with red-hot rocks, leaving deep folds of scar tissue on his chest and stomach.

But one tiny ray of hope still remained: Sis-ki-dee was still directing his remarks toward the place where the steps emerged. Touch the Sky prayed that Maiyun would grant him just enough time—and strength—to climb over that rim and get to that red devil.

He grasped, digging in so hard that blood trickled from his lacerated fingers. Every muscle taut, his face straining, Touch the Sky raised himself up another few inches.

A slight breeze tickled his face like the gentle fingers of a blind person. A breeze! He must be nearing the top.

But this exhaustion . . . he closed his eyes for a long moment to gather and focus his last reserves of will and muscle. He said a brief, silent battle prayer as he touched his personal medicine, badger claws in a small rawhide pouch on his clout. He had no official clan, but Arrow Keeper had presented him with the claws, the clan totem of Chief Running Antelope of the Northern Cheyenne. Running Antelope had been killed in the year the white man's winter-count called 1840, the year Touch the Sky had been born. Arrow Keeper called this chief Touch the Sky's Indian father, and when had Arrow Keeper ever spoken bent words?

Thinking of Arrow Keeper calmed his mind and prepared him.

His groping fingers finally reached the brim. Touch the Sky inhaled deeply, pulled himself up, and managed to hook his elbows to hoist himself up even further.

Abruptly, something smacked into his face,

looped over him, draped weight onto his limbs. A foot smashed into his face, knocking him backward. But instead of falling, he felt himself caught, then reeled in like a gut-hooked fish.

A net! Touch the Sky groped for his lance point, trying to get his arms free of this restraining trap. He must cut himself fr—

"It is finally over, Cheyenne," Sis-ki-dee whispered, and then the hard stock of the North & Savage slammed into Touch the Sky's right temple.

It was the Indian way to boast after a victory, especially a clever one. But despite saving their camp yet again, no one in Touch the Sky's band felt like bragging.

"Your boy saved us," Little Horse assured Honey Eater shortly after the Bull Whips broke for the surrounding trees. "And I hope that I live long enough to someday laugh at the memory of Swift Canoe throwing down his rifle to flee like a scared rabbit. But a thing troubles me greatly."

He and Tangle Hair had ducked in to check on Honey Eater and Sharp Nosed Woman and the baby. Two Twists was keeping watch outside, as were various armed Bow Strings. This situation felt far from resolved—more like the lull between harsh squalls.

"I suspect I know what troubles you," said the perceptive Honey Eater. "I know Cheyenne men well enough to know that they feel it deeply when they think they have lost face in front of the tribe."

"And this night," Sharp Nosed Woman threw in, "the Whips lost face. Oh, did they lose face! They fled from nothing but their own fear, and the entire tribe saw it."

Tangle Hair, too, pitched into the game. "And now they will be implacable in their rage and shame."

"Even now," Little Horse agreed, sticking his head outside the entrance flap to watch the Whips slowly return to camp, one by one, their faces sheepish. But they were not returning to their tipis.

Fear probed its point into Honey Eater. "They will strike again," she said. "And this time nothing will stop them. They are humiliated and will fight like Mandan Berserkers to reestablish their manhood."

"All true except on one count," Little Horse corrected her. His gaze shifted across to the Panther Clan circle. "One thing would stop them."

"Will you be coy like the girls?" Tangle Hair demanded. "What thing? Speak it or bury it, buck! Time is nipping."

"There is only once chance left to us," Little Horse said. "There is one brave who serves as the queen for all these low-crawling workers. Seize the queen, and they will have no hive. So I am going to seize him. And I am going to hold him until Touch the Sky returns. And if our shaman does not return, then I mean to kill this queen of theirs."

His rage had passed quickly, leaving Wolf Who Hunts Smiling filled with a cold, hard determination.

His attempts to stop the Bull Whips had been futile once the rumor flew round that Medicine Flute was supposedly dead, yet walking. Now he sat alone in his tipi, trying to determine his best course of action.

He was weary of this constant cat-and-mouse game. He and Touch the Sky had tested, tormented, and probed each other's vulnerable places while they waited for the right moment to close for the kill. Now, even with his archenemies gone and presumably dead, the cat-and-mouse madness continued.

How long could he tolerate frustration heaped on frustration? Wolf Who Hunts Smiling had powerful dreams of glory. When he was still a child playing war with willow-branch shields, he used to watch the chiefs and soldier-troop leaders ride at the head of the Sun Dance parades. Their war bonnets, heavy with coup feathers, trailed out behind them. And they held their faces stern and proud as the people pointed in awe—for were they not warriors who must maintain an aloof dignity around women and children?

Long ago those dreams had ceased to be sufficient. There was this rat gnawing in his belly, a cankering need for power and respect. Now he must—

Lost in rumination, never expecting trouble so soon after a failed strike, Wolf Who Hunts Smiling looked up hopefully when the entrance flap was thrown back.

But it was Little Horse. And he was aiming his flintlock shotgun at him.

The new arrival's free left hand tossed a hunk of jerked meat at Wolf Who Hunts Smiling. The brave barely caught it before it smacked into his face.

"Settle in and enjoy a meal," Little Horse said

affably, inviting himself into the tipi and setting cross-legged near the center pole. "I have moved in with you, buck. And neither I nor my gun will be leaving until our shaman returns. As soon as your brave 'men' return from hiding in the woods, put out the word: At the next sign of rebellion, your guts go out the back of this tipi."

Pain pulsed through every fiber of his being, white-hot, insistent. Wave after wave, washing over him, each one pulling him closer to awareness.

"Look, pretty!" Sis-ki-dee's voice rang out. "Your red champion comes sassy once again. No time to finish our sport now. But I will take care of it after we have had some diversion with our Cheyenne visitor."

Sis-ki-dee had just finished untying Gliding Hawk, preparing to mount her, when Touch the Sky finally arrived. For the Red Peril, it was most important pleasures first. A woman could always be had, but how often did the tall Bear Caller offer himself up?

While Touch the Sky was still unconscious, he had removed the net and bound him with strips of green rawhide at the ankles and wrists. Now, as the prisoner's eyes eased open, Sis-ki-dee howled his savage cry of triumph.

"All of heaven and earth will shake this day! The equinox will be knocked off schedule! The Yellow River will run clear! All these things and more, for today I skin the face of Touch the Sky!"

The pearl-handled bowie was already in his hand. But Sis-ki-dee did not hurry. Touch the Sky watched him there in the shifting firelight, tall and terrible as he loomed over him. Every effort against the rawhide strips only cut deep into his skin, adding to the pain.

"It is an art we Blackfoot warriors prize," Sis-ki-dee said. "Taking off a man's face, I mean. You Plainsmen can have your scalps. We will not waste good rope hair for trophies. Done correctly, the face can be removed in one fast slice, followed by a sharp tug."

"Your mother meant to have a man," Touch the Sky said. "Instead she had this girl who tries to scare her betters to cover her fear."

"One fast outline cut," Sis-ki-dee said, bending closer and prodding the point of the bowie into Touch the Sky's forehead near the hairline.

Touch the Sky winced when, all of an instant, Sis-ki-dee sliced hard and cut his forehead open for most of its length. Blood poured into his eyes, and despite his will to be strong the thought of his face being literally sliced off nearly panicked him.

But Sis-ki-dee stopped after that first swipe, howling with delighted laughter.

"Look! Look, pretty! Your brave hero has turned as pale as a fish belly. If I slice his face off now, it will be a white man's face."

"You will need to cut off more than my face," Touch the Sky taunted him, "if you would be a man."

Sis-ki-dee grinned, appreciating this. "Buck, you are a man! Look at you! Even now, as I peel back your visage to leave raw, red meat, you defy me. Do you see why I will indeed boast about this kill? Wolf Who Hunts Smiling has already promised me a string of ten fine ponies just for your heart."

Bloody Bones Canyon

Touch the Sky could hardly keep his eyes open, so much warm blood streamed into them.

Sis-ki-dee probed the point of his knife close again, and it took all of Touch the Sky's great strength to refuse to pull back or show fear.

"I am going to continue the outline cut," Sis-ki-dee explained. "Once I have made a fairly shallow cut all the way around, I can peel it off. But be ready—sometimes an eyeball will pop out when the skin is removed."

The blade sliced down the right side of his head, just in front of the ear from the hairline to the hinge of his jaw.

"Good work, Red Peril!" Sis-ki-dee congratulated himself. "Your face will come off in one fine piece. Wait until you see yourself."

Now blood streamed down Touch the Sky's chest, too. He is going to do it, he realized. He is stealing my very face!

"You know me, buck," Sis-ki-dee told him. "You know I will have to kill you this time. But I want you to cross over knowing something else: I am packing your face on salt to preserve it, and then I am sending a runner to your Honey Eater with it. She will have something to remember you by."

Completely intent on finally enjoying this moment, Sis-ki-dee had forgotten about his Crow prisoner. He was forcefully reminded, however, when she suddenly seized his oak war club and ran forward, slamming it into his head.

That blow, Touch the Sky realized, would have killed most men. But Sis-ki-dee was not even out. He folded to the dirt-covered basalt, stunned but not unconscious.

"Hit him again!" Touch the Sky said, but Gliding Hawk was hysterical with fear and threw the club down, trying to avoid Sis-ki-dee.

"Hit him!" Touch the Sky roared, but she didn't understand or couldn't comply. He cursed in English, watching Sis-ki-dee shake his head to clear it.

"Then cut me free!" he commanded in Sioux. "Get the knife from him and cut me free!"

"No!" she said, shying back from the monster struggling to stand up. "I can't!"

"My sash!" Touch the Sky managed. "In my sash! Hurry! Get the lance point and cut me free!"

Sis-ki-dee lost the glaze over his eyes. Slowly, the sick smile began to take over his face again. But now, finally, Gliding Hawk was taking orders, slapped to her senses by the authority in Touch the Sky's tone.

She pulled the lance point out, but her trembling fingers dropped it twice before she managed to start cutting with it.

"Faster, Gliding Hawk!" Touch the Sky urged her. "Faster!"

With a snap, his wrists were free. His hands were far too numb and swollen to be of any use yet, so she moved down to start on his ankles. Touch the Sky helped by applying all the pressure he could. The rawhide was about to give, he could feel—

With a roar of triumph, Sis-ki-dee rose and leaped on Gliding Hawk, knocking her away from Touch the Sky.

Chapter Sixteen

Touch the Sky was helpless to stand and fight when Sis-ki-dee leaped on Gliding Hawk. The huge Blackfoot's momentum rolled him and the woman well beyond the grasp of Touch the Sky's untied hands.

Sis-ki-dee was no fool. Although Gliding Hawk had surprised him by showing unexpected spirit, she was not the chief threat to his life. So as soon as she was out of his way, he turned, bowie held low for the upward thrust to vitals, and rushed at Touch the Sky.

Though he could not stand due to his still-bound ankles, the tall Cheyenne tucked his chin to his chest and rolled hard. His movement saved his life, the ten-inch blade ripping a piece of his shirt as he flashed out of its path. But the roll carried him closer to the edge of the basalt turret—closer to a

161

sheer drop of some two-hundred feet to the hard rock floor below.

Sis-ki-dee snarled and turned on him swift as a civet cat. This time Touch the Sky was forced to meet the charge. His still-swollen hands flashed out, deftly caught the charging renegade by both ankles, and lifted hard even as he rolled backwards.

His timing was perfect. Sis-ki-dee flew, tumbling head over heels and landing near his hobbled claybank. He hit hard enough to shake him up again.

Touch the Sky, his face wild with desperation, spotted the lance point still in Gliding Hawk's hand.

"Throw it to me!" he commanded, and she responded immediately, tossing the chipped-stone point to him.

Sis-ki-dee had struggled to his knees, starting to turn around as Touch the Sky desperately sawed through the stiff rawhide binding his ankles. With a determined roar, the death sheen in his eyes, the Red Peril raised the bowie again and rushed him.

The last strands still hadn't quite broken. With blood surging into his brain, Touch the Sky was forced to drop the lance point to once again meet the charge. This time Sis-ki-dee feinted and swerved at the last second, and Touch the Sky felt white-hot fire rip into his shoulder as the blade sliced it deep.

He couldn't throw his enemy this time, so Touch the Sky did the next best thing: he seized him for the death hug. The two big Indians howled and grunted and cursed and gasped, first one up, then the other, leaving each other's blood smeared everywhere as they poured their fury into this battle.

Again and again the bowie sliced him with the quick pain of snake fangs. But Touch the Sky managed to fend it away from his vitals, taking cut after cut to the face, arms, and hands. He was at a serious disadvantage, however, without the use of his legs. Slowly, as they rolled ever closer to that deadly edge, Sis-ki-dee was wearing him down. And now the Blackfoot sensed, at long last, the final victory.

His twisted, scar-pocked visage was only inches away from Touch the Sky's. Sis-ki-dee grinned. His blade was about to sever his victim's windpipe.

"Feel it, Bear Caller? Feel your last reserves of strength giving out? You are using both arms to hold my knife back, and look—here it comes anyway!"

He howled again, and indeed Touch the Sky could feel the steel pressing deeper. If only he could free his powerfully muscled legs and put them into this fight!

"Gliding Hawk!" he screamed. "It is our last chance! Cut my ankles free!"

Sis-ki-dee could do little when she scrambled forward and began doing as ordered—every cell of his being was focused on getting that blade into his adversary's neck. It pressed deeper still, hurting terribly, and Touch the Sky's muscles just couldn't hold on—

Gliding Hawk cried out in triumph when the last strand gave out. It was only a heartbeat's work for Touch the Sky to raise both strong legs, scissor them around his attacker, and throw him over that edge.

But even then the Red Peril fought back.

As he felt himself going over, Sis-ki-dee groped wildly, seized Gliding Hawk's arm, and pulled her over with him. Her scream alerted Touch the Sky just in time for him to seize Sis-ki-dee's sash. Thus, though she hung completely over, Sis-ki-dee managed to catch himself with one hand and one leg clinging to the edge. Touch the Sky held him while Sis-ki-dee's free arm held the girl.

Nonetheless, Sis-ki-dee hardly held the advantage, for Touch the Sky was the only one left on solid ground. And now Touch the Sky saw something in his enemy's face he had never seen there before: raw, savage fear of dying.

"Touch the Sky!" he shouted desperately. "You see how it is! Kill me and she dies. She is innocent!"

"So? You are right. She is innocent. Hear her singing her death song? She will cross over this day and be with the High Holy Ones. As for you, dungheap, you killed my chief! Your time has come, and it hardly matters if *you* sing a death song."

Touch the Sky loosened his grip on the sash, and Sis-ki-dee sagged dangerously lower. His copper face blanched.

"No!" he shouted. "By the directions, no! You are a shaman, a man of honor. You cannot kill her to get me!"

"I cannot? Blackfoot, only watch me."

In fact Touch the Sky had no intention of letting Gliding Hawk die if he could help it. Yes, Cheyenne law-ways called for the death of Sis-ki-dee. But a higher law protected innocent life. He could not break a greater law to satisfy a lesser.

"No!" Sis-ki-dee cried, and this time there was no

other word for it—he was pleading. "No, Touch the Sky! I beg you, Cheyenne, show mercy! Do not kill me, *please!*"

In that moment Touch the Sky felt a near-total triumph. Never, not once, had this insane renegade ever showed a sign of humility or cowardice. Now listen to the white-liver!

"Quit your blubbering, Sis-ki-dee, and hang on to Gliding Hawk. I am pulling both of you up."

But only a moment later, Sis-ki-dee's panic passed. And he realized what he had just done and what was about to happen. The hateful Cheyenne had just humiliated him—Sis-ki-dee!—and meant to kill him as soon as the girl was safe.

"Hold!" he commanded even as Touch the Sky started tugging. "I swear by the earth and the sun—I will drop her and let you drop me if you do not listen!"

"I have ears, Contrary Warrior."

"Then use them well, for this is how it stands. Before you pull me up, swear this thing on your honor: that you will leave with the woman and not harm me."

Frustration roiled inside him, for Touch the Sky saw how it was. No Cheyenne worthy of the name ever gave his word and broke it, even to an enemy. Unlike white men, red men could not "cross their fingers" to cancel a verbal promise. Words were holy, and Indians hated a liar above all else.

"Swear it, and quickly! I cannot hold her much longer!"

There was nothing else for it. Once again, as so often with Sis-ki-dee, he had reached the conclusion where little was concluded. But even now, his disappointment so keen it hurt like a stab, he savored it again: the sight of Sis-ki-dee with panic in his eyes, begging like a cowardly Ponca!

"You have my word," he said. "And also this promise, I will kill you next time we meet."

And this time, Sis-ki-dee was too relieved to insult him. But even as he began hauling both of them up, Touch the Sky saw it written clear in his enemy's face. From here on out Sis-ki-dee's wrath would be implacable, for this Cheyenne was the only man alive who had ever made him beg for mercy.

"Brother," Little Horse said, "I am sorry past all sorrow that the Red Peril lives on. But seeing you ride into this camp on his claybank was joy enough for me. I was sick of Wolf Who Hunts Smiling's tipi and his smell. In truth, I had almost given you up for dead, and I meant to kill him."

"Buck, I should have waited a day!"

All three of his companions and Honey Eater joined in the laugh that followed this joke. But their mirth was quickly contained. For Little Horse's words, spoken just before Touch the Sky rode north, still held true: *The tribe is between dog and wolf.*

Touch the Sky and Gliding Hawk had left Sis-ki-dee to his own devices, taking both his horse and his saddlebag stuffed with food. The Crow Tribe had honored him with a scalp dance when he returned Gliding Hawk to them. But though he was relieved to be back and to have found his family and friends safe, Touch the Sky felt the nagging pressure of an unfulfilled promise. For he was the

Arrow Keeper, and those sacred arrows remained stained until Sis-ki-dee was sent under.

Little Bear crawled into his father's lap, trying to seize the pretty bear-claw necklace Honey Eater had given Touch the Sky as a wedding gift. Touch the Sky lifted his boy up, tossed him high into the air, and caught him on the drop. Little Bear roared for more of the same.

Honey Eater had described, in vivid detail, how the baby had saved the tribe by roaring out a warning. Yes, thought Touch the Sky, hard times and tearful trails lay ahead for the Shaiyena people. But as this little packet of courage proved, stout warriors would not be lacking when the Last Battle loomed.

His eyes met Little Horse's across the firepit. Touch the Sky then met the eyes of Tangle Hair and Two Twists.

"You three jays," he said proudly. "While I was wasting my time in the north country, you held this camp from the traitors. Trouble has met his match in you three. Good, for trouble is the range we ride. Now stuff a pipe and let us smoke to friendship."

RENEGADE
SIEGE

Prologue

Although Matthew Hanchon bore the name given to him by his adopted white parents, he was the son of full-blooded Northern Cheyennes. The lone survivor of a bluecoat massacre in 1840, the infant was raised by John and Sarah Hanchon in the Wyoming Territory settlement of Bighorn Falls.

His adoptive parents loved him as their own, and at first, the youth was happy enough in his limited world. The occasional stares and threats from some white settlers meant little—until his sixteenth year brought a forbidden love for Kristen, daughter of the wealthy rancher Hiram Steele.

Steele's campaign to run Matthew off like a distempered wolf was assisted by Seth Carlson, a jealous, Indian-hating cavalry officer who was in love with Kristen. Carlson delivered a fateful ultimatum: Either Matthew cleared out of Big-horn Falls for good, or Carlson would break the Hanchons' contract to supply nearby Fort Bates, thus ruining their mercantile business.

His heart sad but determined, Matthew set out for the up-country of the Powder River, Cheyenne territory. Captured by braves from Chief Yellow Bear's tribe, the youth was declared an Indian spy for the hair-face soldiers. Matthew was brutally tortured over fire. Then, only a heartbeat before he was to be scalped and gutted, old Arrow Keeper interceded.

The tribe shaman and protector of the sacred Medicine Arrows, Arrow Keeper had recently experienced an epic vision. This vision foretold that the long-lost son of a great Cheyenne chieftain would return to his people and lead them in one last great victory against their enemies. This youth would be known by the distinctive mark of the warrior, the same birthmark Arrow Keeper spotted buried past this youth's hairline: a mulberry-colored arrowhead.

Arrow Keeper used his influence among the tribesmen to save the youth's life. He also ordered that Matthew be allowed to join the tribe and train with the junior warriors. This action especially infuriated two braves: the fierce war leader Black Elk and his cunning cousin Wolf Who Hunts Smiling.

Black Elk was jealous of the glances cast at the tall young stranger by Honey Eater, daughter of Chief Yellow Bear. And Wolf Who Hunts Smiling, proudly ambitious despite his youth, hated all whites without exception. This stranger, to him, was only a make-believe Cheyenne who wore white man's shoes, spoke the paleface tongue, and showed his emotions in his face like the woman-hearted white men.

To help Matthew become accepted by the tribe, Arrow Keeper buried his white name forever and gave him a new Cheyenne name: Touch the Sky. But the youth remained a white man's dog in the eyes of many in the tribe. At first humiliated at every turn, the determined youth eventually mastered the warrior arts. Slowly, as his coup stick filled with enemy scalps, he won the respect of more and more of his people.

Touch the Sky helped save his village from Pawnee attacks. He defeated ruthless whiskey traders bent on destroying the Indian way of life. He outwitted land-grabbers intent on stealing the Cheyenne homelands for a wagon road. He saved Cheyenne prisoners kidnapped by Kiowas and Comanches during a buffalo hunt. He rode north into the Bear Paw Mountains to save Chief Shoots Left Handed's Cheyennes from Seth Carlson's Indian-fighting regiment. He ascended fearsome Wendigo Mountain to recover the stolen Medicine Arrows. And he saved Honey Eater and many others when he risked his life to obtain a vaccine against the deadly Mountain Fever.

But with each victory, deceiving appearances triumphed over reality, and the acceptance Touch the Sky so desperately craved eluded him. Worse yet, his hard-won victories left him with two especially fierce enemies outside the tribe: a Blackfoot called Sis-ki-dee and a Comanche named Big Tree.

As for the Cheyenne warrior Black Elk, he was hard but fair at first. When Touch the Sky rode off to save his white parents from outlaws, however, Honey Eater was convinced that Touch the

Sky had deserted her and the tribe forever. She was forced to accept Black Elk's bride-price after her father crossed to the Land of Ghosts. But Touch the Sky returned.

Then, as it became clear to all that Honey Eater loved Touch the Sky only, Black Elk's jealousy drove him to join his younger cousin in plotting against Touch the Sky's life. Finally, Wolf Who Hunts Smiling's treachery forced a crisis: Aiming at Touch the Sky in heavy fog, he instead killed Black Elk. Now Touch the Sky stands accused of the murder in the eyes of many.

Though their love divided the tribe irrevocably, Touch the Sky and Honey Eater performed the squaw-taking ceremony and now have a son. He has firm allies in his blood brother Little Horse, the youth Two Twists, and Tangle Hair. With Arrow Keeper's mysterious disappearance, Touch the Sky has become the tribe shaman. But an unholy alliance between Wolf Who Hunts Smiling, Big Tree, and Sis-ki-dee has given birth to the Renegade Nation. The Nation's chief goal is the destruction of Touch the Sky, who remains trapped between two worlds, welcome in neither.

Chapter One

"Brother," Touch the Sky called out, "come out and help me smoke this pipe."

All Cheyenne lodges were raised with their entrances facing east toward the sun and the source of all life. And now the elkskin entrance flap of Little Horse's tipi was thrown back, letting in the bright coppery sunshine. Sitting just inside the entrance on a heap of soft buffalo robes, the sturdy brave was polishing a beautiful silver dagger.

Little Horse knew from long acquaintance with Touch the Sky's tone and manner that the tall brave had not stopped by to discuss the causes of the wind. But custom dictated that warriors never come at an important subject too directly. So Little Horse stepped outside and joined his friend in the lush new grass that was already past their ankles.

11

Little Horse held his Spanish dagger out in the sunlight, and the brilliant reflection made Touch the Sky squint. The blade was double-honed, fine-tempered steel, the haft pure silver inlaid with an exquisite ruby.

"Time is a bird, buck." Little Horse nodded at the dagger while Touch the Sky lit his clay calumet with a borrowed coal. "You gave me this as a gift when Honey Eater told you she was heavy with child. Now that child has two winters behind him and roars like a silvertip bear. Time is a bird, and the bird is on the wing."

Little Horse's words reminded Touch the Sky that their people were preparing for another uneasy season of their camp being divided against itself. It was early in the Moon When the Green Grass Is Up, and this Cheyenne band under the new chief named River of Winds had recently packed their entire camp onto travois. Facing east, singing the Song to the New Sun Rising, they rode out one morning at dawn from their winter home in the Tongue River Valley.

Their ponies were winter worn, gaunt from a scant diet of cottonwood bark, twigs, and buds. The first of the warm moons would be spent grazing the ponies at this permanent summer camp near the fork of the Powder and the Little Powder. Once the ponies had their strength again, herd scouts would be sent out to locate Uncle Pte, the buffalo. Then would come the annual hunt.

All that was normal, thought Touch the Sky, or so it might seem to the causal observer. But in truth death stalked this camp, watching for his chance like a cat on a rat.

For some time further, the two braves dis-

12

cussed inconsequential matters and kept a close eye on the activity around them. Finally, Touch the Sky laid the pipe down on the ground between them—the sign that serious discussion could begin.

"Look there." He gazed toward the vast central clearing.

Little Horse followed his friend's eyes. Beyond the youths wrestling in the clearing, past the first clan circles of tipis, stood the lone tipi of the brave named Medicine Flute. Only two Cheyennes were permitted, by custom, to live outside of the clan gatherings: the peace chief River of Winds, who had been voted peace leader after the brutal murder of Chief Gray Thunder, and the tribe's shaman, the title held—though under dispute—by Touch the Sky and claimed by Medicine Flute.

"What do you notice about the bone blower's lodge?" Touch the Sky asked. He had used the contemptuous name all in his band gave Medicine Flute, whose so-called flute was a crude instrument made from a human leg bone.

"Only this," Little Horse replied. "That it is quiet of late. Too quiet."

Satisfied, Touch the Sky pursed his lips into a grim straight line. He was at least a head taller than most braves in camp and muscled more like the Apaches to the southwest than like the typically slender-limbed Plains Indians. A strong hawk nose set off an intelligent face. He wore his black hair long, except where it was cut short over his eyes to clear his vision. His scarred chest and arms, pocked by burns and knife scars and old bullet wounds, told the violent history of his life among the red men.

13

"Too quiet indeed, buck. Your thoughts fly with mine. They should all be gathered there, should they not? All of our enemies within the tribe. Medicine Flute, Wolf Who Hunts Smiling, the Bull Whip soldiers. Gathered there and plotting."

"But they are not," Little Horse said, continuing his friend's line of thought. "Why?"

"Because they had all the time of the short white days to plot in our winter camp. And now they have their plan."

"And whatever it is," Little Horse said, glancing west toward the distant ranges of the Sans Arc Mountains, "has something to do with all the word-bringers they have sent to the renegades on Wendigo Mountain."

"Buck, I am called shaman, but you too see which way the wind sets." Touch the Sky gazed toward those distant peaks. Wendigo Mountain could not be seen from there because its tip was always enshrouded in steam that escaped from underground hot springs.

"Their disappointment was keen," Little Horse said, "when you returned from Bloody Bones Canyon up north. They were sure that Sis-ki-dee had sent you under."

"He did send me under," Touch the Sky said, recalling the huge rockslide Sis-ki-dee sent crashing down on him. "But the High Holy Ones did not choose to leave me there. Not only did I disappoint the Contrary Warrior, but you kept our enemies in camp from seizing the reins of power. All winter they have been seething, as frustrated as badgers in a barrel. Now they will come at us with a vengeance."

"But how?" Little Horse asked. "And where? I

see no preparations, no plotting, no gathering of weapons. The Bull Whips have not been working their ponies, and even more ominous, they have actually been civil toward the Bow String troopers, their sworn enemies. Yes, they seem to expect some great event. Yet they hardly seem prepared for it themselves."

"Brother, you have placed the ax on the helve," Touch the Sky agreed, and again his deep-set black eyes cut toward the Sans Arc range. "They expect trouble, but this time they will not be a part of it."

"They let Sis-ki-dee kill our last chief," he mused, avoiding Gray Thunder's name, as one did when speaking of the dead. "And I fear they are depending on him again. Him or Big Tree. Or even worse, both of them with their combined camp of murdering Kiowas and Comanches."

"A strike on our camp?" Little Horse said.

"Anything is possible. I will speak with Tangle Hair and Two Twists. Everyone in our little band must watch with the vigilance of five men. They are both on herd guard now. I will speak to them when they return."

"Speaking of trouble clouds blowing our way," Little Horse said, "look what approaches from the river."

Touch the Sky glanced down the long, sloping bank of grass that ended at the spring-swollen Powder. A small but powerfully built brave approached them at a cautious, oblique angle. His eyes constantly shifted, darted, watched for the ever expected attack.

"No need to take up weapons," Wolf Who Hunts Smiling called over, seeing the dagger glint in Little Horse's hand. "My weapons are back in my tipi."

Touch the Sky's lips curled back in a sneer. "Little Horse, do you smell sweet lavender? Honeyed words from a stinking, murdering snake?"

Little Horse nodded. "As you say. Look how he comes to council. He who has killed our own. He who has tried to kill your wife and babe and each of us in our turn. A worm who grins like a wolf and tries to look you in the eye like a man."

For a moment, Wolf Who Hunts Smiling almost lost honor by showing his rage. But he managed to hold his face impassive as a warrior should. Indeed, it was Touch the Sky's ignorant mistake of showing his feelings in his face—when he was first captured many winters ago—that had earned him the name Woman Face from his enemies.

"Never mind," Wolf Who Hunts Smiling said, still strangely calm, it seemed to both braves. Alarmingly so. This was the confident manner of a man who held the high ground and all the escape trails. "Never mind your blustering and insults. I have a destiny to fulfill and you two jays have irked me long enough. I admit you are both warriors and nothing else. Tangle Hair and young Two Twists also. Four bucks worth twenty, all worthy to wear the medicine hat into battle."

Neither brave said a word to this. Their impassive faces, however, disguised amazed minds. This conciliatory tone and these laudatory words were no part of the wily wolf they knew—unless he had a new plan.

"You are warriors," Wolf Who Hunts Smiling repeated. "I have been unable to kill you. Nor have you killed me, though both of you have tried more than once."

"And will again," Little Horse promised.

"Never mind all this praising of us," Touch the Sky said impatiently. "My boasts are made with weapons, and your praise I do not value at all. I have no ears for it. Crack the nut and expose the meat. I am sick of looking on your putrid, murdering form."

"Just this, Noble Red Man. I need fighters like you. Cross your lances over mine, swear allegiance to my new Renegade Nation, and we will enjoy equal shares of the plunder. Your band, united with mine, Sis-ki-dee's, and Big Tree's! Bucks, why push when a thing will not move? We cannot kill one another, and we are in each other's way. So why not instead profit together?"

"Listen to this jay," Touch the Sky said. "Setting himself up as a Roman Nose and turning us into his Dog Soldiers to slay the old headmen in their sleep. The bravery of the Spaniards and the whiskey traders."

"You have heard me. I will not repeat the offer. Know this. Certain events are even now being set in motion. The outcome of these events will enrich my Renegade Nation beyond any peyote fantasy. Once these riches are mine, I will not need you and your followers. The renegades will be armed with the new paleface repeaters and lavishly equipped for battle."

Wolf Who Hunts Smiling suddenly spat, his gesture showing a glimpse of his usual manner around his enemies. "You can ride with me or continue fighting me. But if you cannot stop us now, how will you when we are stronger than a bluecoat regiment?"

This question, Touch the Sky realized, explained Wolf Who Hunts Smiling's new confidence. The murderous brave and his allies were about to strike at some wealthy hair-face interest, and the thought did indeed alarm Touch the Sky. Wolf Who Hunts Smiling had explained matters with a cold accuracy. Since so many blue-bloused soldiers had been called back beyond the Great Waters, possibly to fight their own white brothers, few soldiers remained.

If the Renegade Nation obtained such equipment as Wolf Who Hunts Smiling boasted of, Touch the Sky knew they would control the West. The fierce Blackfeet warriors to the north had been wiped out by the yellow vomit, and the Crow Nation was unmanned by strong water. No one could stop them.

"At least tell us this fine plan," Touch the Sky replied. "I already know of worse treachery involving you. Why hesitate to say which whites you are attacking? It cannot be my parents this time. They don't have the riches you boast of. So why not tell us like a man instead of hinting like the girls in their sewing lodge?"

Wolf Who Hunts Smiling flashed a cunning grin. "Good attempt, buck, but I will not tell you. Just count upon it. The worm will turn and soon. For the sake of your wife and child, if nothing else, consider my offer."

With those ominous words, Wolf Who Hunts Smiling turned and walked back toward the common clearing. Baffled and worried, Little Horse and Touch the Sky exchanged a long look. And his enemy's veiled words sparked in Touch the Sky's thoughts like burning twigs: *Certain events are even now being set in motion.*

*   *   *

"Last spelling lesson, we talked about mnemonic tricks," Kristen Steele said. "Faith, what do I mean by mnemonic?"

Faith Gillycuddy, one of the brightest pupils in the sixth form, stood up from the long wooden bench where she sat with the rest of the older girls. "It's from the Greek word for memory, and the first m is silent. A mnemonic device is a trick to aid your memory."

Kristen nodded. Tall and willow slender, she was in her early twenties. Her hair was as golden as new oats, and her cornflower-blue eyes were as bottomless as a cloudless sky. "Such as?"

"There's a rat in the word separate. That reminds you not to place an e in the middle of the word."

Kristen started to speak, then caught herself and waited for the big steam auger to quit its grinding roar. Teaching in a mine-camp school had definite advantages. Chief among them was the fact that the kids could not easily play hooky since they lived too close to school. But fighting to be heard above the blasts, digging, and constant mucking of ore made her feel like a sergeant, not a teacher.

"Very good," Kristen said when she could be heard. "On the last spelling test, nearly all of you misspelled the word dessert. You confused it with the word desert. Rather than copying the words over and over in your hornbooks, we can make up a mnemonic device. Just remember that dessert is something sweet."

"Aw, hell, Miz Steele," piped up Justin McKinney, son of the mine foreman. "Now you got my stomach growlin'."

"For swearing in the classroom," Kristen said sternly to check the other students' laughter, "you'll stay after school for one hour and split stove lengths."

"Aw, hell! You're a nice lady and all, but who cares about any ol' stupid spelling rules?" Justin demanded. "I'm gonna be a miner like my old man and his old man before him. My pa can't even sign his name, and he runs this gang—after Mr. Riley, of course. If pa can't cipher or write, why should I?"

Despite his spirited mouth, Justin had a good nature and what Kristen termed a rude sense of honor. His occasional rebellions in class did not usually bother her. Now, as she glanced out the little room's only sash window at the tidy streets of the Far West Mining Camp, she resisted an affectionate smile. For the sake of discipline, she must maintain her dignity.

"For your information, young man, it was your father who first suggested this school to Caleb Riley."

"He did?" Justin looked betrayed and embarrassed.

"He most certainly did. And he told me that he hoped I could make something out of his boy besides a hardheaded, cussing worker. He wants you to be a mining engineer, not just a gang boss."

"Well, I'll be dam—uh—darned," Justin said.

"He also told me," Kristen added, fighting hard to quell her mirth, "that if I had any trouble from you I should just remind you of the cowhide strop hanging on the door at home."

Justin turned pale and quickly opened his hornbook. "Dessert is something sweet," he repeated as he hastily wrote, and the rest of the class laughed again. This time Kristen joined them.

Taking a chance while the teacher was in a good mood, Sarah Blackford raised her hand.

"Yes, Sarah?"

"Miss Steele, is it true that you're going to marry Caleb Riley's brother Tom, the officer from Fort Bates?"

All of the students stared eagerly at Kristen, and she felt the color come into her face. "We are at our lessons right now, not larking about on Fiddler's Green!"

"She's gettin' married!" Justin exclaimed. "Look at her flush!"

Suddenly, anger warmed Kristen's face. But even as she opened her mouth to reprimand her students, an explosion of gunfire rose above the steady din of the mines.

After an instant of frozen shock, Kristen ran to the propped-open plank door and peered outside. The mining camp was established in a tea-cup-shaped hollow about halfway up a mountain. The schoolhouse was centered among the few streets of simple but sturdy houses made with raw planks and shake roofs. The other half of the hollow was taken up by the mining operation itself.

The entire camp was encircled by a high ridge. Kristen glanced upward and felt her stomach turn to ice when she saw that the entire ridge was covered with armed Indian warriors, their faces garish with battle paint.

A teamster was hauling a wagon of ore toward the railroad siding, where a steam locomotive hooked to several long wagons waited on the spur line. Touch the Sky had sighted that railroad through the mountains for Caleb. The warriors' assistance in building the vital rail link to Register Cliffs had made this mining operation possible. Now, as Kristen watched in horror, the teamster rolled sideways off his wagon, one side of his face a red smear.

Arrows were flying in so heavily that the air was blurred from them. Benny Havens, the camp courier, caught one in the neck and crumpled to his knees. Up near the head frame of the mine, a man emptying a slusher bucket suddenly collapsed and rolled down into the camp, bouncing hard off the rock-strewn slope.

A woman was returning from the company mercantile with a basket of goods. It was Tilly Blackford, Sarah's mother. Kristen cried out when the woman's white bodice suddenly erupted with a scarlet stain before she collapsed.

"No!" Kristen shouted when a few of the boys leapt forward to see what was happening. "Down! Everyone, get down on the floor. It's an Indian attack!"

This news immediately prompted a chorus of screams from the girls, and even the boys turned pale. However, no one obeyed the teacher until a bullet shattered the only window and sent shards of glass flying in like tiny spears.

Chapter Two

"Have ears, Quohada!" said Sis-ki-dee, known as the Contrary Warrior among his few friends and the Red Peril among his many enemies.

The huge Quohada Comanche named Big Tree turned his grinning face from the sight below to listen. Both renegades were flushed with triumph as they watched the miners scurrying around, dousing fires, and tending to their wounded and dead.

"It was a good first strike," Sis-ki-dee said. "We have not lost a man, yet they have lost several. And only look."

He pointed to two mobile wagons loaded with equipment for the Beardslee Flying Telegraph, a portable telegraph capable of sending sonic codes short distances without copper wires and insulators. Both wagons still burned.

"Now they cannot send words through the air

to Register Cliffs. Our men have already torn out the rails of the path for their iron horse. So they can neither escape nor receive any supplies. We have them under siege. With our position here on this excellent high ground, we will make their world a hurting place!"

Sis-ki-dee flashed his crazy grin. He sat on a big claybank atop the long curving ridge that surrounded the mining camp. Big brass rings dangled from slits in his ears, and heavy copper brassards protected his upper arms from enemy lances and axes. His face, once ruggedly handsome, was badly marred by smallpox scars. In defiance of the long-haired Blackfoot tribe that had banished him, he and all of his braves wore their hair cropped ragged and short. He had just finished sliding his .44-caliber North & Savage rifle into its buckskin sheath.

"We have them," Big Tree agreed. "And Wolf Who Hunts Smiling was right this time. We would lose too many men in a direct attack and might fail to take them. However, we can destroy them with a siege. We have them between the sap and the bark. They cannot leave or call for help nor can they receive supplies."

"Spoken straight arrow," Sis-ki-dee assured him. "And while we have them trapped, we turn the very Wendigo himself loose upon them! By night our fire arrows will warm the cool air; by day our bullets will hum around their ears like blowflies."

This was all true enough. But Big Tree smiled slyly, watching his companion from caged eyes. The Comanche's face was homely, characteristic of his tribesmen, who were considered the ugliest Indians on the plains—and the best horsemen on earth. An eagle-bone whistle hung around his neck, and a gaudy Presidential Medal was pinned to his rawhide shirt. This bore a likeness of the Great White Father and was one of those that had been presented to the tribes upon the most recent treaty signing—a treaty the hair faces violated before the ink was dry.

"Yes," Big Tree said, "we have them. But, of course, word will travel. And the tall bear caller will soon know that we have his friend Caleb Riley up against it. And that sun-haired beauty your loins ache for—the tall one once held her in his blanket for love talk! He will be here, Sis-ki-dee."

Fury burned in Sis-ki-dee's eyes, and at first, he said nothing. Big Tree was goading him, albeit indirectly because, once again, the tall Cheyenne warrior had eluded Sis-ki-dee's best efforts to kill him.

After murdering the Cheyenne Chief Gray Thunder, Sis-ki-dee had fled all the way north to dreaded Bloody Bones Canyon, his former stronghold in the Bear Paw Country. He knew Touch the Sky would follow him, and he had sworn to Big Tree, Wolf Who Hunts Smiling, and all of their followers that he would dangle the tall one's scalp from his sash. Instead, Sis-ki-dee had ended up humiliated and beaten.

But Sis-ki-dee brooked such treatment from no man. "Yes, he will come. And he will bring trouble when he does. But though I have failed to kill him, Quohada, he has not killed me."

"Not for lack of trying, Contrary Warrior. And how many times has he tried to make my wives widows?"

Sis-ki-dee watched the desperate activities below in camp and said, "As you say. So let him come. I am keen for sport. He will not stop us. He cannot. We two have both traded with the Comancheros in our Southwest homeland. We two know, Big Tree, what the red men here in the north country are only beginning to grasp. The whites place foolish value on the yellow rocks they dig from the ground."

He nodded toward the camp. "The yellow dust below will buy our men more new repeating rifles, more bullets, good white man's liquor and coffee, new scarlet strouding. And once we have wiped them out, their campsite will become our second stronghold, a hidden corral for our herds. With sentinels on these ridges, we would control the Sans Arcs Mountains."

Big Tree thrust his red-streamered lance out, and Sis-ki-dee crossed his lance over it. "From where we sit now to the place where the sun goes down," Big Tree vowed, "our enemies have no place to hide! This place hears me! This camp and everything in it is ours. And any man who means to stop us, white or red, will soon be feeding worms!"

Caleb Riley was a big-framed man presently dressed in buckskin trousers and shirt. Usually he also wore a broad-brimmed plainsman's hat and knee-length elkskin moccasins. But this morning, he had gone into the stopes to run a plumb line down a new shaft; so he had donned his heavy boots and a miner's helmet with a squat candle mounted in a little wire cage. He was still wearing them when the surprise attack began.

"Looks as if they're done tossing lead at us for now," Liam McKinney reported.

The burly foreman and his boss had taken cover behind a pile of shoring timbers. Now both men carefully searched the ridges above them.

"Damn featherheads," Liam added. "They shot down Jed Blackford's wife Tilly. Left him a widower and their girl Sarah half orphaned."

"That's just the beginning of our troubles, old son," Caleb said. The mine owner was still shy of 30, and he sported a full blond beard.

"What? Think they ain't done with us yet?"

Caleb shook his head. "I know they're not."

Liam's big bluff face was divided by a frown. "How can you know it, boss? I don't see one Injun up there now."

"When you can't see them," Caleb said, "is when you start worrying. My brother Tom has been fighting Indians since the Fort Laramie Accords started falling apart. Most tribes up here fight skirmish style. They hate to fort up, like white men. They take a shot at you from behind a rock, then move on to a new rock. They use very little organization or battle tactics. Instead, they rely on individual courage to inspire the rest and turn the battle."

Caleb nodded up toward the distant ridge. "But look here. These are Kiowas and Comanches, that renegade bunch from Wendigo Mountain. They'll turn a white man's tactics against him. And right now, my friend, they have us under siege."

"Siege?" Liam said doubtfully.

"Sure. Look at the Beardslee—first thing they burned. That was planned. Now we can't get word out. Want to wager they've taken up the tracks too at some point between here and Register Cliffs?"

27

Liam looked positively sick. "What in the hell for? What do a bunch of gut-eating savages want with this place?"

Caleb was so worried that his blond brows touched as the furrow between his eyes deepened in a frown. "Touch the Sky told me something a while back. He told me that the Comanches and Kiowas have learned the value of gold dust."

"Why even so, we don't have dust on hand! Hell, all we do is send out the ore to be mercury smelted! Those rocks are laced with color, but they're useless right now."

"They don't know we don't have dust on hand. They've learned the value of gold, but not how it's produced."

"Damn!" Liam exclaimed. "And you think they're layin' for us up there?"

Caleb didn't need to answer. At that moment, a miner broke cover and raced from the shelter of a pile of rocks toward his house and frightened family. He made it, but not without drawing several rifle shots and a flurry of arrows from above.

"Are you convinced?" Caleb asked grimly.

Liam swore quietly. "What do we do?"

"We've got men, and we've got arms," Caleb said. "Trouble is, we've also got one lousy position. Damn it, Liam! I've always meant to start posting a permanent guard up on that ridge. Touch the Sky suggested it almost a year ago. I've been so damn busy with these new stopes and recruiting men that I never got around to it."

Caleb swore again. "Well, they've got us! All these women and children. Anyway, we've got to take control. The only way to break a siege is to slip around them. We've got to somehow get word to my brother at Fort Bates. It's two days' hard ride southeast of here."

"What about Touch the Sky?" Liam suggested. "That red son can do for any grizz ever made, and that band of his is all grit and a yard wide."

"I won't send for him," Caleb decided. "He's put his ass on the line for us too much as it is. Besides that, we won't need to send for him. Nothing goes on around here that he doesn't hear about. We may be seeing him yet." Turning from Liam, Caleb called out, "Dakota!"

"Yo!" a voice answered from somewhere behind the mess tent.

"How's that little chestnut mare of yours?"

"Well grained and rested, boss. What's on the spit?"

"Come around to the office after sundown, and I'll tell you. I want you to run a message for me."

Then Caleb peered cautiously around the corner of the timbers. "Meantime, Liam, we've got to make plans for the defense of this camp. Either we roll up our sleeves and quick, or we're going to lose far more than our shirts. Liam, you know all the men by name better than I do. Draw up a list and divide them into three—no, four guard shifts. Six hours each stint, round the clock.

"Post men at the safest possible points among the houses and near the front entrance to camp. And get the order to all the houses: No one shows his face outside the houses by day until those Indians are cleared out. We've got one damned good woman to bury now. I don't want more. Just cross your fingers that we get a message through to Tom. If not, we'll soon be doing the hurt dance."

Chapter Three

Certain events are even now being set in motion.

Wolf Who Hunts Smiling's ominous promise stayed with Touch the Sky like a cankering sore, nagging at him even when he tried to ignore it.

In camp, the routine went forward, reassuring in its familiarity. Every few days, a hunting party rode out. For the time being, the game was plentiful again on the hunting ranges and near the salt licks. Other braves rode herd guard, tended the crude beaver traps, or formed scouting parties. These last were necessary to keep an eye on the movements of nearby red enemies such as the Crows to the north and the Pawnees to the east. Even more fearsome, however, was the new paleface militia called the Regulators. Now and then, Indian fever struck them, and they rode out to massacre a hunting party or terrorize a camp.

"Enough enemies already surround us," Two

Twists complained one night as he and Tangle Hair and Little Horse visited at Touch the Sky's lodge. "Yet we are forced to live like intruders in our own camp."

He nodded toward the buckskin Touch the Sky and Honey Eater had sewn to the inside of their tipi's thinning cover. Similar to the white man's wainscoting, it kept their shadows from showing in the firelight at night.

"You would talk of intruders to Touch the Sky?" Little Horse demanded. "He who has never known a day's true acceptance since he was first captured and brought in among us?"

Tangle Hair was playing with the rambunctious Little Bear, who was trying mightily to grab the strips of red-painted rawhide binding Tangle Hair's braid. The little one possessed amazing strength already. He was the pride of not only Touch the Sky and Honey Eater, but every brave in Touch the Sky's little band of followers. To an Indian, every adult in camp was parent to every child.

"No, I have never been accepted," their shaman said. "But I married the prettiest woman in this camp, and she gave me the finest son. Who are my companions? Only the best warrior between the Sweetwater and the Marias! Never mind singing a dirge for me. I have a more immediate question, bucks. Who knows why the Shoshone sent up smoke this day?"

The Shoshone, with whom the Cheyennes had a shaky peace, lived to the northwest. They were the nearest tribe to the Sans Arcs, as every brave there realized. Pausing as she steeped yarrow tea for them, Honey Eater watched all of them with great interest. She would not speak up, of course,

31

in the presence of a group of men. These matters did not concern women. But she knew full well who lived in the Sans Arcs.

"You saw their smoke too?" Little Horse said. "I cannot read their sign. But I fear the worst trouble in the world will be found there since the messages went on all during the day."

Touch the Sky nodded. "As you say. Our Sioux cousins read their sign better. Perhaps soon we will see one and can ask."

He avoided Honey Eater's curious eyes. Not only did his worst enemies range the Sans Arcs, but the white woman he had once loved lived at the mining camp there. And she would realize he was worried about her.

"Not just the smoke," Little Horse said. "Do you hear them even now? The Bull Whips, I mean. Their lodge is a merry place this night. They are celebrating something. Not one of them does not smile cunningly at me. Something has happened, and they are very pleased, whatever it is."

"I have even heard some of them," Tangle Hair put in, "claim that they will attend the Renewal of the Arrows even though you are our shaman. Such talk worries me. They only cooperate when they have treachery planned or feel confident that we are entering the belly of the beast."

Despite the great dissension in the camp, the mighty Arrow Keeper had left the mantle of shaman on Touch the Sky's shoulders. Dutifully, he conducted the spiritual ceremonies in accordance with the Cheyenne Way handed down by the High Holy Ones. And before the next sunrise, he would cleanse the Arrows, a symbolic purging of the people's guilt and sins. The four sacred

Medicine Arrows were the center of their metaphysics, and it was his task as shaman and Keeper of the Arrows to keep them forever sweet and clean.

"Never mind them," Touch the Sky said. "Let them come or let them gather around Medicine Flute like flies on dung. I am indifferent. Our allies will be there, and we will renew the Arrows. And timely done, bucks! We will need all the strength and guidance of the Arrows if those smoke signals are as important as I fear they are."

Late the next day, while young women kept time with stone-filled gourds, many in the Powder River camp danced at the Renewal of the Arrows. Touch the Sky's clay-painted face was gruesome yet magnificent in the wavering glow of a huge ceremonial fire. This was a rite for the entire tribe, not just the warriors. All who were old enough soon circled the fire. Their knees kicked high as the hypnotic rhythm of stones and the regular cadence of "Hi-ya, hi-ya" lulled them and put the trance glaze over their eyes.

Not everyone came to support the ancient law ways. Touch the Sky could see the rebels, most of them Bull Whips loyal to Wolf Who Hunts Smiling, gathered around Medicine Flute's tipi. The false shaman was conducting the black-magic ceremony known as Praying A Man Into The Ground, and Touch the Sky knew that he was the man whose death they prayed for.

Touch the Sky's face was painted as for war: forehead yellow, nose red, chin black. He wore his single-horned warbonnet, its tail long with coup feathers. For a moment, Touch the Sky thought of the missing Arrow Keeper. And again he felt the power of his epic vision at Medicine Lake many winters ago—the vision quest Arrow Keeper had decreed so that the young warrior could learn his destiny.

Again those vivid and ominous images were laid over his eyes. Red men, thousands of them from every tribe west of the river called Great Waters, all danced as one people, expressing their misery, fear, and utter hopelessness. And on the horizon behind them, guidons snapping in the wind, sabers gleaming in the bloodred sun, came hordes of blue-bloused soldiers. But that vision gave way to more immediate trouble. Again the worried brave thought of all the smoke signals from the Sans Arcs.

Touch the Sky held the four sacred Arrows in a coyote-fur pouch. After the dancing, he unwrapped them and laid them on a stump in the center of camp. The shafts were striped blue and yellow, the crow-feather fletching was dyed bright red. With the Arrows thus presented, the people lined up to leave their gifts.

One by one, every member of the tribe with more than 12 winters behind him knelt beside the Arrows and left something. The gifts reflected their ability to give. Some left valuable pelts, rich tobacco, even weapons; the poorest among them left dyed feathers, decorated coup sticks, or moccasins with beaded soles.

After the gifts had been left, Touch the Sky recited the sacred Renewal Prayer in his most powerful voice. The words drowned out Medicine Flute's reedy voice and idolatrous murmurings.

Oh, Great Spirit of Maiyun,
whose voice we hear in the winds
and whose breath gives life to all the world,
hear us! We are small and weak. We need
your strength and wisdom.

"Let this be so," the people said as one.

Let us walk in beauty, and make our eyes ever
behold the red and purple sunset. Make our
hearts respect the things you have made and
our ears sharp to hear your voice. Make us
wise that we may understand the things you
have taught the people.

"Let this be so," the tribesmen repeated.

Let us learn the lessons you have hidden in
every leaf and rock.
We seek strength, not to be greater than our
brothers, but to fight our greatest enemy—
ourselves.
Make us always ready to come to you with
clean hands and straight eyes.

"Let this be so," the tribe sang as one.
Touch the Sky made a point of seeking the eyes
of Wolf Who Hunts Smiling. His voice swelled
with the power of a ferocious wind; so even his
enemies stood rooted as he concluded the Renewal Prayer in words that echoed out over the
campsite:

So when life fades, as the fading sunset,
our spirits may come to you
without shame.

Touch the Sky was staring dead at his enemy as he said the word shame. "Cheyenne people! The arrows have been renewed!"

Wolf Who Hunts Smiling and Medicine Flute only stared at him with mocking eyes. *The only god, those looks promised, is the gun and the bullet. Our god will bury yours!*

That night, as the clan fires began to bank, a Teton Sioux rode into camp. And after smoking to the directions with River of Winds, he told all of them what they had been waiting to hear, the reason for all those smoke signals of late. The renegades atop Wendigo Mountain had laid bloody siege to the whiteskin mining camp and clearly meant to annihilate them.

"This is fine news!" Wolf Who Hunts Smiling bellowed loud enough to be heard throughout the common clearing. "Of course, these renegades are our enemies. I lost two uncles at Wolf Creek, both scalped by Kiowas and Comanches raiding together as always. But no enemy is more dangerous than the hair faces! This one"—he pointed at Touch the Sky—"calls the miners his friend. He it was who sighted their path for the iron horse that daily crosses our ranges. He has sold our home to our enemies!"

"Odd," a Bow String soldier called out. "This mighty wolf rages about the miners, yet his stroud, his powder horn, and that steel knife in his sheath all came from the miners' peace price for using our land."

"Odd too," Two Twists said, "how the shifty wolf is so quick to assure us he hates the renegades. Odd, I say, since they are his blood brothers in treachery."

This remark incited an explosion of accusations and counteraccusations. River of Winds quickly interceded.

"We have a private treaty with the miners," the acting chief reminded all of his people, "voted for by the headmen. Only then did Touch the Sky sight their railroad for them. However, this new trouble is not our affair. These renegades are not on our homeland. It is pointless to start trouble in camp now. We are staying away from this fight."

This news clearly heartened the Bull Whips and took the fight out of them. As much as Touch the Sky respected River of Winds, he knew the chief was wrong. It was their fight.

Soon after Sister Sun rose the next day, Touch the Sky called a hasty council of his loyal band. As usual when serious trouble was afoot, they met in the comparative safety of the common corral surrounded by their ponies.

"Brothers," he told them, "have ears. Many in this camp, even among our supporters, take joy in this attack on my paleface friends. But it means far more than the loss of our trade goods. Do you see why Wolf Who Hunts Smiling and his lickspittles are rejoicing?"

Little Horse nodded, his features grim. "It is as clear as a blood spoor in new snow. This is only the first part of the final trail. With the riches they gain from this raid, they will become the best fighting force in the Red Nation."

Touch the Sky agreed. "As you say, buck. Even if this were not so, I would join the fight in the Sans Arcs. Caleb Riley is my friend. So are many of the others there, including Hiram Steele's daughter. However, I would not ask my men to

37

ride with me. These are personal matters.

"I do ask you to ride because the welfare of our tribe is the issue. And I am glad that is true, for I know all of you well. You would ride with me no matter what. I do not place your lives in danger for my friends merely, but for the people. Tangle Hair?"

"I have ears."

"And a stout heart, warrior! I will not leave my wife and child alone in this camp. Nor will I trust any but a man from my band to protect them from these cunning red devils surrounding them. Do you believe me when I tell you it is no feather-bed job to remain behind here?"

Tangle Hair nodded. "They will be protected at the value of my very life."

"You two," Touch the Sky told Little Horse and Two Twists. "Ready your battle rigs. Never mind trying to hide your actions. Nor will we seek sanction of council. We will defy our chief and know that we serve a higher law in doing so. Our enemies will spread the familiar rumor that we have gone off to fight for white men against the interests of our own. Let them speak their bent words. If that mining camp falls, I lose more than good friends. We lose more. This camp will be their next target."

Chapter Four

"Tom!" Corey Robinson called out. "Tom Riley!"

A young towheaded army captain stopped halfway across the cracked dirt of what passed for a parade field at Fort Bates, Department of Wyoming. A redhead working on the new commissary building waved a hammer at him.

"Corey! Hey, boy, does your mother know you're out?"

A smile creasing his sunburned face, the officer crossed quickly toward his friend with his hand extended for a grip.

"So you got the contract for this job?" Tom said. "Good. Now I know the damn thing will stand up for at least a year. Last carpenter we hired used shoddy nails."

Corey flashed his gap-toothed grin. "Where you been, hoss? I been working on this job for two weeks. Ain't seen hide nor hair of you."

"Yeah, nobody has. You heard we have a new C.O.?"

Corey nodded. "Colonel Gilmer. I saw him once. Man looks like he's got a pinecone lodged up his sitter."

Tom glanced around. A working party led by a corporal marched past him, and he returned the corporal's salute.

"Corey, he's got bigger problems than a grouchy temper. We had a courier here last week, a civilian scout from Fort Dakota. He told me a few things. This Gilmer is tight with the Indian Ring back in Washington."

"Oh, no," Corey muttered. "Another one?"

Tom nodded. "He's been sent out here because, evidently, their graft and stealing got so blatant that somebody filed a complaint. And that's why you haven't seen me leading my platoon lately. Gilmer has assigned me to mapping-and-topog detail until further notice."

"What the hell's that?" Corey demanded.

"Mainly it's to get me out of the way. Guess who put him up to it?"

"Seth Carlson?"

"Seth Carlson. A man who parades himself as an army officer but who is, in fact, crooked as they come. So now I wander all over filling in terrain details on training maps of the area. Coffee-cooling detail."

Corey frowned. "Why get you out of the way all of a sudden?"

"That's what I was puzzling out when you called to me. If Carlson simply wanted to make my life miserable—a favorite pastime of his—then why stick me on such easy duty? The point was to keep me well away from the fort and es-

pecially from my men. I'm only back here now
to resupply."

"I'll bet you a dollar to a doughnut," Corey said
slowly, "that egg-sucking varmint Carlson is in
cahoots with them renegades again. And that
damned Wolf Who Hunts Smiling. Matthew is in
for six sorts of hell, I'll bet."

"Not against me you won't bet," Tom assured
him, "because my stick floats the same way as
yours. If Carlson—"

"Sir! There you are, Cap'n. I've looked all over
for you, sir."

A private with his loops unbuttoned, one of the
new recruits sent to Fort Bates without previous
training, saluted awkwardly.

"Salute with your right hand, trooper," Riley
snapped.

"Uh, sorry, sir. This come for you by civilian
messenger, sir. 'Bout two hours ago. I'm company runner, and he left it at headquarters. He
was wantin' to see you really bad, but couldn't
nobody find you."

"No," Riley said, his eyes meeting Corey's as he
took the message. "I'm hard to find these days.
Dismissed, Private."

He unfolded the sheet of foolscap and recognized his brother's handwriting immediately.

*Tom: we're under siege by Kiowas and Co-
manches from Wendigo Mountain. They've
got us surrounded on the high ground. Telegraph out; tracks ripped up. We mean to fight,
but they seem dug in for the duration. Our
supply line is cut. I don't know how long we
can hold out. They're dealing us misery, big
brother. We could sure use soldier blue right
about now.*

41

Corey had swung around to read the note over Tom's shoulder. Now both men locked gazes.

"Carlson knew," Tom seethed. "He knew! Damn his West Point bones! And Gilmer is no doubt in on it with him. It's useless to take this to Gilmer. Caleb's mine camp is just out of our jurisdiction anyway."

"Man alive," Corey said. "That bunch under Big Tree and Sis-ki-dee are the worst red trash on the plains. Kristen is up there."

Riley was already well aware of that fact. It was the main reason he had made so many trips up that way in the past few months.

Corey thought of something else. "Matthew will get sucked into this too."

Riley pushed his black-brimmed officer's hat back farther on his crown. His eyes cut to the quartermaster's office in a nearby whitewashed adobe building.

"Yeah," he said. "Matthew will get sucked into it. And I'm going to the fandango too. But not empty-handed if I can help it."

"I don't know, Tom," Oliver Dunbar said, cupping his goateed chin in one hand and rubbing it thoughtfully. "If we were still under Colonel Thompson, why, I'd do it. But this new C.O.—I don't know him yet. I won't take chances with an unknown quantity. I hear that Gilmer is the type to glance the other way if you catch my drift. But the thing of it is, he's new. A new commander sometimes has to lop off a few heads to establish his place in the pecking order. I'd rather not take any chances until I know which way the wind sets."

Riley frowned impatiently. "Well, I said I'd give you that mare of mine you're so sweet on. And I'll also toss in these."

The two officers sat in Dunbar's small cubbyhole office at the front of the supply building. Riley dipped one hand into his blue kersey trousers and removed a bunch of hard-times tokens—private coins issued by local businesses in nearby Bighorn Falls to combat the nation's critical shortage of specie. Soldiers used them as markers in poker games.

"All your markers," Riley told him, dropping them onto the top of the oak desk. "Almost fifty dollars' worth."

Dunbar's eyes widened and again he rubbed his chin. Clearly the quartermaster was tempted. "I don't know," he said slowly.

Now Riley played his ace. He bent down and unbuckled the beautiful star-roweled spurs that were the envy of every officer on post. He tossed them on the desk.

"Just to sweeten the pot, Ollie."

This offer weakened the last of Dunbar's resistance. He scooped the spurs and the poker markers into the wide top drawer of his desk.

"All right. I'll issue one Parrot muzzle loader. And ten rockets for it. But, Tom, you know damn well a cavalry officer has no legitimate right requisitioning an artillery rifle. So you best have a story made up in case someone decides to investigate."

"Never mind a story," Riley said. "Artillery won the war with Mexico and it's the future of warfare. If I'm questioned, I'll just say I want my platoon up to full capability."

"As for demolitions," Dunbar said, "all I have

on hand are a few one-pound blocks of nitro-glycerin. It's pure nitro oil, very volatile. It's been somewhat stabalized by adding an absorbent called kieselguhr so that it can be handled and transported. But it's still quite touchy—a sharp blow can set them off. Do you know the stuff?"

"No."

"I'll show you how to crimp the fuse and blast-ing cap to it. The main thing you have to watch is the fuse. The black powder in it gets dry out here. It's supposed to burn between thirty and forty-five seconds per foot, but you actually need to cut off a piece and burn it to find out the true rate."

Dunbar stared at Riley. "What the hell you got in mind, Tom?"

Riley was already rising from his chair. "Never mind. The less you know, the safer you are. C'mon. We're burning daylight. Show me how to prepare this nitro and let me sign the requisition. I've got to git and quick."

One day after Tom Riley set off for the north-west with a sturdy packhorse tied to his saddle horn by a lead line, his brother Caleb was still supervising the building of key defenses in his camp.

Working under cover of darkness, though rounds pinged in all through each night now, the miners evacuated the most vulnerable houses. These residents doubled up with those whose houses were less exposed to fire from the sur-rounding ridge.

The occupied houses were reinforced as much as possible. Boards were nailed over the win-dows, and water barrels were filled and set near the corners in case of attack by fire arrows. To discourage any mounted attack in force, they set up pointed stakes at the two vulnerable approaches to the main camp. Caleb and Liam had also supervised the building of breastworks and rifle pits, and now the men were distributed better and under some cover, though still vulnerable to the high-ground marksmen.

Caleb's own house was too vulnerable; so his Crow Indian wife Woman Dress moved in temporarily with Kristen. Her own place, though uncomfortably accessible from above to lone intruders, was sheltered under pine trees and made for a poor rifle target.

"Nobody killed in the past twenty-four hours," Caleb informed both of them, having stopped by Kristen's place briefly to check on them and grab a quick cup of strong cowboy coffee. Kristen kept a pot going night and day now, as did many other women. They also had a plentiful supply of hot biscuits. The men, all standing guard in shifts, had little time for the luxury of meals.

Caleb looked exhausted. He hadn't been out of his clothes in more than two days, nor had he slept more than a few minutes at a time since the siege began.

"Any word of help?" Kristen asked.

Caleb shook his head. "I sent Dakota Boggs with a message for Tom. Dakota got through to the fort all right, but Tom wasn't there. Nobody would tell him where he is either, and they threw him off the post under threat of arrest. He was able to leave my note though. I just hope to God Tom gets it in time. If not—"

Caleb glanced at his wife and Kristen, then stopped before he said anything else about their

45

grim situation. Although her English was halting, Woman Dress understood his tone, and Caleb saw the fear stamped into her pretty features. Her fear wasn't for herself, but for her husband and the unborn child growing in her womb.

"We're strong right now," he amended, letting some light into this dark situation. "Down here, I mean. They'd pay dearly if they tried to rush us."

Caleb didn't give voice to what Kristen suspected really troubled him: the fact that they were completely cut off from resupply. Some things they had in abundance: coffee, flour, sugar, and, thank God, bullets. But this camp included infants, children, and other expectant mothers besides Woman Dress. Fresh milk and vegetables and medicines had been brought in almost daily from Register Cliffs. Now that supply line was cut off.

They had wounded badly in need of a doctor and would surely have more. And though it was a less urgent trouble right now, every day this huge operation was shut down was an enormous cost to Caleb. It wouldn't take that much longer to ruin it completely.

Even while Kristen reflected on these things, a rifle shot split the stillness as a renegade sniped from the ridge. All three of them winced. Suddenly, that lone shot was followed by a barrage and shouting from men in the mining camp.

Caleb ran to the front door and yelled out to a man named Perkins, "What's going on? They decide to rush us?"

"Hell, boss! Two fools are tryin' to ride in to camp. One's a soldier and the other is an Injun flyin' a truce flag! But they're dog meat! They'll never get through the lead!"

46

Chapter Five

The Shaiyena were rich in good ponies this season, having chased down a magnificent herd of wild mustangs from the mountains north of Beaver Creek. Touch the Sky had five on his string back at camp, and he chose his favorite for this sure-to-be dangerous mission. Light tan with an ivory mane and tail, the sturdy mare was of the type the whites called palomino.

With the accusing eyes of many in camp trained on them, Touch the Sky, Little Horse, and Two Twists rode out with their rope riggings heavy from battle gear. However, they had been heartened when many of the elders began the off-key minor chant reserved for warriors riding off to battle. The band still had supporters in camp, even if many of them were too old to paint for war.

Touch the Sky had grown accustomed to suspicious glances from his enemies. But even Honey Eater, though she understood the gravity of the situation at the mining camp, had met his eyes with a searching glance. The people say, that glance told him, that the sun-haired white woman is a beauty, that her eyes spark to life every time she looks at you.

The three Cheyennes made good time on their well-grazed mounts. They rode behind the timbered ridges until they left the tableland; then they struck out across the rolling brown plains after they forded the Bighorn River. Still almost a half day's ride southeast of the Sans Arcs range, they encountered a lone rider, who turned out to be Tom Riley.

The Cheyennes welcomed their friend with hearty bear hugs and thumps. The news that the white man was cut off from his men disheartened Touch the Sky since Riley's platoon was made up of seasoned veterans of Western warfare. But the supplies on Tom's packhorse—especially that artillery rifle—made up for the loss of some of them. Touch the Sky had seen the deadly results of Parrot muzzle loaders after Seth Carlson's platoon wiped out a Blackfoot camp with them.

As they neared the mountains, the flat land began to undulate into the foothills. While still well back from the miners, they began to hear the noises of sporadic shooting—sometimes an intense, sustained string of fire; other times lone, scattered shots.

"By God, Caleb is still fighting," Tom muttered.

Touch the Sky rode abreast him. Little Horse and Two Twists were on the flanks and a little behind, where they scanned the landscape for outlying Indian sentries.

"You expect anything but a fight from Caleb?" Touch the Sky said, the English words feeling odd and stiff in his mouth. It had been a long time since he used the language of his white parents.

"Hell, no! He's the one should've joined the army. Caleb's slow to rile, but once he rises on his hind legs, it's time to send for the undertaker."

Riley paused to backhand sweat from his brow. "But this isn't a fair fight, hombre. Those miners are plucky bastards—not a white liver among them. But they aren't the boys for a shooting war. Most of them never fired a real weapon, just squirrel pieces and such. And they don't know Indians, especially these Southwest Kiowas and Comanches. Worst of all, they're trapped on low ground and surrounded by an enemy on high ground. You don't have to sit on the benches at West Point to know that's trouble."

Touch the Sky nodded. "Speaking of high and low ground, do you know there's only one trail into the mining camp?"

It was Riley's turn to nod. "I wondered when we'd get around to that subject. Only one trail, you're saying, and that one covered by renegades."

"Covered as close as ugly on a buzzard. How do we ride in?"

"After dark?" Riley asked, then said, in answer to his own question, "Bad plan. We lose too much valuable time."

Touch the Sky threw a doubtful glance at Riley's big cavalry sorrel. Like most army horses, it was huge—seventeen hands high—and sleek from good grain. Such animals were strong, but out here in the wastes, they were also spoiled from pampered fort life.

"That animal know about bullets?" Touch the Sky asked.

Riley nodded. "Hates 'em. He's been in several skirmishes and always goes out of his way to duck them."

Touch the Sky nodded. "Good. You've seen how the red man rides when he's under fire. That's how we're going to ride in. Bold and right out in the open. You and I will split the flanks. Little Horse and Two Twists will ride behind us and cover the packhorse. A moving target is hard to hit. Just remember not to ride in a straight line for too long, or else they'll lead us and find their range."

"Brother!" Little Horse called over. "You two jays jabber on all day in the paleface tongue. What are you discussing?"

"Exactly how to get you killed," Touch the Sky called back.

"Good!" Little Horse, famous for his bravado when danger loomed, thumped his chest and let loose a war cry. "I have no plans to die in my tipi!"

At this bragging, Two Twists laughed outright. He stared across at Little Horse, who drew teasing lately because he had begun to grow a little stout. "No, you will not die in your tipi, All Behind Him, because by then you will not fit inside it!"

Little Horse glared back at the younger brave. "See? Take this brat away from his mother's dug and he becomes feisty!"

Bravado, however, was a paltry defense as the four riders drew near the troubled mountains. They were spotted well before they came into rifle range. From the ridges their enemy could see anyone approaching from the east.

"When you see the first dust puffs from their bullets," Touch the Sky called out to his companions, "touch up your ponies and fly like the wind!"

Soon, the first spiraling plumes of dust did begin to kick up all around them. The trail upward was wide to accommodate supply wagons and rutted from their passage. But the fleet, sure-footed mountain ponies bolted effortlessly as the Indians kicked them to a gallop. Riley's cavalry horse was only a bit slower and a tad less agile. The gelding was indeed bulletwise, and it wanted only to reach shelter.

Touch the Sky and his companions slid forward in the classic defensive riding position invented by the Cheyennes: They fell to one side of the pony's neck, hanging on for dear life and pulling their bodies low behind the horse's bulk. However, with their enemy so far above them, the real danger was the large target presented by their horses. The riders held to zigzagging patterns, but the Indian ponies were more adept at this than Riley's mount and the packhorse.

Blood thumped in Touch the Sky's temples as he clung to his palomino and felt her muscles working like well-oiled cables. A bullet creased his back like a white-hot wire of pain; another thumped into his rawhide shield. When the miners could see them coming, with Touch the Sky and Tom Riley out front, Caleb's men sent an offensive volley toward the ridge to take some pressure off the approaching riders.

Hastily, miners exposed themselves to fire in order to pull the pointed stakes clear of the approach. All four riders burst into the barricaded camp, wide-eyed but alive, and the defenders loosed a mighty roar.

"Well, it ain't two platoons of cavalry, but I'm damn glad to see you!" Caleb called out.

Suddenly, a fresh volley from above forced everyone to desperate cover. The new arrivals barely got their horses into the makeshift corral protected by a limestone outcropping and behind boulders or into rifle pits.

"How many you make up there?" Tom called out to his brother.

"Best guess is around fifty of 'em."

Fifty battle-hardened Southwest renegades, Touch the Sky thought. Each capable of getting off perhaps three shots a minute with a percussion rifle. But even more formidable was the fact that each wore a quiver stuffed with at least twenty-five arrows, and no doubt hundreds of spare arrows were held in reserve stacks.

"How many casualties down here?" Tom added.

"Three miners killed, six wounded, so far. And they killed Tilly Blackford."

"Little Sarah's ma? Jesus! How are the rest of the women and kids?"

Caleb and Touch the Sky both knew Tom was really asking how Kristen was doing. Caleb had to wait for the gunfire to slacken before he could answer.

"They're scared spitless—that's how they're doing. Snipers keep them confined to the houses. We've got some of that new canned milk of Gail

Borden's, but once it runs out the little ones are without milk. None of the beef cows can be butchered under fire, nor can we haul in any vegetables."

"Man alive," Tom said. "Talk about being trapped between a rock and a hard place!"

"Any shooting we do from down here is wasted," Caleb added. "If those renegades try to come down, raiding all at once or whatever, we can lay down some heavy fire. But we can't see enough from here to justify wasting the lead while they're up there. Besides, it's a bad angle. You have to break cover to get a bead on anything up there."

"Could a raiding party sneak up there?" Tom asked. "In the dark, I mean."

Touch the Sky answered this query himself. "It might get up there, but it would never get back down. These miners are no cowards; they'll do whatever you tell them. But not one of them is trained in night movement or combat. Those Kiowas and Comanches, on the other hand, are the best night fighters on the plains. They can steal a woman from her bed without waking up her husband."

"Besides," Caleb put in, "that's Sis-ki-dee and Big Tree up there. When it comes to dealing misery after sundown, those two are fish in water."

How well Touch the Sky could verify this fact! He remembered the long, brutal, agonizing night he had spent fighting both of them aboard the derailed orphan train full of terrorized children.

Again Two Twists complained about all their chattering in English. Touch the Sky translated the main points for his comrades. It was the canny Little Horse who first suggested the germ of Touch the Sky's plan.

"Brother," he said, "it is true that we are trapped down here without supplies. But they are trapped up there too."

"Have you become the shaman?" Touch the Sky rebuked him. "Give over with this speaking in riddles."

"Think on it, buck," Little Horse said. "We have both crossed that ridge, have we not?"

"You know we have."

"*Ipewa*. Good. You know that rimrock up there; so you must also know there is no place to establish a base camp on it."

"No," Touch the Sky agreed. "The ridge is really only a narrow stone ledge with heaps of scree all behind it."

"As you say. Which has to mean, does it not, that they are unable to establish a base camp?"

"No," Touch the Sky said slowly, catching on to Little Horse's meaning. "They cannot. I see which way your thoughts roam."

"Damn," Tom complained, reminding Touch the Sky that he was truly at home in neither world, red man's or white man's, "I wish to hell you'd talk in English, Matthew."

"Little Horse was just pointing out that they don't have any room at all up there for a base camp."

"So what?" Caleb demanded. "We supposed to feel sorry for them?"

"That's not the point, yellow beard. This is a siege. A siege means they plan to dig in. That means a steady base of resupply. Without a base camp, and with Wendigo Mountain so close by, it's only logical that they'll get their provisions and ammunition by runners from the nearby camp."

"Yeah, so what? You mean we should gun for the runners?"

"No," Touch the Sky said. "Runners can be easily replaced. But a base camp is another matter."

"You mean—"

"I mean that a strong defense here in your camp won't get it done. Time is on their side, and time will whip you. Yes, you have to mount a strong defense, but there has to be an offensive strike too. We have to get on top of Wendigo Mountain and destroy their camp. Do that, and we destroy the siege."

Silence greeted this conclusion as Caleb and Tom considered it. Finally, Caleb said, "That shines right by me. But, Touch the Sky, you yourself tried to ride up that mountain and never made it. They'll have sentries on that slope, and even a few men could hold off an army from up there."

"Straight arrow," Touch the Sky said. "But they will not be watching the cliffs behind. That is how we will get up there."

Chapter Six

"I knew that White Man Runs Him would come flying this way," Wolf Who Hunts Smiling said, his words tipped with scorn. "His hair-face masters are up against it; so of course he must come to lick their spittle! But how did you let word get to the soldiertown? This blue blouse named Riley is a soldier to reckon with. They will be twice the trouble."

Wolf Who Hunts Smiling had ridden out from camp soon after Touch the Sky and his companions, eager to see how things were going up here in the Sans Arcs.

"You would tell us about this soldier?" Big Tree shot back. "Cheyenne, it was he and his men who dressed like hostages down in the Blanco Canyon country. We traded our Cheyenne prisoners for them only to end up in a hail of bullets."

Sis-ki-dee laughed at both of them. "Listen to

the scared girls huddling in their sewing lodge to shiver and quake! Big plans they had, and now one soldier leaps into the picture and they are ready to ride to the rear with the cowards!"

Big Tree, peering over the ridge to see how things stood below in the dark camp, turned to glower at the Contrary Warrior.

"Words are cheap coins, buck, spent freely by toothless old women. You took a Crow woman hostage when you fled from Touch the Sky into Bloody Bones Canyon. She was the only reason he spared your life. But you made one mistake, swollen boaster. In letting her go, you also spared a witness who has spread the tale of your blubbering cowardice across the Red Nation! 'Please, Touch the Sky!' you begged him. 'Please do not kill me!' "

Sis-ki-dee's scar-ravaged face went livid with rage while Wolf Who Hunts Smiling and Big Tree grinned at this rare show of vulnerability. But they both knew better than to push Sis-ki-dee too far.

"Will we scrap like dogs over meat?" Wolf Who Hunts Smiling demanded. "Now we know how the wind sets. Let us cease snarling at each other and turn our fight to our common enemy." A rifle cracked nearby as one of the renegades took aim below. "The high ground will not be enough. I know Touch the Sky, and I know this Tom Riley. And Caleb Riley too has grit to him. They will come at us. They will not sit down there and build their death wickiups. They mean to fight!"

"These are words I can pick up," Big Tree said. "They will fight. And when they do, it will be the unexpected. Soon it will be dark. I will give orders to double the guard below. They will give us some merry sport, bucks. But this place hears me. We will all string our next bows with Touch the Sky's gut!"

No one knew better than the three Cheyenne braves what it would take to scale those cliffs behind Wendigo Mountain. They had done it once before, and it cost them not only the life of their companion Shoots the Bear—it proved to be the hardest struggle they had yet faced.

So Touch the Sky did not even consider making this an order. Indian leaders did not give orders as whiteskin leaders did; instead, they inspired their men by their own example. When a decision was to be reached, they tried to express the will of the group, not their own desires.

As darkness spread over the mining camp like a dark cloak, the three braves parleyed behind a spine of rocks.

"There are easier ways to die," Little Horse said. His bravado had been shaken from him by Touch the Sky's audacious suggestion. "But if we succeed, it will be important not only to the miners here."

Two Twists nodded. "As you say. The majority of their warriors are up on that ridge. The majority of their horses and equipment are not. We can destroy their ability to wage war for many moons to come. And that takes our camp out from under the shadow of attack, at least for a time."

"I am not eager to return to that death trap," Touch the Sky said. "It took our ancestors and it took our companion. It wants the rest of us too. But I see no use in huddling down here like rabbits cowering in a hole."

His companions nodded, but they also looked solemn at his reference to their ancestors. The Cheyennes, the Lakotas, the Arapahoes, even the mountain-loving Utes—all avoided Wendigo Mountain. It was said that any brave who touched the slope of that place would never leave it alive.

Everyone in the tribe knew the bloody and tragic history of Wendigo Mountain and the reason why it was taboo. A group of Cheyenne hunters, surrounded by murderous Crow Crazy Dogs, had fled into the Sans Arcs. Because it was the most formidable peak, they chose Wendigo Mountain. But due to the mists that always enshrouded it, they did not realize that the opposite side was sheer cliffs.

The relentless Crazy Dogs, highly feared suicide warriors, locked onto the Cheyenne like hounds on a blood scent. They backed them to the cliffs. The Cheyennes used all their musket balls and arrows. Then, rather than giving the Crazy Dogs the pleasure of torturing them, the Cheyennes all sang their death songs. As one, all twelve hunters locked arms and stepped off the cliffs. They were impaled on the basalt turrets far below; their bodies were never recovered.

Because the warriors died after dark and violently, they suffered especially bad deaths. Now all twelve were souls in torment, doomed to haunt Wendigo Mountain. It was said one could hear their groans in the moaning of the wind.

But like Touch the Sky, Little Horse and Two Twists saw the need to risk bad death yet again. They gave this plan grim nods, and Touch the Sky moved, leaping from boulder to boulder, then to the pile of timbers where Tom and Caleb huddled.

Tom was explaining the operation of the Parrot muzzle loader when the Cheyenne brave arrived. Touch the Sky quickly explained his plan.

"It's straight grain," Caleb said when the tall warrior fell silent. "An army travels on its stomach, and that includes an Injun army. Cut them off from pemmican and corn liquor, not to mention bullets and arrows, and they'll lose the sap for fighting."

"It's logical," Tom said. "But not if it's too dangerous to succeed. Can those cliffs be scaled, Touch the Sky?"

"We did it before. It'll be rough. But it's the last thing they'll be watching for. They'll be on that front slope."

Reluctantly, Tom nodded. "I think the risk is too great, but everything I've learned in the field tells me a multiple defense is the best. It's always good to strike at the unprotected flanks. Down here, hell, all we can do is react to what they choose to do. Your plan has the virtue of taking charge of the situation."

As if to verify his thoughts, a bullet struck close and made all three men duck.

"Listen," Tom said. "As long as you'll be sneaking out of camp anyway, any chance you'll put some of these in place?"

Tom nodded toward several nitroglycerin blocks, which were well-protected from bullets behind a pile of rocks. "We can prepare the charges now before it gets dark. I've got a whole spool of black-powder fuse. These should be planted about a couple hundred feet out, spanning the ground those renegades would have to cover if they decided to mass against us from below."

Touch the Sky nodded. Tom carefully removed the blocks from their cardboard containers and slid blasting caps into the cap wells on top of each. He crimped an end of fuse to each cap.

Touch the Sky and his companions prepared for their night mission as they had for so many others. First, Touch the Sky blackened their faces with charcoal. This move was more than practical; to a Cheyenne, the color black symbolized joy at the death of an enemy. Ideally, warriors would paint and fast before such a task, but this would have to do.

Next, each covered his head with a robe or blanket, leaving them wrapped for a long time as Uncle Moon climbed higher in the sky. The time spent doing this was amply rewarded, however, when they unwrapped their eyes. Vastly dilated pupils now squeezed the last particles of light from the air, and they could see shapes and outlines they had missed earlier.

Touch the Sky's companions had an acquaintance with various hair-face explosives. He quickly explained the blocks, and as each man took one, nervous sweat glistened on their faces.

Weapons would be a hindrance for the long climb up those cliffs; so their rifles were left behind. But they took their knives and bows, for they would be necessary to kill the guards up above. Caleb provided plenty of strong new rope, which the Cheyennes coiled securely around their bodies.

It was dark save for the foxfire glow of a quarter moon and the light of a starry dome far above the sawtooth mountain peaks. Up above, the renegades fired regularly to keep the whiteskins nervous. Now and then, a fire arrow flew in and set something ablaze. Then gutsy volunteers ran to douse the flames.

Touch the Sky and his companions fanned out on a line, a double arm's length between them, and slowly moved toward the only entrance into the camp. When they drew even with the last guard post established by the miners and faced the long talus slope to the base of the mountain, Touch the Sky again called his men around him.

"Plant your thunder blocks," he whispered. "Place stones over them. Make sure this"—he pointed to the blasting cap on his, which Tom had secured with twine—"is still in place and the fuse attached. Wait for me to make the owl hoot; then head down the slope. They are out there waiting for us; so keep your blade to hand."

His companions nodded. They were fully aware, as was he, that it was very bad medicine, the worst, to chance any risk after sundown. For the Cheyennes, as for most tribes, night belonged to the Wendigo, to the souls in torment, to *odjib*, the things made of smoke that could not be fought, but would fright a man to death.

Yet Touch the Sky carried the white man's ways in him, and he remembered the sayings John Hanchon taught him. One, especially, occurred to him now: *Needs must when the devil drives.* The whites too sometimes had truth firmly by the tail.

The devil right now was red, and his headquarters was on top Wendigo Mountain. They could stay here and hack at the branches of evil, or they could climb those cliffs and chop into its root.

They fanned out again and hid their charges in the dirt and stones. Touch the Sky then studied the slope in the darkness, his night-prepared vision assisting. He could spot no human shapes, but he knew, against this enemy, that meant nothing.

Fear throbbed in his palms, but he refused to let it master him. Instead, as old Arrow Keeper had taught him, he turned his fear into a thing he could place outside of himself.

He searched, listened, and even sniffed the air. Satisfied, he gave the owl hoot softly, and they moved out.

Every foot of that long, talus-strewn slope was gained in an agony of suspense, waiting for cold steel to cut or a Comanche skull cracker to dash the life out of them.

Crawling low to avoid a profile, moving when the wind picked up and covered his noise, Touch the Sky descended the mountain through the very heart of his enemy's best guards. Twice, he passed so close to renegades that he could smell the bear grease in their hair.

But he avoided any clashes since he knew full well the plan was doomed if Big Tree and Sis-ki-dee learned too soon that the Cheyennes had deserted the mining camp. A shout, or a dead body, would cause the same—failure.

He had not reckoned, however, on the many snakes who were nocturnal hunters. As he lay still at one point, waiting for some wind noise to cover his movement past a renegade guard, a scaly body suddenly tracked across his back!

Startled, he almost flinched, but caught himself. When he felt the weight on his back he realized that a snake had crawled onto him and was pausing to take warmth from him. But what kind of snake? Most up here were not poison, but some were, including the many rattlers drawn to these heights by mice and chipmunks.

Touch the Sky lay trapped, unable to move even when the wind conveniently gusted. If that snake was poison and bit him, he might survive; but he would surely be useless to complete this mission. However, his companions must be well out ahead of him by now. He could waste no more time.

Frustrated, he tried tensing and releasing, tensing and releasing his back muscles. The snake shifted, irritated, and Touch the Sky steeled himself for the long fangs.

However, the snake settled in again. Touch the Sky frowned, recalling all he could about snakes. He pictured this one in the darkness, head lifting, forked tongue sampling the air, gathering in odor particles . . . *odor particles!* He reminded himself that snakes had an especially keen sense of smell, and sudden new odors in their territory were interpreted as danger.

Every Cheyenne carried a few grayish-green leaves of the aromatic plant sage in his medicine pouch, for it was a versatile cooking herb. Moving slowly, cautiously, fearful of those fangs at any moment, Touch the Sky inched his right hand toward the rawhide pouch over his right hip.

He slid a dried leaf out, waited for the wind to pick up, then crumpled it between his fingers. Even he could smell the pungent odor, and the snake surely picked it up. Almost instantly its weight left his back.

He gave brief thanks to Maiyun, the Day Maker and protector of the red men. Then, moving out on his elbows and knees, heedless of the raw, throbbing cuts from rocks and stones, Touch the Sky moved forward to join his companions.

Chapter Seven

Dawn broke over the Sans Arcs range in its full glory, turning the sky over the peaks salmon pink. Kristen Steele, her eyes puffy from the growing dearth of rest and sleep, watched the dawn through a narrow space between her front door and the frame. For the moment, all was peaceful and still, and one might have believed life around here was normal again. Pockets of mist floated between the peaks like gossamer clouds of cotton. The dawn chorus of thousands of songbirds filled the camp with a warbling beauty. The air was still crisp and cool, but so pure it caressed the lungs.

But if this were a normal morning, Kristen reminded herself, the first whistle of the day would blow the signal for work to begin. The workday around here lasted from can to can't, as Caleb liked to say. Men would be streaming down the camp streets, carrying their helmets and joking to each other. And if this were a normal day, Woman Dress wouldn't be tending to two wounded men in her living room. Kristen's house had become a field hospital of sorts, and the wounded lay on cots or pallets of blankets and quilts.

"Tom and Caleb be here soon," Woman Dress said in her halting English. "Make coffee maybe better do?"

"Of course," Kristen said, hurrying to the Franklin stove in the little kitchen lean-to and building a fire under the pot.

As the water heated, she crossed to the back door, lifted the bar, and opening the door just a few inches to peer out. Two gray squirrels were playing on the big stump near the door. Kristen gazed at the long gully winding up through the trees to the ridge above. Maybe, she thought, she'd better mention that to Caleb and Tom. Maybe it—

Loud thumps on the front door interrupted her musings. She hurried back inside to let Caleb and Tom in. Both men looked exhausted. Beard stubble darkened Tom's sunburned face. They had been up all night, keeping an eye on the defenses. They had also found a sheltered spot to set up the Parrot artillery rifle on its big tripod mount. As the men waited, Kristen made sourdough biscuits and fried the last of her bacon.

"Sorry there isn't more meat," she apologized as she served the men. "And the flour will run out tomorrow."

"A lot of things will be running out pretty soon." Caleb closed his weary eyes for a long moment and massaged them with his thumbs. Then he opened his eyes and looked at his brother. "Let's just hope Touch the Sky and his men can pull this off. I'm thinking now that maybe we should have stopped them. It's damned risky."

"What?" Kristen demanded. "Pull what off? Where is Matthew?"

Tom glanced at her sharply for a moment, unable to hide his jealousy. Although he and Kristen had talked all around the subject of marriage, an understanding of sorts had grown up between them. He knew she had once loved the Cheyenne; indeed, their forbidden love was the reason Matthew Hanchon had given up the white man's world for the red. But Touch the Sky was married now, a father; yet Kristen's worried tone made it clear she still harbored strong feelings for the brave.

As Caleb explained the plan to route the renegades, Kristen and Woman Dress both turned pale at the thought of the danger those three Cheyenne faced. But before Kristen could say anything, Dakota Boggs's voice sang out from outside the front door.

"Caleb! Harney Robinson just caught a round in his belly! It's bad. We can't move him. We got him inside my place, but he needs doctorin' damn quick!"

"I'll go." Kristen immediately gathered up her bandages and a little pail of solution of gentian.

"Not by yourself." Tom pushed away from his plate. He clapped on his hat and checked the loads in his Colt Cavalry Model. Then he and Kristen joined Dakota in the fortified camp street.

Everywhere, men were huddling behind barricades and glancing up toward the ridges surrounding them. Here and there, partially burned buildings showed blackened corners or roofs. Dakota's little bungalow hunkered about six houses down the line. As they moved quickly across the open space, Tom glanced overhead constantly. They were about halfway to their destination when the renegades decided to unleash another furious volley.

So many rifles detonated that the barrage sounded like an ice floe breaking apart. Sudden, intense screaming erupted from women and children. Kristen was not one to swoon in an emergency, but the suddenness of the attack made her scream and cling to Tom. As bullets kicked up plumes all around their feet, Dakota leapt for the corner of the nearest house, and Tom pushed Kristen to safety under an abandoned freight wagon.

"Christ!" Tom said. "They're focusing their fire on one of the houses!"

Kristen saw what he meant. After the initial sweep of the camp, the renegades had settled their aim on one house about thirty feet ahead of them.

"That's Dot Perkins and her kids trapped in there!" she cried out. "Terry and Jenny are in my class! Oh, Tom, look! They're sending fire arrows down again too!"

Riley had seen and heard enough. Cursing out loud, he suddenly broke from cover and started running headlong down the street.

"Tom!" Kristen cried out. "Tom! What are you doing?"

Behind her, the door to her house slapped open and Caleb leapt out into the street. He raced after his brother. Kristen watched both of them cut toward the long limestone outcropping that ran like a shelf over the north side of the camp. Then she realized that the artillery rifle was set up there!

Kristen watched Tom sight in while Caleb dropped one of the long shells down the muzzle. There was a roar, followed by a long white trail of smoke; then a resounding explosion knocked a chunk of the ridge loose. Kristen had the satisfaction of seeing several Indians tumble down with the debris. Tom had scored a direct hit on one of the most dangerous nests of snipers.

After that brief moment of triumph, a cheer boiled through the camp, and the Indian volley fell silent. But moments later, another spate of burning arrows poured in from other positions, and the men fell silent as they rushed to douse the new fires.

Once they had negotiated their exit from the mining camp, Touch the Sky and his companions faced a hard journey on foot. Never could they have gotten their ponies out of camp, nor was there any place to tether them at the base of Wendigo Mountain.

Fortunately, both Touch the Sky and Little Horse knew this country well from sighting the spur-line railroad through. Relying on good maps provided by their memory, they were able to avoid many of the pitfalls of this rugged terrain: the huge piles of scree and glacial morraine; the steep ridges that wore a man down and led nowhere; the spring-swollen streams that soaked a man's powder and left him shivering in raw night winds. While the moon clawed higher toward its zenith, they crossed the front slope of

Wendigo Mountain and slogged through scree and basalt turrets. Finally, they reached the sheer cliffs behind even as Sister Sun rose from her bed in the eastern sky.

Chafing at the delay, Touch the Sky nonetheless knew they must wait until late in the day before beginning their ascent. Otherwise, they might break through the protective belt of mist above into sight of an alert sentry while it was still light enough to spot them.

They badly needed rest anyway. The trio pitched a cold camp in a well-protected hollow near the cliffs. But rest could never come easy to a Cheyenne in that unholy place. Not only were they surrounded by the bones of their comrades, but the terrible shrieking of those winds up on the cliffs rubbed their nerves raw. These were not winds at all, but eerie human cries, cries of pain and desolation—and of warning.

How many wise Indians, Touch the Sky could not help wondering, had heard that warning and heeded it? As for his band, not one brave here had ever shown the white feather. All had been tested and tested again in hard battles, even young Two Twists. Each was a warrior; none better could have been found in the Red Nation.

And yet, this climb ahead of them was a different type of foe. Touch the Sky's two companions had grown up believing that Wendigo Mountain was a place of terror, suffering, and death—a place to be avoided at all costs. "If you do not behave," Cheyenne mothers often threatened their children, "I'll send you to Wendigo Mountain." Not just a hard climb and a hard enemy waited above, powerful bad medicine loomed ahead as well.

The three Cheyennes prepared as best they could. Their animal-tendon bowstrings were tightened and inspected for frayed spots. They had no idea what might be encountered above or how long they might be pinned down. So they had stuffed their parfleches and legging sashes with dried venison and strips of cloth Caleb gave them for binding wounds. Remembering how hard the last climb was on their feet, they stuffed their moccasins with dried grass to soften the sharp edges.

Now and then, as they waited for the sun to sink lower in the west, a vagrant wind gust brought them the faint sound of battle from the distant mining camp. When their shadows began to slant toward the east, Touch the Sky gave the nod. Their final preparations could begin.

According to their custom, each brave said a brief, silent battle prayer as he touched his personal medicine and the totem of his clan. Touch the Sky had no official clan, but Arrow Keeper had presented him with a set of badger claws—the totem of Chief Running Antelope of the Northern Cheyenne. He had been killed in the year the white man's winter count called 1840, the year Touch the Sky had been born. Arrow Keeper had called this chief Touch the Sky's father, and the warrior had never known Arrow Keeper to speak bent words.

"Brother," Little Horse said curiously, watching his friend remove the badger claws and pray over them. "I would ask you a thing."

"I have ears."

"Brother, we have saved each other's life too many times to count up. We have fought bluecoats and whiskey traders and land-grabbers and

Pawnees. We have fought all of them side by side and then smeared our bodies with their blood. We have stood shoulder to shoulder at the Buffalo Battle and sent many white hiders' souls across the Great Divide. So tell me only this.

"You know that I have seen the mark of the warrior buried in your hair. That arrow point is so perfect it might have been fashioned by Maiyun, the Day Maker. And I recall when the Bull Whips set upon you during the buffalo hunt and beat you after Wolf Who Hunts Smiling played the fox and accused you of violating Hunt Law. You told them your father was a great warrior, greater than any in our tribe."

Touch the Sky nodded. "Certainly I too recall this. The Bull Whips mocked me for a liar."

"They did. But others did not. You fight like five men. Clearly, you descend from a stout warrior's loins! But, brother, when you sought your great vision at Medicine Lake, was it revealed to you the part you are meant to play in our tribe's destiny? How much was made known to you?"

Touch the Sky thought about these questions for some time. While he did, he sharpened his obsidian knife and listened to the distant gunfire.

"Much was revealed," he finally answered. "But it was like shadow pictures on snow. The shape of things was there, but not the substance."

If this answer confused Little Horse, he did not show it. He merely nodded, accepting these words. "Truly, I have heard that visions and medicine dreams convey great truths, yet little that can be told with words."

"As you say. They are felt more than known. But now, buck, let us both give over with words." Touch the Sky nodded toward the cliffs. "It is time. Wendigo Mountain is waiting for us. We have a hard climb ahead, and no doubt a hard fight waits for us at the top. So from here on out, let our thoughts be bloody and nothing else."

Chapter Eight

Taking a grim revenge for the braves killed by that big-thundering artillery gun, the renegades hammered at the mining camp throughout the day. Big Tree and Sis-ki-dee had learned from the white Comancheros in their desert homeland how to make gun cotton. They simply dipped tow cloth into a mixture of niter, sulfur, and naphtha supplied by the slave-trading Comancheros in exchange for Indian captives. Wrapped around their arrows, the gun cotton could be hurled into the camp below, where it would spew flames everywhere.

All day long, the renegades menaced the camp and forced men from shelter to fight the flames. Then they would open fire on the beleagured hair faces. Several more of the whites had been killed or wounded. Yet return fire directed up toward the ridge was mostly wasted—with the exception of that artillery rifle. That weapon had the capacity to blow the very ridge out from under the Indians' feet. So the renegades showed more caution and spread out even farther apart.

As the sun began to cast fiery embers on the western horizon, Big Tree said, "The big-talking gun has been silent for some time now. Perhaps they are out of shells for it."

"No." Sis-ki-dee shook his raggedly cropped head. "Tom Riley hauled that gun in. He would not have carried it this far just to fire it a few times. He is conserving his shots. By fighting the Sioux he has learned their maxim: One bullet, one enemy."

While Sis-ki-dee spoke, he was straining to see how things looked over among the cluster of houses on one side of camp. One house was still on fire and others smoked from continual assaults of gun cotton.

Big Tree laughed. "Look at the Red Peril! His loins ache for his sun-haired white woman. He is worried that perhaps she was killed before he could top her and sate his lust!"

"And you would not top her, I suppose?"

Big Tree shrugged. "She is just one more woman. All cats look alike in the dark. I value a lame horse over a comely woman."

"She is not just one more woman. The tall one once held her in his blanket for love talk. He has risked his life for her before, and she is one reason why he is here now."

"Never mind the woman," Big Tree said. He too had been scouring the area below, but not to look for women. "Answer this. Why have we not seen one sign of those three Cheyennes all this day long?"

This question made Sis-ki-dee's scar-ravaged face compress itself into a frown. "Why indeed?" he said, watching his companion warily. "And now let me meet question with question. Why has not one arrow flown up here to answer ours?"

Both braves stared below, their cocky smiles replaced by speculative frowns. Finally, Sis-ki-dee said, "We have not seen them because they have sneaked out of the camp."

"But why?"

"It is pointless to come up here," Big Tree said. "They are three against a legion."

"Then where?" Sis-ki-dee asked. Even as he finished asking, both renegades turned their heads to the left toward Wendigo Mountain. A queasiness invaded their stomachs as they guessed the truth.

"They mean to cut off our tail while our teeth are gnashing," Big Tree said. "They have gone to destroy our camp!"

Sis-ki-dee tried to shrug that explanation off. "So? Let them try! They will never get up that slope alive. We left enough sentries there."

"We did," Big Tree said. "On the slope. But what if they have dared the cliffs behind?"

Sis-ki-dee could say nothing to this query. Against all odds, those plucky Cheyennes had climbed the cliffs once before. That they might do so again had not occurred to him until now, and all of a sudden, he realized the danger he and his band faced.

"You have truth firmly by the tail, buck," Sis-ki-dee said. "I will pick a few men and—"

"You will not," Big Tree said. "You had your chance at Bloody Bones Canyon, and you squandered it. It is my turn to make Touch the Sky's life a hurting place. And I will take no men. I will ride alone."

When Sis-ki-dee started to object, Big Tree said, "What about your play pretty down below, stag-in-rut? How will you mount her from Wendigo Mountain? Leave me here, and I assure you, she will be cold as a wagon wheel by the time you return. I will surely kill her along with the rest."

"Then go," Sis-ki-dee said. "But whatever you do, do not let that Cheyenne dog gain our camp. If he destroys our horses and powder cache, we will be grizzly bears without teeth or claws."

Big Tree caught up his buckskin mustang and started across the face of the mountains. Since he stuck to well-known trails his men had blazed throughout this area, he was able to make far better time than he could on foot. By the time darkness had claimed the sky, he had rounded Wendigo Mountain and reached the base of the cliffs.

Slowly, while the wind howled and shrieked around him, he threaded his way through the many basalt turrets, searching for sign. However, if his enemies had been this way, they had covered their trail completely.

Big Tree reined in at the very base of the cliffs and gazed thoughtfully overhead. Had he perhaps guessed wrong? It would have been an agonizing climb. Should he bother to take the time to circle back around and ascend that long slope, just to warn them up above? If his enemies were climbing these cliffs, he could easily beat them. Perhaps he should—

Abruptly, a pebble landed at Big Tree's moc-casined feet. A few heartbeats later, another pebble fell. His huge, weather-beaten face creased in a grin of triumph. The Cheyenne dogs were up there, all right. And since they would not have started until late, they could not be that far up yet. Now there would be some merry sport!

Big Tree grabbed a handful of his pony's roached mane, meaning to swing up and ride like the wind around to the front. His companions must be warned. But something occurred to him. Why not begin the sport right now? Besides, it was better if the three Cheyennes realized they had been discovered. They might abandon their plan and come down. Still grinning, Big Tree reached one hand over his shoulder and grabbed a bunch of new pine-shaft arrows from his quiver.

The winds that buffeted Wendigo Mountain al-ways howled like souls in pain. But added to this misery were intermittent, lashing rains—cold rains that soaked the three warriors and chilled them to violent shivers after the sun went down.

The Powder River Cheyennes were up against it in the truest sense. The arduous climb was dan-gerous and exhausting. So much so that, at the beginning, Touch the Sky had almost called off his crazy plan. But the young warrior had learned one thing well. Trouble never went away on its own if he ran from it. He either had to take it by the horns or suffer a hard goring. If the warriors could not get up there and destroy the ren-egades' base of operations, the Northern Plains would belong to Wolf Who Hunts Smiling and his murdering cohort.

Progress was agonizingly slow. Every finger length was eked out at the cost of unbelievable sweat and toil. Touch the Sky had the longest arms; so he went up first, clawing for handholds, groping constantly for toeholds on the smooth limestone expanse. Each time he reached a spur or occasional stunted tree or bush, he carefully tested its strength. Then he secured a rope to it. Little Horse followed, then Two Twists.

Despite the cold, salty and stinging sweat beaded up on Touch the Sky's scalp and then rolled into his eyes. The fierce winds fanned the sweat, causing him to shake violently.

A few inches, another foot, and now the cliff face was so smooth it seemed as if farther advance was impossible. But Touch the Sky willed himself higher and refused to give up. Fingers and toes seeming to make their own holds, he somehow inched his way up that smooth stretch.

Little Horse and Two Twists were having a rough time. Shorter of limb, they found it even harder than he did to stretch between the scant holds. Touch the Sky knew he had to get a rope tied to something or his plan was smoke behind them. They could not continue to climb on air! Lightning flashed between rain squalls, and the brave could see his companions' faces below, ashen with fear and effort.

"Brothers!" he shouted down to them, his voice sounding tiny in the immensity of the constant wind. "We are the fighting Cheyennes! Hang on a bit longer, and we will reach easier going. I will throw the ropes down to you then!"

Muscles straining like guy ropes, Touch the Sky scrambled for some kind of hold. Above, perhaps ten handbreadths away, he spotted a small rock spur. If only he could reach it in time. But his assurance to his companions was proving easier to shout than to carry out.

"Brother!" Little Horse said in a desperate voice.

Touch the Sky looked down; then he felt his blood seem to stop and flow backward in his veins. Two Twists had slipped, and now he held on by only one foot and one hand. He pressed close to the rock face, but the rapacious wind threatened at every moment to tear him loose and hurtle him to the basalt turrets below.

"Hold on!" Touch the Sky shouted. "I will have a rope down in a little!"

Desperation welled up inside the brave. How many times had young Two Twists faced the Grim Warrior Death to prove his loyalty? How many times had his battlefield bravery, his habit of mocking the enemy to their face, inspired his comrades to the extra effort that decided the victory? And now he was about to plunge to his death right in front of the man he had always served without question.

Touch the Sky grasped, clawed, grasped again, and somehow found holds where none existed. His fingernails had torn loose long ago. Spidery lines of blood spread from his fingertips all the way down his arms. But the rock spur was just above him. And now his bones turned to stone when he heard Two Twists chanting the death song! Touch the Sky, face frozen with desperate urgency, unlooped his rope. Then he flung it up toward the spur—and missed!

He didn't realize it when he cussed in English. He tossed the rope up again and this time snared the spur. Working with desperate haste, willing his fingers to a machinelike efficiency, he knotted the rope.

"Watch out, Little Horse!" he shouted.

Touch the Sky tossed the rope past his companion. It reached Two Twists just as the young warrior lost his battle with gravity. Even as he began plummeting to his death, the rope slapped him in the face. Two Twists instinctively grabbed at it, missed, then grabbed once more. A second later, the rope snapped taut and held, and Two Twists dangled safely though somewhat shaken from the impact when he swung back into the face of the cliff.

For some time, all three braves held motionless, recovering from the near miss and steeling their nerves for more climbing. It was a slow and agonizing process getting Little Horse and Two Twists up to this stretch where, Touch the Sky knew from experience, the going got a bit easier. Little Horse climbed to the level of the rock spur; then Two Twists followed.

"I was in no trouble," Two Twists boasted, showing bravado to cover his understandable fear. "My only concern is that All Behind Him here"—he swatted Little Horse on his ample rump—"might fall on me."

"Once again," Little Horse said, "the calf bellows to the bull!"

Despite his exhaustion and apprehension—or maybe because of them—Touch the Sky flashed a rueful grin. "Never mind the chatter, you two jays. If you survive this, you can kill each other at your leisure."

He fell silent, squinting at a spot just below them. It was foolish, of course. But Touch the

82

Sky could almost swear he had seen sparks fly from the face of the—

There! There it was again. Sparks.

Something tickled his left ear. More sparks flew into his eyes. And then, with a sinking feeling in his belly like a chunk of cold lead, he realized that arrows were pelting them! And the sparks were because these arrows were special Comanche arrows tipped with white man's sheet iron, not flint. Iron tips bent and clinched when they hit bone, making them much more deadly.

Touch the Sky had no time to wonder how the renegades had guessed their plan. A Comanche could launch a big handful of arrows in mere seconds, and the sheer number coming in now, obviously launched from the base of the cliff, turned the air deadly all around them.

Finally, the barrage slowed and seemed to stop. Touch the Sky, holding his next breath, finally began to expel it in relief. Suddenly, one final arrow found them. And Touch the Sky heard the sickening noise, like an ax cutting a side of meat, as the iron-tipped arrow sliced into Little Horse's calf.

Chapter Nine

"Plenty Coups," Sis-ki-dee called out to one of his men. "I am going down below to scout. I will descend behind the houses. They have sentries walking. Have some of the men keep up a sporadic fire until I return. I want them to worry about the opposite end of the camp; so this time direct fire arrows and bullets at that end."

Plenty Coups nodded, though the Blackfoot lackey knew full well his leader had no reason to scout. They had done all the scouting they needed long ago. Sis-ki-dee had fire in his loins, and he was scouting for the woman who would put out the fire.

"Do not hold one position," Sis-ki-dee said. "That will give them a bead with the thunder gun. Shoot and then each time move to a new position."

Plenty Coups and several other braves moved

forward in the darkness, taking up positions at the rim. They were safe now; no one could see to draw a bead on them in this blackness.

Sis-ki-dee left his North & Savage rifle in its sheath, opting only for his bone-handled knife. He moved northwest along the high ridge, nearing the spot where that gully snaked down among the houses. His mastery of movement and hiding had already gotten him close enough to find out where Kristen Steele lived. The Crow Indian woman was staying with her during this emergency.

That thought prompted a smile from Sis-ki-dee. They were both beauties. Perhaps he could enjoy one of them down below and take one with him for later. And when he and Big Tree tired of her, they would let the men line up for her.

As Sis-ki-dee had ordered, his men opened up on the dark, quiet camp below. He watched bright orange flames arc out over the rim and plummet into the wagons, buildings, and numerous stacks of timber dotting the business end of camp. When Sis-ki-dee was sure the roving sentries would be down there fighting flames, he began his descent down the steep erosion gully.

It was hard going, even for one as seasoned to adverse climbs as he. At some points, he was forced to rig a rope to a stunted bush or a fat rock and lower himself foot by foot. He gave up any idea of bringing a woman back up this way. He would enjoy them and then kill them. The scalp of the blond woman, especially, would fetch much praise and trade high.

Soon enough, Sis-ki-dee could glimpse lantern light leaking under the edge of the back door of a house. It was built on a slant with the bottom of the ridge. Now the going was easy, and he had merely to brace his leg muscles against gravity. In the grainy blackness, he moved from rock to rock until he was only a stone's throw from the house. He slid his knife from his sash and settled in for a long moment to watch before he made his final move.

Tom and Caleb Riley, holed up with some of the wounded in Kristen's house, had been grabbing a few minutes of fitful sleep when the latest attack opened up.

"Damn," Caleb said, groping for his rifle. "Don't those featherheads ever sleep? Liam's on watch. Should we leave it to him?"

"I trust Liam," Tom said, peeking out the front door and watching the new flames at the far end of the street. "But we'd better head out. This might be a softening attack before they rush the entrance."

This thought sobered Caleb. After all, his brother hadn't won a brevet promotion for clerking duties. The two brothers hurried down to the sheltered position of the artillery rifle. All around them, men directed by Liam McKinney and others fought the flames with buckets of water and shovelfuls of dirt.

"Liam!" Caleb shouted above the din of shouting men and crackling flames. "Throw up a skirmish line across the front of camp, and dig in good. They might be attacking in force this time!"

Caleb and Tom took up their position at the Parrot, ensconced under a limestone outcropping. Then Caleb said, "Can you get a bead?"

"They won't let me. I can tell from watching the dispersal pattern that they're staying in motion as they shoot. This little puppy has taught them some deep respect for white man's technology. Won't do us much good in the dark, though. Unless—"

"Unless what?" When Tom waited a while before he answered, Caleb said, "Dammit! You've always done that, Tom! Always makin' a man beg you to know what's on your damned mind!"

"Quit whining, little brother, and listen up. They're moving around, all right. But they're confining their movement to that one section of the ridge between the south end and the spot where it forms a notch just off to our right. See? Regular as Big Ben."

"Yeah. Well, so what?"

"You're a damn good miner, Caleb, and you got a hell of a hard-hitting right fist. But you're poor shakes as a soldier. Look at this thing in terms of known facts and possible results. We now know for a fact that a good number of them are concentrated in a finite area—an area we have measured exactly, right?"

Caleb was starting to twig the game, and his temples were pulsing at the prospects. "Right. Don't whack the cork on me now, Cap'n."

"We haven't got many shells. But this gal fires as quick as you can drop ammo down the muzzle. If I traverse this barrel on an exact line with that one section of the ridge while you drop beans down the tube quick, we can blow a good section of the landscape right out from under them. I think four shells will do it. That leaves us with only three rockets, but it's a calculated risk. We not only discourage them from night harassment; we may even take out a good chunk of their man power."

"But if it doesn't work," Caleb muttered, "we're sitting on damn few shells if they attack down here later."

"True. But our friends up topside don't know how many shells we have. By not firing, we drop a hint that we're low. By blasting away now, we create the impression that we've got lots more where that came from."

Caleb nodded. Both points made sense. But he sure would have felt easier knowing they had more shells on hand. The savages obviously respected that gun.

"Dammit," Caleb said. "I wonder how Touch the Sky is doing?"

"He'll do his job or die trying. But we can't count on him. We have to fend for ourselves. Every man has to pack his own gear, or it won't get done. Not against these Indians, Caleb. They wiped out half the white population in Texas before they rode up here."

Reluctantly, Caleb agreed. "All right, big brother," he said, grabbing a shell. "It's time to kiss the mistress!"

Tom wrapped the lanyard around his hand and waited for the shell to slide home solidly. Then he double-checked his elevation and windage settings; he had calculated them during daylight hours and knew the exact setting for this distance. Satisfied, he jerked the lanyard and the first rocket whooshed toward its target, trailing blue-green fire.

Again, again, and yet again rockets were launched, four in total, the explosions so close together they seemed to come as one. As they detonated above, the Riley boys had the pleasure of hearing the miners cheer and of seeing tall gey-

sers of dirt, rock, and shocked Indians blown off
the ridge.

Satisfied that no sentries roamed close by, Sis-
ki-dee had emerged from hiding and covered the
remaining distance to the small lodge. Though
the windows were reinforced with boards, wide
cracks had been left. He peered through one and
studied the interior.

It was hardly more luxurious than some Indian
lodges he had seen, though cleaner and neater.
He glanced past a kitchen with a hand pump and
crossed-stick shelves. In the bigger room, makeshift beds had been arranged on the floor, and
several wounded hair faces occupied them. They
were either asleep or unconscious. And there was
the golden-haired beauty, bent over one of them
to administer white man's medicine from a dark
brown bottle.

How noble, he thought, a sneer dividing his
face in the moonlit darkness. Like Touch the Sky,
whom she probably still loved even though he
had a red wife and babe. Filled with light and
reason and hope and all the other claptrap taught
by their white medicine men who preached
about a loving God. There was only one God
among the white men, and his name was Sam
Colt. The gun was the only deity that mattered
out here.

Woman Dress was nowhere in sight, but Sis-
ki-dee didn't worry about her. Nor would those
wounded men pose much trouble. He moved to
the corner of the house, intending to go round to
the front door. They would expect no Indians in
camp now, and the sun-haired beauty would no
doubt open the door at his knock—if it was even

locked. He could pull her out into the street and take her there on the ground like a common animal to humiliate her even more.

He had just started his final move when the sky overhead and to his right suddenly exploded in blinding light. Startled, Sis-ki-dee looked up just in time to see some of his men thrown from the ridge. Those four quick explosions had been masterfully timed and placed; within moments, Sis-ki-dee heard the shrill piping of an eagle-bone whistle. One of his men was calling desperately to him. His men were not squaws, quick to panic. It must be bad indeed up there.

Sis-ki-dee cursed. If Plenty Coups had been killed, they were without a leader. And in the ensuing panic of those explosions, who knew what mistake they might make? His men feared little, but most of them had been stringing their bows with both hands when brains were passed out.

There was nothing else for it. He would have to forego his pleasure this time. But he swore by the four directions that he would merge his flesh with Kristen Steele's before he slid his knife under that scalp the color of new wheat.

"It has struck bone," Touch the Sky said grimly.

The rains had stopped some time ago, but the wind still howled and raged like berserk warriors. It clawed at them, trying to pry them loose from their precarious holds on the side of Wendigo Mountain.

Going mostly by touch, severely hampered in his cramped and tentative position, Touch the Sky had quickly examined Little Horse's wound. The stout brave had not lost his hold when struck; however, weakened by the fierce pain and growing blood loss, Little Horse must surely be forced to soon let go and plunge to his death.

Two Twists too managed to work in close to his companions. All three of them knew the importance of Touch the Sky's words about the point striking bone. That sheet iron would surely have clinched. Merely snapping off the arrow and pushing it through would be disastrous in this case.

"Never mind," Little Horse said, his voice spiked with pain. "I am dead, brothers, but you are not! Move on, both of you, and take the fight to the cricket-eating vermin above! I have lived well, and I will die well. When I fall from this cliff, I will not scream in terror. I will curse the name of my enemies with my last breath since I cannot fall on their bones."

"Listen to All Behind Him strut and pose," Two Twists said with brash desperation, trying to hide his fear that Little Horse might soon die. "Now that he has to hang on, he regrets all the rich gall bladders and livers and intestines he gorged on all winter."

But even as he spoke, Two Twists wasted no time. While Touch the Sky removed his knife and prepared for some desperate surgery, the younger brave was rigging a rope around Little Horse. It was not easy work on this precarious cliff. But somehow Two Twists got a rope around his friend and then tied it around himself.

"Throw me the other end, buck!" Touch the Sky yelled. He too secured himself to Little Horse. No words were needed. All three knew what they intended. Little Horse would surely pass out at the intense pain, and all of his weight

would become the burden of his companions—
or so they thought.

"Cut those ropes," Little Horse ordered Two
Twists. His friends were barely holding on themselves; he had no intention of dragging them to
their death with him.

"Cut a cat's tail," Two Twists defied him, even
as he tightened the knot.

"Touch the Sky," Little Horse said, "cut those
ropes, or I will not let you cut my leg! I will not
let my companions die."

"The white men have a saying," Touch the Sky
said as he maneuvered into position to make the
first cut. "Teach your grandmother to suck eggs.
I am cutting that arrow point out, and we are
leaving the ropes on. Now hold quiet or I will
push all three of us off to shut you up."

Touch the Sky flinched when, abruptly, another flurry of arrows rained in.

"Arrows fly two ways," Two Twists said an-
grily, slewing around to grab a few from his
pouch. In a moment, he sent them flying toward
the ground.

"Hurry, brother," Little Horse urged Touch the
Sky. "I am keen for some diversion!"

Touch the Sky had only been joking. But now,
as he moved his body into position, he feared he
really might send them all falling. The arrow
point had entered the solid part of Little Horse's
calf, ripping muscle fibers and then clamping
around the bone.

Touch the Sky had once watched a white doctor remove one of these arrows. The trick was to
unbend the clinched metal with the very tip of
the knife, much as one might pry back the little
nubbins holding on a can lid. But he would have

to cut deep and work with brutal swiftness. He had cloths to bind the wound, but already blood loss was considerable.

Each brave wore a leather band around his left wrist to protect it from the slap of his bowstring. Two Twists removed his now and inserted it between Little Horse's teeth.

Touch the Sky pushed his knife into the ragged wound, and Little Horse jerked violently. Showing no mercy, since conditions hardly permitted it, the desperate Cheyenne probed deeper. He was severely hampered by having only one hand available, the other clinging tenaciously to a crevice. This meant that he had to probe with the knife, then stop and use his fingers to feel his way since light was insufficient.

Touch the Sky worked as quickly as possible, praying all the while that Maiyun would bless his clumsy fingers. Little Horse was losing far too much blood now.

Touch the Sky and Two Twists kept expecting sudden weight to challenge them as Little Horse sagged. But though Little Horse grunted hard, flinched often, and came close to oblivion, he fought it off. He had meant what he said about refusing to risk his friends.

At last, Touch the Sky eased the mangled metal point out and quickly bound his friend's wound. Two Twists took the leather band from his mouth.

"When are you going to start?" Little Horse said weakly. "We can't dawdle here all night."

All three Cheyennes mocked death and shared a laugh at their comrade's joke. But before they began their laborious ascent again, Two Twists handed something to Touch the Sky. He glanced down in the dim moonlight, and pride and re-spect swelled his heart at this vivid proof of Little Horse's bottomless courage. The thick leather had been bitten clean through.

Chapter Ten

Big Tree did not count how many arrows he launched up the face of that cliff. It was his habit to always wear two quivers, both stuffed tight with carefully wrought arrows. His first flurry upward emptied perhaps half a quiver.

Big Tree remained well back from the cliff until the last of his spent arrows had clattered back to ground. He hurried forward to salvage those that had not broken because he spent far too much time fashioning each arrow to waste them lightly.

He was stuffing the last of them back into the foxskin quiver when he felt something wet drip onto his shoulder—something wet and still warm. He rubbed some onto his fingertips and smelled it in the darkness. An ear-to-ear smile suddenly divided his face when he recognized the familiar odor of blood. At least one of his arrows had scored!

If the hit had been fatal, his enemies had somehow caught the body. More likely it was a wound. But on that sheer cliff, even a mild wound took on dangerous new facets.

Perhaps he had even wounded Touch the Sky, the one Pawnees called, in hushed and respectful tones, the Bear Caller. They swore by the four directions that he had once summoned a grizzly bear to attack a Pawnee war party. But only look at the Pawnee tribe—once mighty warriors, they were now called the drunken fools of the plains, debauched as they were by devil water.

The mighty Bear Caller too, Big Tree gloated, was destined to be reduced. True, Big Tree mightily enjoyed mocking Sis-ki-dee's recent humiliation at Touch the Sky's hands. But the truth cried out in his inescapable memory. He had supped full of humiliations heaped on by Touch the Sky.

He had sat immobile, taken completely by surprise, when Touch the Sky killed his chief, Iron Eyes, and stole Honey Eater back from the Comancheros. And when Big Tree had launched an arrow into Touch the Sky's chest at point-blank range, the Cheyenne had flinched just enough to keep the point out of his heart. And that first climb the Cheyennes made up Wendigo Mountain—one of them had died, yes. But the other four had broached the renegade camp and got their Medicine Arrows back, killing a score of renegades in the process.

All these reasons, and several more, made Big Tree at least as keen as Sis-ki-dee to rip the Cheyenne's warm and beating heart out. And cataloging all his grievances also inspired Big Tree to empty the rest of one quiver. Big Tree waited for more blood. This time, however, a return flurry of hard-hitting arrows made him duck back, grinning at the sport.

If Big Tree's enemies wasted precious arrows like that, they must be angry. That meant the wound Big Tree had inflicted was serious. Good. He was here to make their world a hurting place, and this was only the beginning.

The three Cheyenne warriors knew they had been discovered, Big Tree reasoned as he caught up his buckskin and slid her hackamore on. But he knew the tall one was resolute of purpose, a trait learned from his white masters. Once Touch the Sky determined on a course of action, he generally completed it.

No, the warriors meant to gain the summit and wreak havoc on that camp. But Big Tree knew he could easily beat them to the top by riding unchallenged up the front slope.

For a moment, he felt as elated as he had when, still a boy, he watched his first torture of white captives in Texas. No tribe took such extreme pleasure at inflicting pain as did the Comanches. The torture of a white child was a festive event that sometimes lasted three days. And the idea of inflicting pain on these Northern Cheyennes held even more pleasure.

Big Tree rubbed his hand in the blood on his shoulder, then smeared it all over his face. Touch the Sky's or not, at least it was Cheyenne blood. Then he kicked his pony's flanks hard with both heels, racing to intercept his enemies.

* * *

97

"Over here," Sis-ki-dee told Plenty Coups. "In the light. I want to show you something."

Plenty Coups had barely escaped death when the whites blew that ridge out from under the Indians. But he had watched at least five companions tumble screaming to their deaths below. Now fear still held him in its grip as he obeyed his leader.

Sis-ki-dee had a small firepit burning well back from the ridge. "Look here. They will brag for days about killing our brothers! We are going to exact the cost of those brags."

"How?" Plenty Coups asked. "You said we must conserve bullets until the situation at our camp is resolved. And we are running out of gun cotton to hurl on them."

"Buck, we have an ample supply of primer caps and black powder. We are going to turn a favorite Cheyenne trick against their white masters. We are going to make their famous exploding arrows—the same arrows Touch the Sky used to defeat us in the Sans Arcs. Watch. It is simple."

Sis-ki-dee's copper brassards gleamed in the light as he worked. First, he used a length of buffalo sinew to tie one of the primer caps to an arrow point. Then he poured black powder from his flask into a little rawhide pouch and tied that around the cap.

"They fail about half the time," he said. "So have the men make a generous supply of them. We are going to launch them as one man, and you will see how we will make them pay. But this is only the bloody diversion. We are going to attack!"

Plenty Coups stared at him. "Attack? Contrary

Warrior, do you mean to go below and rush their camp?"

Sis-ki-dee threw back his head and roared his insane laugh. "Would you place a woman on the other side of camp if you meant to top her? You fool, how else can we attack them? Stop gaping and listen. They think they are safe. They have shaken us with the big-thundering gun. They won't expect an attack. We are going to rain exploding arrows in on them. Then while they are distracted with the fires, we will swarm on them. Make your thoughts bloody, buck, and nothing else!"

"Shh," Kristen said, trying to hush a crying child. "It's all right now, Mattie. Things are quiet outside now. It's all right, sweet love. Shush now."

Kristen rocked the little four-year-old in her lap. Other children too had taken shelter with their schoolmarm, a result of this most recent spate of fires. Now Kristen's house, one of the safest in camp, was crowded with wounded men and morose children.

Woman Dress, exhausted like everyone else, tended to the wounded miners as best she could. In the corner, hunched and deeply depressed, sat poor Sarah Blackford. Her mother Tilly lay dead, cruelly murdered, and so far they had not even been able to give her a proper Christian burial.

Justin McKinney, as plucky as his dad, stood guard near the front door with a shotgun under one arm. Some of the other older boys were armed too. Enough miners had been killed or wounded by now that they faced a very nasty prospect. Either the oldest boys would have to stand in for men, or this whole camp was doomed.

There was the noise of approaching feet from outside, and Justin brought his scattergun quickly up to the ready.

"Hello, the house," Caleb called out, knowing the nervous boys were armed and probably jumpy with fright. "Friends approaching. Lower your hammers!"

Kristen heaved a sigh of relief when Caleb and Tom, both exhausted and powder blackened but otherwise unharmed, entered the crowded room. Tom met her eyes and they exchanged a long look, then a smile. But his expression turned to a deeply worried frown as he surveyed the room with its grim and unhappy occupants.

"I'm hungry," Mattie wailed.

Kristen could barely hold back tears of frustration and rage. Mattie's mother and father were both missing and presumed dead. As for feeding all these hungry children, not to mention the men who were fighting this hard battle, she was helpless. The last of her flour and bacon had disappeared quickly, and even the coffee was gone.

"How does it look?" she asked Tom, who shook his head. Riley was not good at sugarcoating the truth, nor did he want to upset this woman whom he was falling in love with.

"They're quiet for now," he said. "Which worries me. They've got something else planned. I feel it in my bones. We've got the worst of the fires out now, but the men are dead on their feet with exhaustion. One more hard attack, and I don't know how long we can hold out."

Tom spoke low so none of the wounded or the

older kids would hear him. He glanced at Sarah, alone in her corner.

"She spoken to anyone yet?" he asked, pity clear in his tone.

Kristen bit her lip to keep from crying outright. She shook her head. "The poor thing is still in total shock. She doesn't understand it. Why would anyone kill her mother? And how will any of us explain it?"

"We won't," Tom said. "It's a scar that'll never heal. She'll carry it for life if she survives this."

He met Kristen's eyes again. "I just hope to God Matthew can get up to that camp in time and make enough catarumpus to pull them off us. If not—"

He broke off, unwilling to say what Kristen already knew without the words being spoken.

The four braves, two Kiowas and two Comanches, held counsel in a tight group at the top of the front slope of Wendigo Mountain. Below them, about halfway down, a huge belt of mist circled the mountain like a sash. Actually it was steam released by the underground springs, then trapped by wind currents. In the dim moonlight, they had just watched a lone rider come out of the steam and head for the top. They could not make him out clearly in the moonlight.

"It is Big Tree," said Sioux Killer, one of the Comanches. "Light is gleaming from his medal and the silver conchos on his saddle."

His companions were Sun Road, Bull Hump, and Scalp Cane. Good fighters all, they had been selected to protect the camp while the main body was dealing misery to the miners. The rest breathed easier at Sioux Killer's report and lowered their weapons.

"Something is on the spit," Scalp Cane said. "Big Tree is pushing his mount hard."

Soon enough their leader was within hearing distance, his tired mount blowing foam. "Look lively, brothers! Three Cheyenne bucks are on their way up to beard the lion in his den. Only the lion is going to rip their meat from their limbs."

Big Tree reached the camp, swung down, threw his bridle, and let one of his lickspittles lead the buckskin to the water trough that was kept filled from one of the underground streams.

"Are they fools?" Bull Hump scoffed, searching the slope below. "We can pick them off from here easier than lice from a blanket."

"We can pick them off easy enough," Big Tree said. "But not from here—from the back of camp. They are coming up the cliffs."

This evoked two chief emotions from the sentries: anticipation because this should be some lively sport and a rugged determination because each of them recalled what happened the last time they had let Cheyennes reach the summit of those cliffs.

"Is one of them the tall Bear Caller?" Scalp Cane asked.

When Big Tree nodded, the rest exchanged apprehensive glances in the moonlight. Big Tree mocked them with a sudden burst of laughter.

"Look at the squaw men on the feather edge of panic at the mere mention of his name! Follow me, bold warriors, and I will put the strength back into your limbs! Poke your fear into your parfleches. I tell you that he is still far down and will never make it. We are going to make sure of that right now."

Big Tree led them past the wickiups and lodges and storehouses to the rim of the steep cliffs on the backside of the mountain. "Start rolling boulders to the edge. Make many piles about a double arm's length apart so that we have the entire cliff covered. They are still below the steam; so we will not spot them. Nor is there much light down there even when they break through. But we will not have to see them to cause them the worst trouble in the world."

Indeed, Touch the Sky and his companions faced enough bad trouble as it was. The climbing was a bit easier now as hand- and footholds were more plentiful. But Little Horse had lost much blood, even though his wound was now well bound. There were times when, despite his heroic efforts, his companions were forced to carry his weight along with their own.

But worst of all, Touch the Sky realized, their enemy now knew they were coming up. The element of surprise had been ruined. They had only so much room to maneuver; so getting over that rim up above was going to prove a bloody piece of work, if it was even possible.

But it must be done! They had not come this far only to show the white feather and climb down. Look at Little Horse, Touch the Sky told himself—weak from blood loss, but carrying the fight forward anyway as he had always done. For he too knew the grim truth. Either they ruined that camp and thus cut off their enemy's supply line, or nothing would stop the formidable Renegade Nation.

These marauders had murdered Spotted Tail, leader of the Bow Strings. They had murdered Chief Gray Thunder. And now they meant to kill Chief River of Winds. Slowly, inexorably, they were chipping away at the rock of Cheyenne leadership and stability. Not just the white miners and their families were in peril. The Powder River Cheyennes were next.

So Touch the Sky fought on. His arms trembled with weariness. The three warriors inched closer toward the belt of steam. Once again, the nimble young brave covered a smooth expanse of cliff while his companions hung on for dear life and waited for the rope. Touch the Sky's eyes met Little Horse's. The plucky brave showed the great strain of his wound and lost blood.

"This is a better place to die than in your tipi!" Touch the Sky shouted down to him above the sound of raging wind. "But this is not a good night for dying! Death has another day reserved for you, brother. Your shaman feels it in his bones!"

Touch the Sky rarely invoked his status as a shaman, but doing so gave special credence to his words. Seeming to take heart, Little Horse renewed his efforts against the gray slate of the cliff face.

Touch the Sky reached a tiny ledge the width of perhaps three fingers. He hauled himself up, hugged the stone face, and again snubbed the rope around a rock spur. He knotted it and had just tossed it down to his companions when disaster struck.

Even as Touch the Sky looked up to gauge their distance from the roiling belt of steam, massive gray shapes came hurtling out of it. The deadly cascade livened the air all around them, and then a huge, solid boulder struck Touch the Sky hard on the forehead and tore him loose from his hold. For a moment, he almost recovered, with his hands and feet scrabbling for a grip. But he had been hit hard and his reactions were slowed. A solid ball of ice replaced his stomach when he began hurtling toward the deadly points of the basalt turrets far below.

Chapter Eleven

Sis-ki-dee could not make out the contours of mountain peaks in the darkness, only their shadowy mass. But he stared in the direction of the Wendigo Mountain camp, visualizing those cliffs. He had climbed them once himself—down only; and he had emerged from an emergency escape tunnel that opened on the cliff. Rather than face down Touch the Sky, he chose those cliffs.

His men worked all around him in the darkness, preparing the exploding arrows. Sis-ki-dee had heard nothing from the direction of Wendigo Mountain. That silence bothered him.

True it was, four stout bucks were guarding the camp. And Big Tree was even more trustworthy as a fighter. Still, this Touch the Sky grew meaner and more wily as his desperation increased. Sis-ki-dee had been gone to the south country when the Cheyenne's woman and child were kidnapped by Hiram Steele. But the widows left wailing after that particular mistake convinced Steele never to try it again.

And if his cunning foe reached that camp, Sis-ki-dee knew that his five fine ponies were dust behind him. So was his cache of fine white man's tobacco and coffee, not to mention his handguns and other personal effects. Such a loss would destroy not only the Renegade Nation's ability to wage war; it would leave him and Big Tree as poor as their most dissolute braves.

So he knew his present plan was best. Never mind waiting for Touch the Sky to counter this strike. They must win with what supplies they had and return to their camp. With a victory, they could massacre the men below and ransom the women and children to the Comancheros. That would add to their riches. At least they could then afford to replace their goods if Touch the Sky's reckless plan worked.

"Contrary Warrior," Plenty Coups called out from a group of braves working in the light from the pit. "The arrows are ready."

"Stout buck! Divide them equally among all the men. Then line up at close intervals along the ridge. Don't worry about that thunder gun. You are not going to be on that ridge long enough to end up like our comrades. No one launches an arrow until my command."

"What targets?" Plenty Coups asked. "Only the mining equipment?"

"No, I want them concentrated on the houses too. We want fires, plenty of them. But have ears, brother! No one fires on the house I showed you earlier—the one at the end of the camp road."

107

* * *

"Jesus, it's damn near four a.m.," Tom muttered. "They've been quiet for too long now. I wonder how Touch the Sky is doing?"

The children were mostly asleep now. Nonetheless, Kristen found time to admonish Tom. "Now see here, Captain Riley! You are in my bad books!"

Riley's exhaustion gave way for a moment to genuine surprise. He sat up straighter against the wall that supported him. He watched Kristen rolling bandages she had soaked in gentian.

"Your bad books? What have I done?"

"I realize you're a soldier and you're used to a . . . vivid vocabulary in the field. But please watch all the cursing around the children! They already swear like little troopers as a result of the miners. You needn't encourage it, sir."

Though he was thus roundly rebuked, Tom could not resist a smile. Even caught between a rock and a hard place, this pretty girl insisted on the rules of civilized society.

"Sure is hard to sleep with my back to this wall," Tom said. "Caleb over there has the right idea."

Kristen, who was also worrying about what Touch the Sky was up to, didn't need to look to know that Caleb over there was asleep on the floor with his head in Woman Dress's lap.

"Hmph!" she said, glad Tom couldn't see her blush in the dark. "There's a pillow on the Boston rocker."

"Faith Gillycuddy is asleep on it. You wouldn't want me to wake her up, would you?"

"Well," Kristen said, "long as I have to sit and

do this anyway, I suppose it wouldn't hurt if you—"

Sarah, only half asleep, screamed at the sudden loud impacts all around them followed by popping explosions. Caleb shot up and clawed for his gun. Tom, halfway across to lie in his lady's lap, spun on his heel and raced toward the door.

"Damn!" he said. "What the hell are they doing now?"

Tom held the door slanted open enough that Kristen could see out into the camp street and beyond. Bright clusters of orange sparks seemed to leap off the houses. Some of them caused bad fires immediately as the little explosions spewed chunks of flaming wood everywhere, starting more fires—especially on the vulnerable shake roofs.

"C'mon, Caleb!" Tom roared above the din of terrified children. "Let's get to that Parrot gun before they burn this camp down around us!"

Little Horse and Two Twists, like their comrade, had been caught flush with surprise when those boulders suddenly showered down out of the band of mist above them. Touch the Sky was perhaps a double arm's length above them. The two of them were roughly side by side below him. Two Twists waited for the rope to be tossed down so he could assist Little Horse to the next ledge, where they might rest a moment.

Hurtling rocks barely missed both of them, but brushed by so close they could feel the breeze from them. Then before either of them could even blink, Touch the Sky flew past them. Little Horse's right arm speared out and managed to grab Touch the Sky by an ankle; Two Twists' left hand shot out and barely gripped his comrade's red sash.

"Hold on, brother!" Two Twists roared out to Little Horse. "I only just have a handful."

"I have plenty," Little Horse said in a horribly strained voice. The plucky brave normally had the strength of a young burro. But much of that legendary strength had drained out with his blood. "Too much, buck! I cannot hold him much longer!"

"Try! He dropped the rope too," Two Twists said, "but it is tied above. Hold him just a bit while I see if I can get it tied around him."

However, this was far easier to say than to do. Two Twists had a reasonably good position, with his feet wedged into a fissure in the rock. But one hand had to hold Touch the Sky while he desperately tried to snare that rope with the other. Howling winds buffeted them and made his task harder, especially by blowing the rope just beyond his grasp.

"Touch the Sky!" Little Horse shouted. "Can you hear us?"

Their friend was ominously still, and they could see a gash opened to the bone where that rock had smashed into him.

"*Ipewa!*" Two Twists cried in Cheyenne when his fingers seized that errant rope. "Good!"

"Work fast," Little Horse urged him, desperation spiking his voice. "I am losing him, Two Twists!"

His face pinched with urgency, Two Twists managed to loop the dangling rope around his comrade and fix a knot on it just as Little Horse let go because he had to to save himself from falling. Unfortunately, there were still perhaps four feet of slack in the rope, which made a hard, fast snap as it tightened and Touch the Sky slammed into the granite facade of the cliff.

And thus things stood. The three of them, two exhausted and resting, the third unconscious, brought to a halt on that bare gray and hostile immensity of stone. Although Touch the Sky was safe for the moment, his companions did not even know if he lived.

The attack with those horrible arrows, Kristen quickly realized, had not lasted long. Clearly the savages up above had no intention of providing another target for the artillery gun. But though the actual attack was over quicker than a bad dream, the results had become a nightmare that wouldn't go away. Nearly half the houses were on fire, and the screams of frightened women and children drowned out the crackling flames.

Kristen and Woman Dress were under strict orders to remain in the house. But Kristen could not obey those orders, not with other women outside forming a bucket brigade despite the potential danger of a massed enfilade fire from above. A huge cistern at the back of camp collected rain water and snow runoff. Now a line snaked forward from it, and the desperate residents fought to save their homes and possessions.

Kristen asked Woman Dress to stay with the children and wounded; then she ran outside to assist the effort. She joined the far end, toward the direction of the mine itself. The Riley boys held their usual post at the Parrot artillery rifle. But both men, she could see in the eerie, bright orange glow of fires, scowled with frustration. The Indians had struck and then quickly retreated, leaving them nothing to draw a bead on.

Dakota Boggs's house, just to Kristen's left, was aflame, but still salvageable. She accepted bucket after heavy bucket, passing them on to the last woman in line, who doused the flames over and over. They were just beginning to make some headway when a hideous shriek, rivaling all the devils loosed from hell, assaulted Kristen's ears.

Startled, she glanced toward the entrance at the front of camp. A score or more of garishly painted savages, wielding every conceivable type of weapon, boiled up the slope, the kill cry distorting their faces. They fired their first volley, and Kristen heard a man scream as a bullet found him. But the savages had not yet spotted the Rileys under that limestone shelf. Even as the renegades poured deeper into camp, the last three ten-pound rockets whooshed in among them.

Too awed to take cover or scream, Kristen watched as powerful blasts literally blew redskins toward the heavens. Tom aimed with deadly skill, and the Parrot slowed the charge considerably. But an ugly leader she recognized as Sis-ki-dee himself rallied the last group of Indians coming up the slope.

Tom and Caleb's fighting fury was unbelievable. What they did next, Kristen realized later, saved the camp. A few miners had been all but routed by the Indian's massed charge. Bellowing commands in a voice louder than any plebe popping off at West Point, Tom organized and rallied them.

"Full front face!" he screamed to a ragged squad on his left. "Full front face and fire!"

Both Riley brothers deserted the gun, which was useless now. They ripped their sidearms out of their holsters and entered the melee at point-blank range. The other miners, watching Tom and Caleb rear up like grizzlies, were inspired to quell their retreat and join the fray in hand-to-hand fighting.

Kristen's life on the frontier had ever been perilous. But never had she witnessed a battle like this. It was awful, utterly terrifying, and yet it held her spellbound. Tom Riley looked like one of the berserkers she had read about in history books. His pistol empty, he used it as a club to smash at the invading horde.

Then, abruptly, a scream was torn from Kristen when a renegade shot Tom in the stomach and he folded to the ground. But at least Sis-ki-dee had decided this price was too heavy for the pleasure of exterminating these whites. Kristen saw him and his braves retreat down the slope even as she rushed forward to see if Tom Riley still belonged to the land of the living.

Touch the Sky dangled helpless on the feather edge of death as his mind played cat and mouse with awareness.

Brother! Brother, can you hear?

Yes, he wanted to say, tried to say. But could he really hear, or was it just a dream voice, part of his vision in the Black Hills? Memory flexed a muscle, time suddenly shifted, and he was back on Massacre Bluff where the white eyes held Honey Eater and Little Bear.

Shaman! Can you hear?

None of it held. Memory succeeded memory like geese flying in formation. Now he heard the voice of Old Knobby, the former hostler at the feed stable in Bighorn Falls: *The Injun figgers he belongs to the land. The white man figgers the land belongs to him. They ain't meant to live together.*

The melodic voice of Kristen Steele: *It scares me, all the enemies you've earned, all sworn to kill you.*

The hateful voice of Hiram, her father: *Now I've finally got this red son of a bitch pinned in the dirt. Let me see him squirm a little before I step on him.*

And now other, more familiar voices, even nearer: *Brother! Wake to the living world!*

Touch the Sky's eyes eased open.

"Brother!" Two Twists bellowed again above the piercing howl of the wind. "Can you hear me?"

"Pipe down, jay. I hear you," Touch the Sky said weakly. "Your shouts are like kicks to the head."

Thunder exploded, a rain squall slapped at them, and ghostly tines of lightning shot down from the sky.

"I will kick your head," Little Horse promised him gamely, "if we survive this unholy lump of misery. When I climb behind you, buck, I take my life in my hands! You almost flicked both of us off too. With a name like Touch the Sky, you'd best live up to it."

"Listen to All Behind Him," Two Twists scoffed, his voice implying that they were up against nothing more than a day in their camp. "That arrow should have hit you where you sit. You never would have felt it."

Touch the Sky was bruised and battered, but he could not resist a grin. His friends didn't fool him. Their brave banter was proof that now, more than ever, they were up against it. The code of the warrior was clear, and his band never deviated. Bear pain in silence; meet death with defiance.

"Bucks!" he shouted above the din of rough weather. "They are not done with us yet. Look sharp. Not only do we have to get up the rest of this cliff. We have to get over it. Now let's get it done. And if we cannot, then let us show them how well a Cheyenne can die!"

Chapter Twelve

"Those boulders made things lively for them," Big Tree said. "Count upon it. Those three noble red men will soon regret their rash impulse to beard the lion in his den."

The last of the rocks had been rolled over the cliff. The weather had cleared up, and a huge raft of clouds had been blown away from the moon. Now Big Tree's battle scars stood out in the moonlight as he scoured the camp, hatching more misery for the hapless Cheyenne interlopers. His four minions surrounded him.

Scalp Cane stared downward. "Very little light makes it down there. If they have climbed out of the steam yet, I cannot see them."

Big Tree gauged the time by judging the height of the dawn star in the east. "They will be up here soon. They will have to be. They know they will

116

never stand a chance if they let Sister Sun catch them on that cliff face."

"A chance?" Sioux Killer gave out a harsh bark of laughter. "Quohada, light or dark, how can they have a chance of getting up here? Only think on this thing. I can almost toss a stone from one end of this cliff's rim to the other. If they go too far left, they will never get over that huge pile of rimrock. Go too far right, they encounter tra-prock shelves that would stop a mountain goat, let along two-footed men."

"I have ears," Bull Hump said. "The five of us can cover this rim secure in the knowledge that we have clear shots at trapped men who can hardly fire back while climbing for their lives."

"Clearly," Sun Road said. "Either they have been killed already by Big Tree's arrows and our rocks, or they have wisely climbed down."

"Listen to me," Big Tree told them severely. "You are good men—men to ride the river with, bucks! But false pride is dangerous where this Touch the Sky is involved. What kills a normal man only makes him more dangerous. Yes, our position is excellent here. But I do not think the Noble Red Man will give up his quest. And I agree that they can hardly clear that cliff while we are here. But I have no intention of hunkering down and biding my time until they appear to do battle. We are not done sporting with them!"

He pointed across camp to a spot where a wagon sheet had been staked out to cover several casks. They had been stolen from a whiteskin pack train passing through the Little Bighorn country. They contained chemicals long familiar to the Southwest tribes—the chemicals used to

117

make white man's Greek Fire or gun cotton. Big Tree did not know how to pronounce the whiteskin names painted on these casks: niter, sulfur, and naptha. But he knew that the last of the three was highly inflammable by itself.

"Bull Hump and Sioux Killer," he ordered. "Go get that casket with the yellow signs on it. You, Sun Road and Scalp Cane," he added, pointing to a long wooden watering trough they had fashioned for the horses by splitting and hollowing a tree much as they might for a dugout. "Carry that to the edge of the cliff."

His comrades grinned and nodded, seeing which way the wind set. But Big Tree exhorted them, "Have ears, brothers! That exploding water will blaze at a moment's touch from a burning coal. We pour it into the trough, ignite it, and dump it over. Repeat this perhaps four or five times, and we can cover the entire length of the cliff. Hurry, bucks! The Cheyennes call this Wendigo Mountain. Now let us remind them why."

"Oh, merciful lord, he's lost so much blood," Kristen Steele muttered.

The pretty schoolteacher caught her lower lip between her teeth as she unbuttoned Tom Riley's military tunic to expose the ugly blue-black swelling where the bullet had pierced his stomach. The bleeding had finally slowed, but not before Tom passed out from blood loss.

"Belly shot," Woman Dress said sadly, shaking her head. Both women knew it was far better, if one had to be shot, to catch a bullet in the rib cage than in the stomach. Gut shots bled internally, and in a land where doctors were usually far off, that meant slow death.

"If this siege ends soon enough," Kristen mused out loud as she bathed the wound with a camphor-soaked cloth, "we can get him to Register Cliffs. Even without the train. We can use a buckboard. But it has to end soon."

Woman Dress looked worried at these words. Caleb was outside fighting fires with the rest of the able-bodied men. But she feared he would insist on trying to get his brother to help whether those Indians were gone or not.

"Maybe so better not go," she said in her halting, confused English.

Kristen let her head drop for a moment and massaged both her tired eyeballs with her fingers. How exhausted and spirit broken she felt! The children had finally cried themselves into a fitful sleep, and soon the sun would crest the mountains. What a night it had been! Tom lay dying, and what was Matthew's fate? If he hadn't gained the peak of that nearby mountain, they were all doomed here.

All of it was just so unfair! Kristen, forced to flee from her father's wrath like an antelope before a prairie fire; Tom, caught between the corrupt Indian Ring back in Washington and a sense of duty that forced him to fight secretly for his so-called Indian enemies; and Matthew, trapped between two worlds bent on his utter destruction. Hot tears welled up behind her eyes, but she fought them down. She would be of no use to anyone if she let herself break down.

Kristen went into the little slope-off kitchen and pumped up some fresh water. As she reached for the basin, however, her skin suddenly turned cold and grained with fear.

She glanced at the boarded-up window, thinking of the erosion gully that led down from the ridge above. But it was so steep at its beginning. And besides, why would any of the renegades pick on this house of all houses?

She was exhausted, she reminded herself. And nerve frazzled. She had to go take care of Tom Riley because until he got some help she was all that stood between him and death.

Sis-ki-dee unlooped his rope from the sapling, having finished the steepest part of his descent. From here, it was easy going to the back of the house. He paused behind the boarded-up window to listen. He heard men snoring and a child's cough. A sudden, metallic squealing made him flinch. Then he realized it was just one of the women pumping up some water. Sis-ki-dee reminded himself that some of the wounded might be able to fire at him. So he must work fast.

Moving silently, his moccasined feet feeling carefully to avoid dried sticks that might snap, he worked his way around the east wall of the wooden lodge. Cautiously Sis-ki-dee poked his head around to look into the main street. The sight gratified him. Although some buildings still smoked at this end of camp, most of the fires were concentrated farther down, and so were the men fighting them. A defensive line of riflemen, he could see in the ruddy glow of flames, guarded the entrance to camp.

As usual, he had timed things well. But like all battle leaders who had survived on these perilous plains, Sis-ki-dee knew that speed and surprise were essential. His blood sang in his veins, and if at all possible, he meant to take the white beauty outside and shame her in the dirt. But if he was discovered before he could get her mouth covered and drag her outside and around to the blind side of the lodge, then he would at least kill her on the spot.

No, she was not the proud Cheyenne beauty Touch the Sky had married. But the murder of this sun-haired woman would leave the Noble Red Man grieving for many moons. Perhaps, Sis-ki-dee thought with a sudden spurt of inspiration, he could even send him her scalp by a runner!

He checked the street again in the last of the night's dim blackness. Then Sis-ki-dee eased around the corner of the lodge, ducked under a window, and reached the split-slab door around front. He pushed against it. It resisted, but not before easing open an inch. It was only held by a latch string inside.

He checked the street once again, hugging the front of the house. Then, brass earrings glinting in the moonlight, he slid the bone-handled knife from his sheath. It was a mere heartbeat's work to slice through the rawhide thong holding the door. Sis-ki-dee pushed the door open a foot and peered inside.

He saw her immediately, bent over someone—Riley! He recognized the blue kersey tunic. She was wiping Riley's forehead with a damp cloth. The wounded lay here and there, interspersed with sleeping children.

Kristen Steele was absorbed in watching Riley and never thought to glance toward the door. Sis-ki-dee rose from his crouch and eased inside. Her beauty, seen close up in soft lantern light, made him pause for just a few blinks in his fast charge. Just long enough for the young girl sleeping in the rocking chair to wake up and scream loud enough to wake snakes.

Sis-ki-dee cursed. The rest happened faster than a digger could shoot an ox. Kristen Steele glanced up, started to scream, then took on a fighting scowl Sis-ki-dee could only call a war face.

Her right hand shot down to the officer's side and came back up holding his Colt Third Model Dragoon—or trying to anyway. This was one of the heaviest Colts known, the steel of its case-hardened frame weighted even more with a metal back strap.

Even as she lifted it, Sis-ki-dee saw the muzzle waver, then plunge. She fired, the sound deafening in this close lodge, and a big chunk of floor kicked up in front of him. He was only a few steps away now, closing fast, and he laughed outright at her comical attempt to kill him.

Then came a sudden shriek as unnerving as the kill cry of a Mexican lancer. Sis-ki-dee glanced right just in time to see the Crow Indian squaw lift her calico dress and slide a thin knife from her stocking. Her throw was not exactly grace-full, but a moment later he felt fangs rip into his right shoulder as the knife caught him just above his protective brassards.

He roared, as much in anger as in pain. But by now Kristen Steel had better control of that Colt Dragoon. Sis-ki-dee wrenched the knife from his shoulder and leapt for the door even as the gun exploded behind him.

"When we come out of this steam," Touch the Sky told his companions, "all three of us are going to pause for a moment and see how the wind sets. It has been hard to this point, brothers. Even now blood runs in my eyes, and it feels as if I have been mule kicked in the skull. Little Horse has lost so much blood he looks like a whiteskin. Only double braid here has not suffered a wound yet, and I fear his time is coming."

"I may skip the wound this time," Two Twists boasted between grunts of strain as he hoisted himself up. "I may skip it and go right to my death!"

The three Cheyennes had nearly passed through the belt of escaping steam that circled the entire mountain. Although half the climb still remained, it was the easy half—plenty of hand- and footholds. Unfortunately, Touch the Sky reminded himself, those delays caused by arrows and rocks had wasted valuable time.

"Never mind dying, buck," he told Two Twists as his companions came up beside him to counsel. "Not until I'm done with you. Now have ears, both of you. It is lighter than I thought. They will not be able to spot us just yet as we emerge. But I will guess they will have enough light to draw beads on us while we are still half this last distance down."

"So what?" Little Horse said. "It means that somehow we must cover the last distance while also firing at them to keep them respectful. It is possible to launch arrows from here on up by planting your feet good."

"It is," Touch the Sky said. "It is also possible to stand up in a canoe on the Snake River, but only a fool does it."

Both Little Horse and Two Twists exchanged a puzzled frown. Then Two Twists said, "Are you hinting, shaman, that we should go back down?"

"Go ask your mother for a dug! I will leave hints to the old squaws in their gossip circle. I will say it bold. With luck, we will neither go back down nor climb this cliff the rest of the way."

"Somehow," Two Twists assured Little Horse, "our comrade has found peyote growing up here and gnawed on it too long."

But Little Horse had finally seized his friend's meaning by the tail. "You mean the secret cave! The one Sis-ki-dee used to escape when we came up here to get our Medicine Arrows back."

"I mean just that, yes, and nothing else. Only think. We know he has one. He and Big Tree would never camp anywhere that had only one road in or out. We also know he got away from us somehow when we were in those caverns above us. They are not deep tunnels. One of them comes out somewhere up there. It has to."

They had begun moving upward again, and they cleared the swirling steam cloud even as Touch the Sky spoke. All three braves, thinking of that hidden cave mouth, stared upward—just in time to watch a roaring wall of deadly fire come hurtling down at them!

Chapter Thirteen

At first, time and place became confused. As that sheet of flame hurled down toward them, Touch the Sky was sure he was back on the prairie, caught in a grassfire. But the moment of stunned immobility passed in a blink, and the will to live instinctively asserted itself.

Just to Touch the Sky's left was a slight protrusion where the rock had buckled. Little Horse was already under it. Touch the Sky grabbed Two Twists and by sheer dint of will and muscle pulled him as he crowded in close to Little Horse.

"Press tight against the cliff!" Touch the Sky shouted. "Pretend it is your mother's breast!"

But speech was impossible as the roaring, air-borne inferno engulfed them. That protrusion just above them was their only defense. It served as a sort of dam, channeling this lethal flow slightly outward from the face of the cliff. All three Cheyennes grimaced with maddening pain as the passing heat seared them. A few drops of flaming naptha clung to their skin, the pain worse than a thousand fire ants biting them at once. But the fiery juggernaut dropped past them, turning the mist below to hissing steam. They held their positions, burned and shaken but afraid to move just yet. Several more times a wide line of fire flowed down, each time tracking along a different part of the cliff.

"They are sweeping the cliff for us," Touch the Sky called out.

Two Twists finally found his voice. "Brother, what manner of white man's devil is that?"

Touch the Sky shook his head, casting another worried glance topside. "Does it matter what name it goes by? Arrow Keeper always said that if it chops wood you may call it an ax. Whatever it is, it will surely kill us if we are caught in it. All the more reason to find that cave entrance."

"That and Sister Sun," Little Horse threw in, nodding toward the east. A band of sky over the plains was turning rose colored just atop the horizon.

"The burning water seems to have stopped for now," Touch the Sky said. "It is risky to break cover, brothers. But I fear greater danger if we hide here any longer. Fan out. Two Twists, climb up through that black lava rock and watch for openings. Little Horse, do the same through that belt of banded rock just overhead. I will search the rest of the cliff. And remember that whoever has been trying so cleverly to kill us may be waiting in the cave. So if you find the cave, signal by hand!"

*   *   *

"Brothers," Sioux Killer boasted, "if they survived that they are not mortal warriors. We did not miss any part of the front of the cliff. Shall we dump more, Quohada?"

Big Tree shook his head. "Save the rest. Sis-ki-dee and I have a bloody campaign planned for it once we have taken the mining camp. As for their death, believe it when we stack their bones and not before. More than once they have turned up from the dead after we have given a victory dance to celebrate killing them."

"Quohada," Sun Road scoffed, "the Bear Caller has salted your tail too often and turned you into a nervous old Ponca. Only think. You emptied a quiver full of arrows and got blood for the effort. We loosed half a mountain of rocks down on them and followed it with murderous fire."

"We have," Big Tree said. "Enough danger and death to wipe out a Pawnee camp. But have you forgotten what he did to us down in Bighorn Falls when we had his white parents surrounded? How many of our comrades may we no longer mention because Touch the Sky sent them under unclean? I say it again, and this place hears me. Only when I have taken a bite out of his warm heart will I pronounce him dead!"

"Big Tree speaks straight words," Bull Hump said. "But if they are coming, they will have to clear this rim. And already I can see the sun's glow on the horizon. The tall one will need all his shaman's tricks to elude our shots this time."

"Shaman's tricks," Sioux Killer said, "or a secret way up."

That chance remark suddenly sent ice into Big Tree's veins. A secret way up! What if Touch the Sky knew about the cave? Back at the front of this camp was a huge cave that all the men knew about. It was periodically used as a den by local mountain lions. What the men didn't know, and he and Sis-ki-dee did, was that a smaller maze of tunnels spun off from this central cave. And one of them ended at the cliff. It was just a tiny opening, barely large enough for a man and disguised well in black lava rock at the extreme left edge of the cliff face.

Touch the Sky would never spot the cave if he didn't know about it. But what if he did? He had chased Sis-ki-dee through those tunnels, but that was long before Big Tree and his braves came north. Big Tree didn't know if Touch the Sky had guessed about it or not.

Big Tree couldn't take the chance. Nor could he, with only four braves against Touch the Sky and his men, dare to split this small force. Yet there was no other way to guard both this cliff and that cave.

"Scalp Cane," he said. "You stay here and guard carefully. If you see them, fire your rifle to summon us. The rest of you, come with me. I have thought of something. There may by chance be a cave down on that cliff—one that connects with the cave up here."

Big Tree led his men toward the cave. An old wagon box sat in the middle of camp, the legacy of a raid on a whiteskin pack train. He had his men drag it along with them to the cave. Set up on end, it neatly covered the opening.

"Good." Big Tree picked up a huge boulder—one twice the size of any his companions could manage—and thumped it down in front of the wagon box. "Pile on the rocks, bucks! We must be sure they will not be able to come out this way.

If they are still alive, the only way into this camp will be by that cliff."

Touch the Sky, battling fierce winds and hard climbing, scoured his section of the cliff. But no opening bigger than his fist penetrated the solid rock. He glanced to his left just in time to see Two Twists desperately signaling to him and Little Horse.

"I found it, brother," he whispered when his comrade joined him. The youth pointed. Sure enough, the opening was small and, in the black lava rock, almost impossible to see from more than a few feet away. Truly, it was not much bigger than the smoke hole of a lodge. But a man could get through it, Touch the Sky realized. And three men would get through it.

But who was harassing them? If it was Sis-ki-dee, they were very well marked for death. He would have a trap waiting.

"You hog all the sport," Little Horse said when Touch the Sky started to worm his way into the entrance. "Let me go first."

Touch the Sky ignored him—and the fearful pounding of his own heart—and wiggled farther into the hole. His body dropped through onto cold, damp stone. He moved in farther and his companions came in after him.

"If they mean to spring a death trap on us," Touch the Sky said quietly, "it will come later. Keep both eyes to the sides. I have never been in this tunnel, but closer to their camp there is a confusing maze of them. I only hope I can recall the way out."

Normally, Two Twists or Little Horse would have added some bold comment and scoffed at death. But what they were doing right now, crawling trapped in an enclosed space, was contrary to their nature as Indians. Even from their tipis they could always see the sky. In here, all was cold, dark, and cramped like a premature grave.

Soon they had other troubles. The small tunnel gradually widened, allowing them to stoop, then stand upright. But it connected with other tunnels, and each one they followed seemed to double back around on itself. Finally, however, they entered one vaulted chamber and Touch the Sky felt the back of his neck tingle. His shaman sense was telling him he had been here before.

"Here," he said in the darkness. "We are close to the way out."

"How can that be?" Little Horse said doubtfully. "I remember that cave you mean. It had a tall, narrow entrance that let much light pass. All is darkness here, yet outside the new sun is coming up by now."

"They have blocked the entrance," Touch the Sky said with certain dread. "Search the walls! If they have blocked us in, there is nothing else for it. We will have to find our way out and finish our climb in daylight."

"Here!" Little Horse called out after a little time had elapsed in desperate searching. "I feel wood. And I can feel a faint breeze."

"This is the entrance," Touch the Sky said. "And they have blocked it. Brothers, I know you are tired, especially you, Little Horse. That wound in your leg would have a lesser man groaning in his robes. But now we must set our shoulders to this wood and see if we can budge it."

The warrior did not expect the job to be easy. However, the moment he strained against that wood Touch the Sky knew it was blocked from behind by plenty of weight.

"It does not even begin to budge," he said, fighting off a wave of dizzy nausea. The effort took its toll after that long climb up and the injury to his head.

"We can burn it," the resolute Little Horse said. "Burn the wood, I mean, and see if we can move what is behind it?"

"They may see the smoke," Two Twists said.

"So what?" Little Horse said. "They may see our smoke, and they will see us coming up that cliff. Would you rather be told you might die or you will die?"

"Now All Behind Him has become a logician," Two Twists said.

"Yes," Touch the Sky said, breaking out his flint and steel. "And a persuasive one, at that."

All of them always carried crumbled bark in their parfleches and legging sashes for tinder. Touch the Sky sprinkled some at the base of the dry, weathered wood. Then he struck flint to steel, throwing a few sparks downward. Soon the bark caught, and he carefully fanned it to life. The wood slowly caught fire, sending a brighter and brighter orange glow to light up the cavern.

"It is an old wagon box," Touch the Sky said, recognizing the forged iron bands around it.

All three braves were forced to back up as the flames and smoke increased. Any moment, Touch the Sky expected shouts from outside. But soon the flaming wood crumbled inward under the weight of boulders, and a little window of dull light appeared at the top of the heap.

"We have some work ahead, Cheyennes," Touch the Sky said. "But they should all be gathered near that cliff at the rear of camp. If we work quickly, we are free of this place and in their camp! Hands to the work, bucks!"

Once again, Touch the Sky's days among the white men stood them in good stead, and he organized a quick system for clearing the heap. Little Horse was the weakest of the trio, and the least able to move around agilely. So Touch the Sky put him at the end of the line and Two Twists in the middle. Then the tall brave climbed onto the heap and began rolling the boulders down to Two Twists. He heaved them back to Little Horse, who rolled them aside and out of the way.

The window grew until it was big enough to let him squeeze through. Touch the Sky's companions followed him out, Two Twists and Touch the Sky helping Little Horse.

The sun was up now, and all of them were drenched with sweat from their efforts. For some time, they crouched in the heap of rocks and kept a wary eye on the deserted camp while they regained a little of their strength.

"I can see no one," Little Horse said.

"Nor I," Touch the Sky said. "But they are all up at the cliff. We can't see it from here until we go through the camp."

Go through the camp they did only a few moments later. Cautiously, in single file, they crossed from tree to rock. They passed through the deserted lodges, past the hut storehouses, and up the rest of the mountain until the rim of the cliff eased into view. Using hand signals, Touch the Sky called his companions up to his side.

"Look," he whispered. "Maiyun lined them up for us."

He pointed off to the north. Four figures were crouched at various points along the rim of the cliff. Each one stared intently down, rifle or bow to hand.

"Are there more?" Little Horse wondered.

"If so, where? We have come through the camp."

Even as they spoke, all three warriors notched arrows into their bows and pulled the buffalo-sinew strings taut.

"Today is a good day to die!" Touch the Sky shouted out in Sioux, knowing the renegades understood it.

The three Cheyennes waited until their startled foes had spun around, bringing their weapons up as they did. Fletched arrows hissed through the morning mist, and cries of pain followed as the expert archers skewered their targets in their vitals. Two dropped dead above, and two more fell back off the cliff, one of them screaming so hideously he made the hair on Touch the Sky's nape tingle.

The tall warrior thrust his bow in the air and shouted, "Hi-ya, hii-ya!" His brothers joined his victory shout.

But even as their exalted voices split the mountain stillness, Touch the Sky spotted something in the corner of one eye. He glanced quickly to the left toward the front slope that led up Wendigo Mountain. He was just in time to see a lone figure leap out from behind a rock and tear off down the slope. Then he realized their terrible mistake. The massive size of that figure meant it could be only one Indian: the Comanche war leader Big Tree.

Chapter Fourteen

"Burn it, brothers," Touch the Sky said to his companions. "Every lodge, every cache, every weapon except those you claim as trophies. Make piles and heap them high. Once the flames are licking, use robes and wagon sheets to make plenty of smoke. We want the rest at the mining camp to see and know their siege is ended. Their enemies have lost their base of supplies!"

Little Horse, limping and tired, but also eager to begin the destruction, glanced at his comrade. He and Two Twists had not seen the figure leap from behind a rock.

"Shaman," Little Horse said. "Whenever you place your hand on the haft of your knife like that, bloody business is close at hand. What do you know that we do not?"

"You called me shaman, buck, and you said

right. Listen to the birds, and they will tell you what I have in mind."

"What birds?" Two Twists demanded. "There are no birds up here."

"There are two puzzled jays," Touch the Sky said. "Named All Behind Him and Double Braid. Just set to work, brothers. I have a piece of work out on the slope. I have just seen a wild longhorn. You know how the wild ones are. The Mexicans call them *ladinos*, the sly ones. Sometimes they seem to run away, but they hide and then attack."

"Longhorns?" Two Twists asked. "The cows down to the south in the land of sagebrush and greasewood? Why would one be in the mountains?"

Little Horse, who knew Touch the Sky's indirect ways better than most, said, "Never mind, tadpole. Swim down to the camp and let us set to work."

"Kill the ponies," Touch the Sky said as he headed toward the slope. "But lead out three for us. I like that grullo and that blood with the white forelegs. And find me a good weapon for the ride back."

"Don't let those longhorns gore you," Little Horse called out behind him.

Touch the Sky had no desire to tangle with Big Tree right now. He was far from good fighting fettle, and a man who locked horns with that superb Comanche warrior had best be in top form or expect to feed worms.

But Little Horse had immediately understood what the less experienced Two Twists had not. Touch the Sky's reference to the famous man-killing cattle in Texas did indeed fit Big Tree. It was one of his favorite tricks to be seen fleeing a trouble spot; then he would double back and score surprise kills while his quarry celebrated or rested. Touch the Sky had no plans to chase Big Tree down the mountain. But he would at least cover that slope while his friends destroyed the camp. Otherwise they were at risk from the back-shooting Comanche.

Even as he braced his leg muscles for the downward slope, Touch the Sky heard an eerie, hideous trumpeting noise behind him. He realized that his friends had wisely decided to start with the horses since the destruction and fire would spook them. That noise was air rushing through the slits in their windpipes. It saddened him greatly. These wild mustangs were fine mountain stock descended from the best Spanish breeds. Like the best Indians, the best mustangs had freedom in their blood and resisted conquering by the hair-face invaders.

But the warrior chastised himself for such distracting thoughts. He recalled one of the first lessons in survival that Arrow Keeper had taught him. At moments of danger, a warrior must stop the inner flow of words called thoughts and attend only to the language of the senses.

The sun was well up, but still cut off from this south face of Wendigo Mountain. As Touch the Sky let his gaze cross the entire slope, he studied and read the shadows. Then he turned sideways and studied it with his peripheral vision. Sometimes that could reveal movements that direct vision could not.

Touch the Sky moved a little way down and searched behind the bigger rocks as he did. Behind him, a sudden burst of sustained gunfire made him wince until he realized it was ammo stores burning. He hoped his friends got out of the way in time. Already, it sounded like a full battle.

Good! Let the noise shake the very sky, for they had been forced to endure the sounds of battle from the mining camp. Now let Sis-ki-dee hear some of the same.

Touch the Sky took a few more steps, paused, then heard a faint metallic click. A less experienced man might have stopped to puzzle that sound out. But the Cheyenne recognized it without needing a moment's reflection.

Blood surged into his face, and Touch the Sky tucked and rolled just as the gun went off. There was a sharp tug at his rawhide shirt when the bullet passed through the folds under the armpit. But he got to a stack of rocks and hunkered behind them.

Big Tree's harsh laughter barked. "Bear Caller! You would be dead right now if only I followed Sis-ki-dee's advice. He always carries his rifle cocked with a bullet in the chamber. I leave my hammer on an empty chamber. I will not ruin another shot at you by cocking a weapon and warning you!"

"I cannot wish the fault undone, Quohada. And neither will you undo the damage my comrades are doing to your camp and horses. Hear it? Smell the burning stink of it? The Renegade Nation will live like lowly, filthy Diggers, grubbing for roots and sleeping in holes. And while you do, thank three Northern Cheyennes who made all of it possible for you."

These words were shot straight. Big Tree and Sis-ki-dee were able to play the big Indians, in part, because of the wealth they had amassed over the years, booty seized in countless raids. Now that sign of their status was going up in flames along with everything else. Touch the Sky could tell, from Big Tree's wooden tone, that his goading words just now were barbs landed in vitals.

"Boast, White Man Runs Him! Your masters in the mining camp are not out of trouble yet. And by now, Sis-ki-dee has left his seed in your paleface cow. As for you and your lickspittles up in my camp—you have a long ride down, and I will be playing with you!"

Keeping a careful eye on his back trail, Touch the Sky returned to the camp, or rather, the blazing inferno that had been the camp. The destruction was complete. And after that harrowing climb up the cliffs, it was a gratifying victory. But Big Tree would be as good as his word. They were in for a dangerous ride down.

"Count upon it, brothers," Touch the Sky assured his companions as they hurried to set out. "It isn't just a hard ride ahead for us. We have destroyed their camp and thus their ability to hold siege. But Big Tree, puffed up with his pride, will want one last chance to destroy the miners. By now Caleb and Tom and Liam, if even alive, will need all the fighters they can count."

Little Horse had cut out a fine grullo, a solid blue-black mare, for Touch the Sky. The Cheyenne often rode off-color breeds, but had discovered that the solid hues were most durable. Touch the Sky salvaged a hackamore and blanket from the ruins of the camp.

"Here," Two Twists said, handing his tall comrade a Colt Model 1861 musket. "They have left no repeaters in camp, but this came from Big Tree's lodge. A fine weapon, and very similar to the one you had when our tribe captured you. The one Wolf Who Hunts Smiling stole and never returned."

Touch the Sky nodded and lay the .58-caliber weapon over the grullo's withers at the ready. Little Horse had selected a dun, Two Twists an ugly little paint with powerful haunches. Both braves had found rifles too, Little Horse a brass-frame Henry and Two Twists a North & Savage revolving percussion rifle.

"The trail is wide until we reach the belt of steam," Touch the Sky said. "We'll ride abreast. Once we hit that belt, throw caution to the winds and goad your steeds! Trust in their instincts to place their feet on that trail and ride full out. Big Tree must not have a slow-moving target in that mist."

His companions nodded. The ponies, muscle cramped from the small corral, were eager for exercise and difficult to control, especially with new riders on their backs. These mounts were hardly tamed, and that wildness almost made Touch the Sky wish they had bits in their mouths. Sometimes the white man's cruel ways made sense.

They had barely gained the slope before a gunshot from a hidden position reminded them of their danger. Two Twists's paint crow hopped wildly, and he fought her down only with hard effort.

Another shot rang out a few moments later; this one hummed past Touch the Sky's ears. But Little Horse thought he caught a glimpse of muzzle flash. He fired down the trail at a little niche in the solid wall of rock to their left. Sure enough, Big Tree flashed into view for a second as he moved to another position.

"Brothers," Two Twists said, "a thing troubles me. Why would Big Tree have left camp without a mount?"

"We frightened him out too fast," Little Horse boasted.

But Touch the Sky shook his head. "Big Tree is a Comanche. He would take his chances in camp before he would flee without a horse. They have ponies cached in several grazing spots closer to the bottom. Big Tree knows all the shortcuts and defiles and cutbanks. He can get down there on foot almost as fast as we can mounted."

"And this way," Little Horse said, seeing his friend was right, "he can make our lives a hurting place from hiding."

"Eyes to the side," Touch the Sky said again.

However, Little Horse's shot had sent Big Tree ahead for now, and they reached the edge of the wide steam belt without further incident. Now, using hand signals to minimize the warning to Big Tree, Touch the Sky formed them in a single file. The path here, as it entered the blinding steam, not only steepened its grade but narrowed. It would make for a perfect ambush.

"Remember," he said in a low tone. "Let the horses feel your heels! Ride close to their necks with weapon to hand. Two Twists, stop pulling your pony's nose up. Let it sniff the ground. That is how they feel danger. They will obey better if you let them feel the ground."

They nodded, and he kicked the grullo's stout-muscled flanks hard. The mare had been waiting for a chance to run, but this blinding mist held her to a frustrating trot. Touch the Sky rode first, followed by Two Twists and then Little Horse.

Once again Big Tree proved the Comanche skill at terror and menace. Mocking shouts, seeming to emanate from all around them, soon rang out in the swirling white confusion.

"Bear Caller! By now Sis-ki-dee has topped your white woman and cropped her ears to mark his victory! And I had your Honey Eater when she was our prisoner at Blanco Canyon. She resisted at first, but when she experienced a true man, she cried out and begged me for more!"

Touch the Sky tried to locate the source of the voice. But wet air confused sounds, and it came from any direction he cocked an ear toward.

"Woman Face! You have a fine son. I mean to hold him by the ankles and brain him against a tree. I will dry his skin and use it for a parfleche."

Another shot rang out, the bullet splatting from rock to rock as it ricocheted. Touch the Sky's horse began sidestepping dangerously close to the right side of the trail, where it dropped off precipitously into nothingness. Touch the Sky leaned far forward and bit her savagely on the left ear. The ancient trick worked. She gentled enough for him to muscle her back onto the trail.

But the next shot brought more trouble. Touch the Sky heard a heavy crash behind him as Two Twists's paint dropped dead. He whirled just in time to see the youth barely lift his leg out of the way in time to avoid being trapped.

"Two Twists!" he shouted, extending a hand. Two Twists gathered up his weapons and swung

up behind his comrade. Touch the Sky was about
to urge his mount forward again when something caught his eye up ahead. Barely visible in
a cleft between two rocks was a man in hiding.

The tall warrior reached one arm out to stop
Little Horse as he too rode up. Touch the Sky
nodded silently toward the form. His two friends
saw it and nodded back.

Keeping his voice to a whisper, Touch the Sky
said, "Big Tree has finally found his own grave,
bucks. He does not realize the mist is thicker up
here than down there. We can see him, but he
cannot spot us yet. Wait here and draw a bead
on him. I am sneaking around behind the rocks.
When you hear my musket speak its piece, take
your shot also. We have three chances to finally
kill him."

Touch the Sky chewed off the paper end of a
cartridge that contained the powder and ball. He
poured the powder down the barrel of his Colt,
then pushed the bullet in with his thumb. He
drew the ramrod from its mounts and pushed the
projectile down the barrel. He pulled back the
hammer and seated a percussion cap on the nib
beneath it.

His weapon ready, he eased off the trail and
behind the piles of scree that had been cleared
away long ago when the renegades made this
path. Touch the Sky fought down the frantic
pounding of his heart. This was not just any or-
dinary kill, but an attempt on Big Tree. Many
good men had gone under trying to kill the Red
Raider of the Southwest country.

The mist swirled and eddied all around him.
He moved from rock to rock, praying to Maiyun
that he would not make any telltale noise. And

soon, with the Day Maker's help, he had taken up an excellent position above the crouching figure.

Against an honorable warrior, Touch the Sky would never have accepted a surprise kill. A brave who upheld the warrior code deserved to face his enemy in a fair fight, a fair test of wills and courage. But this was a murderer of women and children, a back-shooting criminal lower than the bloody Utes who massacred whiteskin wagon trains in the mountains. Killing this red criminal was a duty, not an honor.

The figure held still. Touch the Sky drew a bead dead center, then eased his finger inside the trigger guard and took up the slack. The musket bucked in his hands, and he had the intense satisfaction of seeing the figure below suddenly flinch as the bullet caught him.

Two more shots rang out to Touch the Sky's left as his companions opened fire. Both shots scored hits, and Touch the Sky cried out with eager gladness.

But his joy died when he reached that niche and discovered the cruel hoax Big Tree had played on them. The man they had just stalked and shot was a buckskin shirt stuffed with grass. Even as they stared at each other, Big Tree's mocking voice called out below them. "Good shooting, Cheyennes! You have just shot *odjib*, the thing of smoke! Will you scalp him too and tell the brothers in your lodge how you counted coup on twigs and grass? Mighty red men!"

His mocking laughter was followed by the fast thudding of unshod hooves.

"You were right, brother," Little Horse told Touch the Sky. "He had a pony cached."

Touch the Sky nodded, already hurrying back

to his own mount. "Big Tree has foxed us again. And now you do not need your shaman to tell you what comes next. They mean to mount a final strike on the miners and, if possible, before we get there to interfere. Now we ride, brothers. The battle of all battles is coming."

Chapter Fifteen

"You mocked me," Sis-ki-dee said bitterly. "Threw it back in my face that I failed to kill him at Bloody Bones Canyon. This time, you swore, it would get done because Big Tree himself, the Big Indian, would take care of it. Now you crawl whipped from our ruined camp, swallowing back your own prideful words. Admit it, Quohada! He is the better man."

Sis-ki-dee and Big Tree stood well back from the long ridge overlooking the paleface camp below. Even now, with their shadows slanting eastward in the declining sun, they could still see black smoke boiling from Wendigo Mountain as the last of their camp smoldered.

Rage sparked in Big Tree's dark eyes. "I admit nothing of the kind, Contrary Warrior. And if you are a better man than Big Tree, bridge the gap. I am for you."

For a few tense moments, the two braves, both bitter with frustration, squared off. Menace seemed to mark the very air between them. Then, abrupt as a thunder clap, Sis-ki-dee tossed back his head and roared with laughter. A bloody cloth was wrapped around his right arm just above the brassard—the legacy of that Crow squaw's accurate knife-throwing arm.

"Look at us, Quohada! Ready to gut each other, and over what? It is not just you he made a fool of. Once again, he goads all three of us: you, me, and Wolf Who Hunts Smiling. But do you not see it? If we kill each other, the tall one wins. Who will be left to kill him?"

For a long time, Big Tree, still smarting from his failure, brooded. But slowly, he began to nod his head. "Spoken straight-arrow, buck. He wins indeed if we two clash. Wolf Who Hunts Smiling is right. We must cross our lances as one until that tall one is sent over. Then we can turn to the task of killing each other."

"He has ruined us," Sis-ki-dee said, glancing again at that roiling smoke. "My ponies and weapons and liquor are all smoke now."

"And all my fine battle trophies," Big Tree added. "Along with all our food and stock."

"Our men know what happened, Quohada. And they blame us! I have heard them complaining among themselves. They too have lost everything—the results of many winters of raiding and hard work."

"Good. That anger," Big Tree said, "can work in our favor. You know that the fight here is almost over?"

Sis-ki-dee nodded. "Indeed. That is why those three brazen warriors climbed those cliffs."

"As you say. We must give it one more bloody effort. How is our ammunition?"

"Plenty of arrows. Not so many bullets. We are low on pig lead."

"Enough," Big Tree asked, "to sustain one more charge?"

Sis-ki-dee nodded, the brass rings in his ears glinted in the setting sun.

"Good," Big Tree said. "Those Cheyennes must still ride back into the camp below. I was well ahead of them. That means we have one more chance at killing them when they ride in. But kill them or not, we must make preparations to strike one last time."

"Buck, we tried once while you were on Wendigo Mountain. We almost breached their entrance. But it was a bloody business, and many good braves did not come back. Now we are too few, I fear, to mount an attack in force, especially if Touch the Sky and his minions return first."

Big Tree pondered all this. "If only we had another way down. Some other way that would let us split our force. A diversionary group could hit the entrance slope again. When all the miners rushed there to defend it, we could slip the second group down."

"There is a second way down," Sis-ki-dee said. "It is steep at some places and requires a rope. But once past those places, it is easy going. It is a runoff gully that ends among the houses."

"I have ears for this! A man can swat one mosquito, but two can drive him crazy. We will talk to the men first and get them breathing fire for this kill. They are angry at us, but we must direct that anger at our enemies."

"Sis-ki-dee!" Plenty Coups yelled from a position to their left, overlooking the entrance slope. "Here come riders on our ponies!"

"They are returning," Big Tree said. "Grab your rifle, Contrary Warrior. Now is our chance!"

Sis-ki-dee pulled his North & Savage from its sheath and hurried to the south end of the ridge. Now they could spot three riders on two horses boldly racing toward the slope.

"Plenty Coups!" Sis-ki-dee called out. "Roan Bear, Hawk Nose, Battle Road!" he shouted, naming the best shots among the men. "Now is our chance, bucks! Let daylight into their souls!"

"It is working, brother," Little Horse said, peering out from his hiding place just below the slope. "They are killing us now!"

"Good," Touch the Sky said. "Run for it, brothers! Keep to the right. They are all watching the horses on the other side."

How fitting, Touch the Sky told himself, that his enemies were falling for the same trick Big Tree had just played on them. Those Indians on those ponies were buckskin suits stuffed with grass, complete with feathered headdresses. From so high above, they looked real enough.

"Caleb!" Touch the Sky shouted out in English. "Caleb, Tom, Liam! We're coming in on foot. Hold your fire."

"Now!" he told his comrades, and all three made a break for it.

They fanned out wide of each other, all of them running a zigzag pattern. Little Horse, with his wounded leg, had a rough time of it, but he lumbered along as best he could. At first, as they skirted boulders and clumps of bushes, the going was easy. Their enemy were distracted and did not notice them. Then a shout from above changed all that.

All of a sudden, Touch the Sky heard bullets and arrows chunking into the ground and trees all around them. They were almost safe, and he could see Caleb and Liam desperately running from cover to move a line of stakes out of the way. But Little Horse was falling farther and farther back. Blood loss had finally caught up to him and sapped his last reserves of strength.

"Brother!" Touch the Sky yelled to Two Twists. "Catch!"

Still on the run, Touch the Sky flipped one end of one of his ropes to Two Twists. The youth caught it. Working with perfect coordination, they flipped the rope back and behind the flagging Little Horse's back. Both braves pulled the rope taut, propelling Little Horse with it. When his feet were finally swept out from under him, the game warrior merely grabbed the rope and let his comrades pull him in the last few dozen yards. It was a rough finish, giving him a few bruises and cuts. But he was safe.

Caleb loosed a whoop. "By God, no Texas wranglers could fancy rope better than that. Am I glad to see you boys. We knew you got their camp when we seen all that smoke. And just in time. It's coming down to the nut cutting around here. Signs show they're going to try at least one last strike."

Caleb, Liam, Touch the Sky, and his comrades had all taken quick shelter behind a stack of shoring timbers.

Touch the Sky glanced around. "Where's Tom?"

Caleb's elated expression sank into a worried

frown. "Tom's stove up. Bad. Caught a slug in the gut. Kristen and Woman Dress are doing what they can for him. But if we don't get him to a doctor pretty damn quick, he's a goner. We almost lost Kristen too. But Woman Dress ran a knife into Sis-ki-dee's arm."

"Kristen's all right?" Touch the Sky demanded sharply.

Caleb looked startled. "Yeah, she's all right. The thing of it is, nobody knows how he got down here. Kristen thinks maybe behind her house. There's an erosion ditch there, but I think it looks too steep farther up."

"Judging from those dead renegades we saw coming in," Touch the Sky said grimly, "Tom made them pay for the privilege of shooting him."

"Tom saved our bacon while you were gone," Liam said. "I never saw a man stay so frosty under fire! He rallied all of us and kept those bastards from taking this camp. Damn savage Indians—uh, sorry, Touch the Sky. Didn't mean you and your bunch."

"Brother," Little Horse complained between chews. He and Two Twists were both working away on strips of pemmican since there had been little time to eat lately. "Will you talk hair-face talk all night? What are you saying?"

Touch the Sky told them Tom Riley was shot and perhaps dying. This news sobered his friends and settled them from the elation of their latest victory over the renegades. In general they despised the *Mah-ish-ta-shee-da*, the Yellow Eyes, as their tribe called white men, because the first whites they ever saw were mountain men with severe jaundice. But Tom Riley, like Touch the

Sky's boyhood friend Corey Robinson, spoke one way to the red man. Whites who did not speak from both sides of their mouths were rare. And Tom Riley had placed his life in danger to save their tribe. In fact, he was doing so now. Once this camp fell, Powder River would be next.

"Either Tom will soon get to a doctor," Touch the Sky said, "or he will be dead along with the rest of us. Our mission to Wendigo Mountain has cut short this siege. But as you said, they'll try one last strike."

The words of Honey Eater's father, Chief Yellow Bear, came back to him now from his vision at Medicine Lake: *When all seems lost, become your enemy!*

"What are your plans for the defense?" Touch the Sky asked Caleb.

"Well, I figure they'll try an attack in force. But then again, that didn't work last time. And now they've got fewer braves to do it. So to tell you the honest-to-God truth, Touch the Sky, I don't rightly know. With Big Tree and Sis-ki-dee, how the hell can you?"

"You can't," Touch the Sky said.

"So I'm mainly calling it by good ol' gut hunches. What you red sons call medicine."

Caleb pointed toward the stakes. "This bunch is different from you Northern Plains warriors. You boys like to hunker round the fires at night if you can. This bunch loves to strike after dark, and that's when I figure they'll play their ace. You agree?"

Touch the Sky shook his head. "No, I don't. Everything you're saying is smart and logical and the best possible deduction based on their past

151

behavior. But they know you know that. Understand me?"

Caleb looked confused, but some light began to glimmer in his eyes. "So you're saying they'll bluff me?"

The Cheyenne nodded. "I think so. I'd say the attack will come anytime now, but before dark. And as for the attack in force, it didn't work last time. I predict they'll fake it, but try something else."

Caleb glanced at the main line of his men, dispersed along the entrance to camp. "You suggesting the men be moved?"

"First of all, are those explosive charges still buried out there?"

"They need to be checked," Caleb said. "They might have been disturbed during that last attack. We had no time to light the fuses then."

Touch the Sky nodded. "We'll check. Assuming the nitro packs are still in place, I'd leave you here in charge of lighting them and a light force up front. No more than five good shots to hold back the decoy group long enough for you to get the explosives lit. I'd include Little Horse if he can still stand. With that revolving-barrel shotgun of his, he can clear out a canyon."

"It's risky, buddy. Damned risky if you're wrong. If they storm us from the front again, I can't stop all of them with two explosions. Well, where would you put the main force of men?"

"Nowhere," Touch the Sky said.

Caleb looked like a man who had gone to bed in one country and woken up in another. "Nowhere? You want to spell that out plain?"

"Glad to. You give up white man's tactics for

once and fight like Indians. These are Indians attacking us, aren't they?"

Caleb was getting interested. "Hell, don't whack the cork now. What do you mean by fight like Indians? Whoop and use arrows?"

"Funny, paleface, real funny. No, I mean that for once quit thinking that all you can do is fort up and take one position. The main point here is that we don't know what they'll do this time, right?"

"Sure, but—"

"And since we don't know, we don't want your men pinned to one spot."

Caleb was catching on. "You mean, keep the main group as roving skirmishers, ready to hustle anywhere? Hell, yes! Like the Green Mountain Boys and Rogers' Rangers."

"I had the Apaches in mind," Touch the Sky said dryly, and Caleb grinned.

Both men looked around as Touch the Sky translated the main points for his comrades.

"They'll try to find another way in," Touch the Sky assured Caleb. "And they'll send at least a light force at the front. So we have to have a built-up position and skirmishers on the move. And just in case, we had better tell the people in the houses to arm themselves with what they have."

Caleb nodded, his face grim. "I've already got all the boys twelve and over out on guard. We've lost too many men."

"And you'll lose some more," Touch the Sky said. "Bear in mind, Caleb, that neither one of those bucks brooks humiliation. It's not just the defeats here. Their camp is a shambles. I know the ritual by now. Right now, those Kiowas and Comanche devils are getting nerved with liquor and corn beer, the last they have thanks to us. This next strike is not going to be a strike for booty. It's bloodlust now, and a hard fight is coming."

Chapter Sixteen

Touch the Sky's predictions proved right. However, Big Tree and Sis-ki-dee added some cunning twists to their strategy, and fate intervened, ensuring a pitched battle whose outcome would hang in the balance until the last bloody charge.

Working quickly, Touch the Sky and Two Twists risked fire from above to verify that the nitroglycerin blocks were still in place, blasting caps and fuses attached. Touch the Sky recalled something Tom had mentioned about how sharp, concussive impacts—such as from a bullet—might also detonate them. On a hunch, he had Two Twists follow his example in exposing one corner of the blocks aboveground. Not enough to make them obvious, just enough to offer a bare target.

"None of them shot at us while we were exposed," Touch the Sky told Caleb when the two braves returned to the relative safety of the built-up area. "That troubles me."

Little Horse, under strict orders from his comrades, was lying on his sleeping robes, resting. But he had his shotgun and captured Henry rifle to hand.

"They are quiet now," Little Horse said after his friend switched to Cheyenne and repeated his remark, "only because they are busy preparing the attack."

"I've got the men distributed like you said," Caleb told Touch the Sky. He nodded toward the light force nearby. Five adults were backed up by an equal number of boys, Justin McKinney among them. "That's all we got defending the front. If the men are killed, the boys have strict orders to rush forward and fill in. The rest are in two skirmish groups farther back. I hope you're right, hombre."

"If I'm not," Touch the Sky said grimly, "we had better hope that those boys become men quick and that the skirmish groups can respond quick to plug the gap. You just make sure you live by those fuses. Those nitro blocks could be the key to dispersing the forward attackers. You got the timing down?"

"I think so, but that part'll be tricky. Tom said something about testing the fuse because the powder can dry out."

"Too late now," Touch the Sky said, glancing up at the ridge. "If they see us fooling around with it, we'll ruin the surprise. You can't quite see it from here, but we left the blocks exposed to gunfire from a little closer. Bullets will detonate them. Remember that in an emergency."

"An emergency?" Caleb muttered. "That's all we've had around here."

"Double braid," Touch the Sky said to Two Twists. "We are going to cut our horses out from the corral. Little Horse will be up here with the defending force at the entrance. You and I will watch how things develop and take the fight where it is needed."

Two Twists approved of this strategy. It was a fitting way for an Indian brave to fight, not hunkered down behind breastworks.

"Look!" Caleb pointed down the slope. A line of braves was descending the ridge by a narrow trail, streamered lances held high.

"Here comes the fight!" Touch the Sky called out in English, then Cheyenne. "One bullet, one enemy!"

"You might have called it right," Caleb said, counting the descending braves. "That ain't near half their force. But, dammit, it's still more than we can hold back if they all rush at once."

Soon, however, all discussion ended as the attacking renegades took up positions and began firing into the defenders.

"Hold your first shot!" Caleb roared out to his men. "They want to charge while most of us are reloading!"

As if sensing the presence of those nitro blocks, the attackers held back from a main charge in force. Touch the Sky could see Big Tree directing the attack from this end, which meant Sis-ki-dee and the rest were somewhere else. But where?

"Should I call some of the skirmishers up front?" Caleb bellowed out, his face set tight with worry.

"No," Touch the Sky said. "We can hold here."

But that was not at all clear to the defenders. Big Tree cleverly drew off their fire with several feints. Then, abruptly, a knot of perhaps ten renegades threw a line of stakes aside and rushed them.

Little Horse's shotgun roared, rock salt tearing faces to red smears. Touch the Sky emptied his Sharps and his captured musket, and Two Twists fired too. This sent the surviving renegades reeling back while Touch the Sky charged his weapons. But a tenacious Big Tree, realizing the defenders were reloading, sent another line of men almost immediately.

"Justin!" Caleb screamed, desperately thumbing rounds into his pistoi. "All you boys, on the line and fire!"

The frightened but determined boys, several armed only with small-caliber squirrel guns, darted forward and discharged their weapons. Fear made their aim careless, but they bought a precious few seconds for the Cheyennes to grab their bows from their rope riggings. Still mounted, easy targets, they nonetheless unleashed a firestorm of deadly arrows.

This stopped the attack once again. But the victory was costly. Half of the defending line were dead or wounded; others were out of ammo. The boys moved up onto the main line of defense. But Touch the Sky feared they would not hold one more assault.

The momentary lull in this fight only drew attention to the abrupt explosion of battle noises behind them. Touch the Sky whirled around in his saddle and saw a score or more of braves pouring down that erosion gully behind Kristen's house. But this part of the plan he had antici-

pated brilliantly. Liam McKinney had formed
the skirmish groups to meet them, and renegades
were dropping like flies as they descended into a
hail of lead.

No, it was this end of camp that stood in danger. More than he had allowed for. And now
Touch the Sky could see that Big Tree had decided to unleash the final assault. Two Twists
saw it too; so he dismounted, giving up the Indian style for the white man's as he forted up
beside Little Horse. Touch the Sky's shaman
sense, however, warned him not to follow suit.
He must stay mounted, ready to move.

"Caleb!" he shouted desperately above the din
of battle. "Here it comes! Light the fuses!"

A wall of lead slammed into them as the attackers hurtled forward. Caleb bent down, fum-
bling for a match; a moment later, Touch the Sky
watched in horror as blood blossomed from his
chest and he was slammed backward.

From where he sat, Touch the Sky was closer
to the charges than he was to those fuses. And
besides, enough time had been lost that the fuses
might not burn quickly enough. There was only
one hope. He had to get close enough to shoot
those nitro blocks.

The warrior knew it meant sure death for his
pony and probably for himself. But the determined Cheyenne tugged his hackamore hard left
and kicked his palomino into motion. He
charged into the very teeth of the oncoming renegades.

Now he risked being killed by his own side,
especially those inexperienced boys behind him.
He could hear Little Horse and Two Twists
mocking their enemy with shouts. Closer still

Touch the Sky pounded, bullets whistling past his ears.

The main force of the attackers was rapidly drawing even with those nitro blocks. But a heartbeat later, Touch the Sky felt his pony crash beneath him as she caught a round in her lights.

The first renegades reached him. He had his lance to hand and skewered one; another felt the obsidian blade of his knife. But Touch the Sky refused to fire his recharged rifle and musket, each looped over a shoulder. A few more braves streamed past him, and the roaring Two Twists rose with knife in hand, leading the miners and the fired-up boys in desperate hand-to-hand combat. They were fighting like she-grizzes with cubs, but if many more of those attacking renegades got past Touch the Sky, he knew his friends were doomed.

The tall Cheyenne searched desperately for sight of one of the charges. When he found it, he shrugged his Sharps off his right shoulder. He needed to get a little closer, but death could find him at any moment if he waited. As the main body surged over that charge, he fired and missed!

So desperate he cursed in English, Touch the Sky shrugged the Colt musket off his left shoulder. Now, even if lucky, he could only set off one of those blocks. It would have to be enough, or the battle was all over.

Touch the Sky drew a tight bead, took in a long breath, and willed his muscles to relax as he took up the trigger slack. The musket kicked in his hands. Then there was a whip-cracking explosion like an ice flow breaking up, and the air was filled with flying rocks, dirt, and bloody chunks of Indians.

That explosion broke the back of the beast. The attack down the erosion gully had already failed, and the remainder of the renegades fled back up to the ridge. Liam's skirmishers set up a lusty cheer at the same time as the survivors up front, who watched Big Tree and his defeated men retreat in a rout.

" 'Earth to earth, ashes to ashes, dust to dust,' " said Levi Carruthers, a miner who had been a Methodist preacher back in St. Joe. " 'In sure and certain hope of the Ressurection unto eternal life.' "

Quietly, as the victims of the renegade siege were finally laid to a decent rest, Touch the Sky translated the solemn words for his curious friends. They both paid strict attention. Like most red men, they were in awe of all matters spiritual. It fascinated them when Touch the Sky explained that white men too believed in an afterlife for worthy warriors.

The three Cheyennes stood respectfully at the front of the gathering because the miners had insisted their heroic friends be prominently placed. Caleb and Tom were absent; they had both been rushed into Register Cliffs by buckboard as soon as the siege lifted. Though they were missed today for the burial of their friends, at least the news was good concerning their injuries. Tom had lost much blood, but he would recover. Caleb was in even better shape, and he should be back on the job shortly.

Meantime, things were up and running. The telegraph had been repaired, the tracks soon would be, and as soon as possible, Liam planned to get at least one shift working in the mine. Caleb had payroll to make, and it was time for these big galoots to start earning their breakfast again.

Kristen Steele, severely pretty in a black bombazine dress and a wide-brimmed hat, stood among the braves, her eyes glistening with tears as Tilly Blackford's pine coffin was lowered and the ropes were pulled out from under it.

"Brother," Two Twists said awkwardly to Touch the Sky, his voice low, "not one of these miners is a coward. But why are many of them crying like the women?"

"White man's customs permit it at funerals. It is not considered a loss of manhood. Whites believe that if grief is not expressed now it may hurt them more later."

Two Twists and Little Horse exchanged glances. This reasoning was curious, but contained a hard nugget of truth. Perhaps these hair faces knew something, after all.

The Cheyennes had waited instead of returning to their camp right away—waited to make sure the renegades were truly gone and waited so that Little Horse could recover his strength. The delay was not crucial. Touch the Sky had heard from a camp runner that Tangle Hair had performed his job admirably. Honey Eater and Little Bear were safe.

But the renegades were indeed gone. They had returned to their ruined camp to lick their wounds and nurse new grudges. No one was foolish enough to think them finished. However, it would be many moons before they could again seriously threaten anyone in these parts.

Nor, as Touch the Sky gazed around this gathering of mourners, could he forget what else that word bringer from camp had told him—a message from Wolf Who Hunts Smiling, who had obviously heard the news about the renegades' failure. "Blood will beget blood, Woman Face. We offered to share the spoils with you, but you refused. Now dig in for the fight."

Let it come, Touch the Sky thought grimly, looking at all these sad faces. He belonged to no clan, to no soldier society; and his enemies claimed he carried the stink that scared away the buffalo. But who among them could also say he feared any warrior?

Touch the Sky's eyes met those of his comrades, and no words were needed. All shared one thought: *The next fight is coming, and we have been promised a share in it.*

CHEYENNE

JUDD COLE

Follow the adventures of Touch the Sky as he searches for a world he can call his own!

CHEYENNE

DOUBLE EDITION
JUDD COLE

One man's heroic search for a world he can call his own.

Arrow Keeper. A Cheyenne raised among pioneers, Matthew Hanchon has never known anything but distrust. The settlers brand him a savage, and when Matthew realizes that his adopted parents will suffer for his sake, he flees into the wilderness—where he'll need a warrior's courage if he hopes to survive.

And in the same volume...

Death Chant. When Matthew returns to the Cheyenne, he doesn't find the acceptance he seeks. The Cheyenne can't fully trust any who were raised in the ways of the white man. Forced to prove his loyalty, Matthew faces the greatest challenge he has ever known.

___4280-0 $4.99 US/$5.99 CAN

CHEYENNE

Spirit Path
Mankiller
Judd Cole

Spirit Path. The mighty Cheyenne trust their tribe's shaman to protect them against great sickness and bloody defeat. A rival accuses Touch the Sky of bad medicine, and if he can't prove the claim false, he'll come to a brutal end.

And in the same action-packed volume . . .

Mankiller. A fierce warrior, Touch the Sky can outfight, outwit, and outlast any enemy. Yet the fearsome Cherokee brave named Mankiller can snap a man's neck as easily as a reed, and he is determined to count coup on Touch the Sky.

___4445-5 $4.99 US/$5.99 CAN

Dorchester Publishing Co., Inc.
P.O. Box 6640
Wayne, PA 19087-8640

Please add $1.75 for shipping and handling for the first book and $.50 for each book thereafter. NY, NYC, and PA residents, please add appropriate sales tax. No cash, stamps, or C.O.D.s. All orders shipped within 6 weeks via postal service book rate. Canadian orders require $2.00 extra postage and must be paid in U.S. dollars through a U.S. banking facility.

Name_____
Address_____
City_____State_____Zip_____
I have enclosed $_____ in payment for the checked book(s).
Payment <u>must</u> accompany all orders. ❑ Please send a free catalog.
    CHECK OUT OUR WEBSITE! www.dorchesterpub.com

CHEYENNE

WENDIGO MOUNTAIN
DEATH CAMP
JUDD COLE

Wendigo Mountain. A Cheyenne warrior raised by white settlers, Touch the Sky is blessed with strong medicine. Yet his powers as a shaman cannot help him foretell that his tribe's sacred arrows will be stolen—or that his enemies will demand his head for their return. To save his tribe from utter destruction, the young brave will wage a battle like none he's ever fought.

And in the same action-packed volume . . .

Death Camp. Touch the Sky will gladly give his life to protect his tribe. Yet not even he can save them from an outbreak of deadly disease. Racing against time and brutal enemies, Touch the Sky has to either forsake his heritage and trust the white man's medicine—or prove his loyalty even as he watches his proud people die.

___4479-X $4.99 US/$5.99 CAN

WILDERNESS

#27
GOLD RAGE

DAVID THOMPSON

Penniless old trapper Ben Frazier is just about ready to pack it all in when an Arapaho warrior takes pity on him and shows him where to find the elusive gold that white men value so greatly. His problems seem to be over, but then another band of trappers finds out about the gold and forces Ben to lead them to it. It's up to Zach King to save the old man, but can he survive a fight against a gang of gold-crazed mountain men?

___4519-2 $3.99 US/$4.99 CAN

WILDERNESS

BLOOD FEUD

←——————————→

David Thompson

The brutal wilderness of the Rocky Mountains can be deadly to those unaccustomed to its dangers. So when a clan of travelers from the hill country back East arrive at Nate King's part of the mountain, Nate is more than willing to lend a hand and show them some hospitality. He has no way of knowing that this clan is used to fighting—and killing—for what they want. And they want Nate's land for their own!

___4477-3 $3.99 US/$4.99 CAN